YESTERDAY COMES AROUND

LINDA E. KEELER

Order this book online at www.trafford.com/07-0636
or email orders@trafford.com

Most Trafford titles are also available at major online book retailers.

© Copyright 2007 Linda E. Keeler.

All rights reserved. No part of this publication may be reproduced, stored in a retrieval system, or transmitted, in any form or by any means, electronic, mechanical, photocopying, recording, or otherwise, without the written prior permission of the author.

Artwork by Ray F. Seaford

Note for Librarians: A cataloguing record for this book is available from Library and Archives Canada at www.collectionscanada.ca/amicus/index-e.html

Printed in Victoria, BC, Canada.

ISBN: 978-1-4251-2235-5

We at Trafford believe that it is the responsibility of us all, as both individuals and corporations, to make choices that are environmentally and socially sound. You, in turn, are supporting this responsible conduct each time you purchase a Trafford book, or make use of our publishing services. To find out how you are helping, please visit www.trafford.com/responsiblepublishing.html

Our mission is to efficiently provide the world's finest, most comprehensive book publishing service, enabling every author to experience success. To find out how to publish your book, your way, and have it available worldwide, visit us online at www.trafford.com/10510

Trafford
PUBLISHING

www.trafford.com

North America & international
toll-free: 1 888 232 4444 (USA & Canada)
phone: 250 383 6864 ♦ fax: 250 383 6804
email: info@trafford.com

The United Kingdom & Europe
phone: +44 (0)1865 722 113 ♦ local rate: 0845 230 9601
facsimile: +44 (0)1865 722 868 ♦ email: info.uk@trafford.com

10 9 8 7 6 5 4 3

TABLE OF CONTENTS

	Page
Synopsis	2
Why Us?	3
The Convent	16
Down South	28
Teenage Years	38
Victory	53
Moving On	69
The Fifties	77
Wine and Roses	92
Running with the Big Boys	111
On the Moor	135
Footloose	151
Back to the Smoke	162
Tarts and Hearts	181
Turn up for the Book	195

SYNOPSIS

'Yesterday Comes Around' is the title I have chosen for this book.

The story's main character is Harry Creedy. Harry's mother, Kathleen, had been left a widow with four young daughters. Her first husband was killed in a building accident. John Creedy came into her life a year later, and she was more than happy to accept his proposal of marriage. She went on to have three more children, Harry being the eldest of the three.

Sadly Kathleen died at a young age, leaving John with seven children. John had no other choice but to send his stepdaughters to board at a convent school.

Then through the poverty of war, life became hard. This led Harry to steal; he began with stealing sweets, and as the years progressed he went on to rob banks, from there he became a safe-cracker.

Prison became a way of life for him. There were times when it all became too much to bear. This prompted him to make his escape across the misty open land of Dartmoor.

What kept Harry going through all this were his many love affairs along the way.

Throughout his life he thought a lot about the daughter he had lost contact with because of his life of crime. UNTIL...

WHY US?

Palmerston Road was busy on that warm June morning in 1929; the smell of the soap from the many laundries filled the air.

The sound of a new born baby crying came from number 19, Kathleen Creedy had just given birth to her fifth child, a baby son named Henry John, who they decided would be called Harry. The four elder girls had just left the house to set off for school; their names were Kathleen, Nora, Biddy and Ruby.

Life was tough for the family, Kathleen's first husband died in a building accident; she found life hard bringing up four girls on her own. When John Creedy came into her life a year later, she was more than pleased to accept his proposal of marriage. John, a stocky-built man, with a rugged complexion, was a good hard working man, who was happy to take on Kathleen's girls. Today was a proud day for him, as he now had his own son.

Kathleen, known to everybody as Katy, was a woman with an erect bearing and slim figure. She wore her long shiny hair piled high on her head; she had an elegance about her. Katy was certainly a beautiful woman, heads would turn as she strolled confidently down the street.

John, a carpenter, came from an Irish family that had settled in London when he was a boy. Their small terraced house was situated just opposite the station. The couple of rows of houses were out numbered by the many laundries in the area; it became known as Soap Suds Island.

The Creedy household was always busy, Katy spent her days cooking and cleaning. Looking after the children was hard work, the house was kept perfect, with sparse but highly polished furniture. John would light his treasured oil lamp each evening, to read his books.

Sundays he spent cleaning and polishing it, his lamp was special to him, for it once belonged to his mother. On the dresser stood a basket, with a red check cloth, Katy kept this to take food to her neighbours when they were unwell. Evening time, Kathleen and Nora would sit and sew, chatting away merrily. Biddy and Ruby often sat with Katy, brushing her long dark hair until their arms ached. Katy loved this more than anything: her beloved daughters pampering her.

In less than a year, Katy gave birth to her second son Patrick. She looked at her growing family with pride. John was working all hours, with more mouths to feed; now with six children, Katy's days were full. Tiredness began to set in, making sure the children and John were well fed; she often forgot about herself, her petite figure had become even slimmer. Most of the families, in this area were just as poor, but somehow, they managed to keep their spirits up, and went about their daily life.

Almost a year later, Katy realised she was going to have another child, again, worry took over. How was she going to cope? John tried to comfort her. "Never mind Katy, we'll get by," he said, putting his arms around her to reassure her. "You know I love you more than anything."

As the weeks progressed, Katy's health went down hill. The ward was cold and clinical; John glanced around in the dim light at the sleeping patients, all to be heard was the odd cough. Gently he touched Katy's face her breath was fading rapidly. His heart began to thump heavily, he knew she was slipping away and there was nothing he could do. He frantically looked around, hoping an angel would appear and give him some kind of comfort. Suddenly Katy's body began to shudder and there was complete silence. Then came a hand resting on his shoulder, "Mr Creedy, I'm sorry, it's the end."

The wind blew fiercely as he made his way back home from the Middlesex Hospital. He pulled his collar up around the back of his neck to protect himself from the cold bitter February wind. The clock chimed two as he made his way through the market square. The silence was almost frightening; wearily he looked up to the rolling clouds that were moving so fast it was as if they were being chased.

Angrily he punched his fist into the air, and wanted to grab hold of one of the clouds because this is where he sees his Katy now floating up there with the angels.

Nervously he turned the key into the door; the gas light on the wall gave out a slight glow. Silently he crept along creaky passage, wanting desperately not to wake the children. His hands were still trembling as he pushed the door open to go into the small parlour. The embers in the fireplace somehow gave him a feeling of comfort. His arms felt heavy as he brought them up to his face as he rubbed his sore tired eyes. He felt as if he hadn't slept for days, what with the worry of his beloved Katy and seven children to care for, he felt done in. Wearily he grabbed a coat from the hook on the door and slumped into the armchair. There he spent the night drifting in and out of a fitful sleep.

Slowly his eyes opened, a shiver went across his body, he gazed across to the window; through the crack in the curtains he could see a small glimmer of daylight. Was it all a dream? Suddenly he was feeling confused. No, no, it couldn't possibly be true; never in a million years would his Katy have left him in this mess with seven children to care for.

His thoughts were broken by the turning of the handle on the door. Quickly he rubbed his tear-stained face, as if to put some life into it. It was the moment he had been dreading there stood the two elder girls, Kathleen and Nora. Slowly Nora touched him on the shoulder. "What is it, what has happened to Mum?"

Caringly he put his arm around her, "I'm sorry girls, your Mother passed away peacefully in her sleep. I held her hand tightly just to let her know I was there."
He bowed his head not wanting to show the tears that began to stream down his face.

Kathleen nervously twirled her long dark hair around her fingers, "But what about the younger ones, how are they going to take it? This will break Biddy and Ruby's hearts."
"I know girls, you don't have to tell me, it is something that is weighing deeply on my mind. Harry and Patrick won't really understand, and as for baby Margaret, well she is just months old. Dear oh dear girls, what am I to do?"

The days running up to the funeral were desperate, Katy's death had affected them all badly. Bibby and Ruby were inseparable; it was as if they were joint at the hip. Kathleen and Nora helped by taking care of the smaller ones.

On the day of the funeral John woke early, he looked at the tattered shreds of wallpaper that were peeling from the damp bedroom wall, he sighed to himself, yes he had been promising Katy for months that he would do something about it. At that moment in time he wouldn't have cared if the house fell down around him. Wearily he pulled the curtains and looked out to see a thin layer of snow on the ground.
He sighed wistfully, oh how his beloved Katy had loved the snow. As he tied his black tie, he felt a great surge of resentment, he looked up wrenching his fist into his chest, feeling angry with God for taking her in the prime of her life.

A knock came on the front door; Nora had already answered it as he made his way down the stairs. It was Lilly Brown, the next door neighbour, she bowed her head as she handed him four small posies for the girls to carry to their Mother's graveside. Across her arm she had a black coat that she had made for Ruby as she didn't have one suitable for a funeral.
Gently she touched John on the shoulder, "You know it's a sad day, Mr Creedy, I say a very sad day indeed. How would you like me to look after the three young ones? Its no place for them to be, I say it's no place for them to be."
"Well thank you very much Mrs Brown, it is much appreciated."
He called the girls one by one; they stood in a line in front of him. The overwhelming sadness showed on their solemn faces, it was as if the blood had been taken from their young bodies.

Nervously he took a deep breath, finding it hard to choose the right words. "Well girls it's going to be very hard for you, are you ready to come into the parlour to say goodbye to your Mother?"
They didn't answer but looked down to the ground sheepishly. Slowly they entered the cold dark room, with just one lonely flickering candle on the mantle shelf. Next to it was a photograph of John and Kathleen on their wedding day.
One by one they walked around their Mother's coffin, not wanting to catch sight of her dead body. Each put in small keepsake. Amidst the sobs John knew he had to stay strong.

Suddenly came what he had been dreading most, the hearse arrived. Caringly he led the girls from the room, for the coffin lid to be screwed down by the undertaker. In the passage they came face to face with the tall sullen looking man, dressed in a black coat and hat. He nodded across to John to indicate it was time for Katy's coffin to leave the house.
John turned to look down the dark passage, and there stood little Harry, he was just three years old. He walked towards his young son, picking

him up and holding him closely to his chest, as the young boy cried out, "I want my Mummy!"

John led Kathleen's girls out into the street. The fresh white snowflakes came to rest on their dark clothing. A handful of neighbours gathered round to pay their respects as the family set off for the burial. In the snow-covered graveyard, they linked arms as Kathleen's coffin was lowered into the ground.
The uneasy silence was broken by the continual sobs, and the whistling of the wind as a near blizzard erupted.

Slowly life began to return to normal, with the help of Lilly Brown who looked after Harry, Patrick and little baby Margaret, while John returned to work. The four girls tried desperately hard to look after themselves, but life was difficult, knowing the Mother they loved so much would never return.
Months passed, but it was no use, Lilly Brown done her best to help out, but it all proved to be too much for John. The only choice he had was to keep the three small children and send his four stepdaughters off to board at a convent school for girls. It was only a few miles away, so he knew he would be able to visit often.

Kathleen and Nora settled in quite well, for they knew it wouldn't be too long before they could make their own way in life. Biddy found it difficult; she was not getting over the death of her Mother.
Often when John left Biddy, he would look at her red curly hair and pale freckled skin, and see the sadness in her big blue eyes.
Ruby kept her feelings to herself and found her comfort praying in the chapel.

John arrived early, he sat in the reception room, looking out onto the large garden surrounding the convent; he waited nervously, as the girls walked towards him. They sat themselves down around a big old wooden table.
He tried desperately to bring a smile to his face. Slowly he studied the girls one by one, wondering how they were going to react to the news he was about to give them.
He loosened his tie as he began to speak. "Well girls, it's bad news. I'm sorry it's your little baby sister Margaret, sadly she died last night, she had pneumonia."
He rested his head in his hands and discreetly wiped away the tears.
John peered around at their gentle faces; all he could see was heartache. They had lost their Mother and now their baby sister, how much more could they take? he asked himself.

That night Ruby went to the chapel and prayed, for praying was now helping her cope with the harsh realities of life.

John tried to get back to as normal life as possible, but still with his two young sons to care for it was still hard. He was now in his fifties, his thick dark hair turning grey, and he no longer had the energy of a younger man.

Yes there was no doubt about it, he was still missing Katy more each day, and she was almost twenty years younger than him, that is why he found it a cruel twist of fate that she should be taken first. No he could never reason why this beautiful woman should be taken so young.

The time had finally come for John to move on, so he decided to leave the house in Palmerston Road; he could no longer live with all the sad memories. After giving it some thought he decided to rent a ground floor flat in a three-storey house. It was just a few streets away and the rent was much cheaper.

Park Road became the perfect place for them. He glanced around the small flat, looking at the dreary, drab walls. But, he reassured himself, with a lick of paint, he would having looking cosy in no time.
Mrs Masters lived upstairs with her husband and sons, Dickie and Tommy, and the very top floor was occupied by her parents.

Finally the day had come for little Harry to start school. Gently he pulled the covers back from the bed, "Come on son, it's a big day for you, it's your first day at school."
He took him by the hand and led Harry into the warm scullery, took him over to the sink, and picked up an old wooden chair.
"Here you are son jump up on this."
Harry stood on the rickety chair and splashed his hands around in the warm water. John handed him a bar of soap. "Come on son; let's see you looking spick and span."
He rubbed his little son's blonde curly hair, as he handed him over to Mrs Masters. Harry gripped Mrs Master's hand firmly, as they walked up the steep hill to the school, as the school bell rang out, he knew even at this young age, he didn't want to be with anyone else's Mother; he just wanted his own.

In the year that followed it soon became noticeable, that Harry was much brighter than the other children, he was already showing keen interest in his school work. He was a waiflike little character with blonde hair and big blue eyes. Often looking ragged and worn. Patrick was a boisterous child often getting into trouble.

The boys often came home from school to an empty house; while John was busy out earning a living, his young sons would often go without food and roam the streets. It didn't take long before young Harry soon became streetwise. It wasn't long before he was sending his younger brother Patrick into the sweet shop, to distract the shopkeeper, while he stuffed the ill-gotten gain up his jumper.

John woke early, he put on his best suit, and eagerly told the boys to make themselves look smart, they were going to visit their stepsisters, at the Convent School. They left the house, and walked briskly along the lane, to catch the trolley bus for the remainder of their journey.

They arrived at the old convent building, they were greeted by a nun, who escorted them along the silent passageway. Harry disliked it here; he always found it cold and unwelcoming. An overwhelming sadness rose up in his body, the thought of his sisters having to regard this awful place as their home.
He gripped his father's arm, feeling thankful that he hadn't been sent away as well.

Patiently they sat in the waiting room, waiting for the girls to arrive. John felt a flutter in his heart, feeling pleased to be there, as he always did, for he knew he was doing the right thing by Katy.
The girls finally arrived, John handed them their sweets as he always did. He studied them one by one, yes Katy would have been very proud of them, he thought.
Kathleen cleared her throat nervously as she broke the news that she and Nora had been offered a chance to work and live on a farm in Devon.
John rubbed his hands over his face, as if to give it some consideration. The very idea of them being so far away disturbed him somewhat, but he couldn't stand in their way, after all they had been given a golden opportunity, and he must let them take it. For he had nothing to offer them. He took their hands and wished them well for their future life.

Harry was sitting at his desk with his head bowed down, deeply engrossed in a book. The bell rang out it, was the end of the school day, everyone else had left, and he looked up and there stood Mr Hearn.
"Come on Harry, don't you want to go home?"
"Sorry," said Harry.
"Don't be, who knows, one day Harry, you could be here teaching children yourself."

Harry walked down the hill, with his hands in his short grey trouser pockets, staring down at the uneven pavement, trying desperately hard not to tread on the cracks. He was about to pull the key from the letterbox, when he had second thoughts, what was the point there would be no one there, so he turned and went on down the street. Tirelessly he searched the streets for someone to play football with, but had no luck. Wistfully he carried on walking until his legs tired.

He looked over to the greengrocer shop, on the corner, he noticed a display of apples on a stall outside. Quickly he crossed the road, and checked that no one was watching, and ran and took some and stuffed them down his shirt.
Hastily he turned the corner, and ran down a narrow cobbled street, until he came to rest at a derelict building. He pulled away an old bit of fencing that was propped up against the porch and sat himself down.

He took one of the apples from his shirt, and vigorously began to rub it on his trousers. Happily he held the perfect apple up in front of him, and was ready to take a much wanted bite, when a voice shouted, "Give me one then! Or I will go and tell that man I just seen you nick them."

Feeling bewildered, he looked up, to see a young girl walking towards him, he held the shiny red apple up for her to take. She smiled and thanked him. He looked her up and down, and asked her name, she replied, "Laura."

Yes he liked her straight away, he liked her cheek. He thought how pretty she was, her long dark hair, hung thick on her shoulders, her big blue eyes stared boldly at him. Her ill-fitting clothes looked ragged and tattered. She sat herself down beside him, and they got to know each other.
Suddenly she jumped up in panic. "I must go, or I will be in trouble with my mum."

Happily they walked to the end of the street together, before parting company. As he made his way home, he was feeling pleased he had met her.

John made his way over the railway bridge in one of his melancholy moods. Instead of heading towards Park Road, he made his way to the Victory. Well the boys are hardly ever in these days and one pint would do no harm, he thought.

He sat at the bar; his problems were weighing on his mind, how his life had turned out. When his thoughts were broken by his friend Michel Donavan, well, one pint led to another. Michel was a jolly-looking man, around fifty. It wasn't long before Michel began to play his piano accordion. John looked up at the clock, time was ticking by, but his melancholy mood had disappeared, the music was lifting his heart.

As he looked across the smoky haze, he caught sight of Mary Grady, tapping her feet on the wooden floorboards. Suddenly she got up and began to do the Irish jig; he was mesmerised by this beautiful woman, as she swung her skirt in time to the music. He looked at her tiny feet, as they jittered from heel to toe when the light caught her highly polished black shoes.

He felt his heart beating fast as she made her way towards him. She grabbed his arm and pulled him up to dance. He was now gaining confidence, as she led him around the floor, to a hooray of cheers. Yes, he thought to himself, he couldn't remember enjoying himself like this, since dancing with Katy on their wedding night.

Mary was a well-known character in the pub; she always managed to gather the men around her table. Her happy-go-lucky personality shone through. The men found it hard to keep their eyes off her voluptuous figure and her flame red hair.

The bell rang out for the last orders of the evening; sadly the night had come to an end. Mary was just about to leave, when John took her by the arm. "Mary would you like me to walk you home? It's along my way after all." She agreed.

As they walked along unsteadily, he found himself putting his arm around her shoulder. He gazed up to the clear deep blue sky that was full of stars, thinking that he hadn't been this happy in ages.
Finally they arrived at Mary's house, he clasped her hand. "Well goodnight Mary, see you soon."
Hastily she pulled him towards her, and kissed him on the cheek. The closeness of her body, sent a tingle over him; he had almost forgotten what it was like to hold a woman so close. She turned the key in the door and gave him a cheeky wink, "Why don't you come in for a drink?"
He didn't hesitate, "Well I'll just have a quick one then," he replied nervously.

Mary led him in to her cosy room, that had a perfect woman's touch to it, yes that was something else he missed, the smell of lavender polish and flowers on the table.
She began to pour them each a rather large brandy, then she invited him on the sofa to sit next to her. They talked about the evening, what fun it had been, but in his heart he was now beginning to feel it was not

right being in this situation, it was too late, there wasn't much he could do about it now.

Mary leaned across to him and began to touch his knee, gently moving her hand towards his crotch "You know John I have always liked you, I'll say this, you're a real gentleman."
This took him by surprise, he felt uncomfortable, and then she kissed him forcefully, on the lips, and pushed him down.

She spread herself across him, he was about to resist, when she put her tongue into his mouth, he felt aroused, he touched his dick, it felt hot and hard, at this moment, he wanted Mary more than anything, and there was no way he was going to fight her off.
She began to unbutton his shirt, almost pulling it apart, "Come upstairs with me." Taking him by the hand, she led the way up the narrow dark staircase. They entered the dark room, hastily they began to take off their clothes, as they lay naked on the bed he gently fondled her body.

There was no turning back now, the passion between them was almost unbearable, he had forgotten just how good it could be. It felt like his whole body would explode at any minute, to feel this woman next to him, was sending him wild. He wanted it to go on for ever as they both groaned with pleasure, he jerked up and down, faster and faster on top of her body, then at last he sighed breathlessly, he had come; he lay there motionless. They didn't speak, both lay in each others arms, drifting off into a contented sleep.

He woke to the sound of clinking bottles; the milkman was on his round. He tried to gather his thoughts as he turned to Mary, she was sleeping soundly. He began to panic he felt he should not be there, it was wrong. His thoughts turned to the boys; they had been on their own all night. He asked himself what sort of a father was he, and now he felt despair, and ashamed.

In sheer panic he searched the dark room for his clothes, dressing himself quickly he crept out of the room, tiptoed down the stairs, and gently shut the front door behind him.
On his walk home, he recalled the passion of the night before; she definitely was a wild woman, and an experience he wouldn't forget for a long time.

He entered his house very quietly, he peeped into the boy's bedroom; they were still sleeping; a feeling of relief came over him. He went into the scullery to make himself a cup of tea, and suddenly Harry appeared from nowhere.

He stood innocently looking up at his father, his blonde hair was dishevelled, "You're up early Dad," he said.
John felt happy, he had no explaining to do about the previous night. He ruffled his son's hair, and felt an overwhelming love for his young boy in front of him, after all he was part of his Katy. But at this moment in time, he felt he let her down, he had betrayed her.

He walked across the room to the larder, finding it empty, he asked Harry to go across to the corner shop, to get eggs bacon and bread, and he would cook them all a hearty breakfast. He put a ten shilling note in his hand he told him to hurry.

Harry stood at the counter waiting to be served, he looked around the shop there was were no customers, it was empty. He breathed in the savoury smell of the bacon and cheese. Then he spotted the bars of chocolate on the tray in front of him.
Swiftly he put two bars in his trouser pocket, he felt himself turning hot, with fear as he noticed the shopkeeper busily putting his stock away on the lower shelf behind the counter. He prayed he hadn't been spotted.
A cheery voice poked his head up from behind the counter, "What can I do for you young man?"
Nervously he told the grocer what he wanted, and left the shop in a hurry, with his groceries tucked under his arm. As he ran back to his house he raised his fist towards the sky, feeling happy that he had got away with it again.

John looked across at the dresser, there lay an unopened envelope, picking it up, he knew it was from Ruby, by her small neat handwriting. "When did this come?" "I picked it up off the doormat yesterday," replied Patrick, as he yawned wearily.

John opened the envelope very carefully; he always treated the opening of a letter with the greatest of respect, after all the sender had taken time to put pen to paper.

Ruby's news came as no surprise; she had now become a novice and would soon be leaving Nazareth House Convent and she would now be moving to Saint Vincent Convent at Watford. She hoped they could visit once she had settled. She wrote that the convent had found Biddy a post, as a mother's help, in Chiswick.
This pleased him, it meant he could still keep in contact with Biddy; Chiswick was only a short distance away. She signed off in her usual way, "God bless you."

He put the letter on the dresser, feeling content that the girls, who were now young women, had chosen their paths in life, his concern now was that Harry and Patrick should grow into fine young men.

John spent Saturday afternoon in the back garden, with Harry's help they set to tidying it up.
"You know Harry our summer's coming to an end," he began to break the brown heads off the marigolds. "And what with the talk of war..."

Harry looked up at his father showing concern, his heart began to race, "Please Dad, there won't be a war, will there?"
"I hope not son," he replied, not wanting to worry his son.
Harry carried on putting the dead foliage in the wheelbarrow, feeling bewildered, his mind filled with frightening thoughts. When the gardening was finished, he asked his father if he could go across to the park.
John readily agreed. He looked down at his fair haired little son, his knees and hands were caked with earth from the garden, yes, he thought, he was all you would want a son to be.

Harry wandered along the street, the late afternoon sunshine was hurting his eyes. His thoughts started to run riot in his mind. What if there was a war, soldiers fighting, bombs falling, and what if the whole world was blown apart?

A sudden shiver went through his body. What if he was the only human being left in the whole wide world, and only monsters survived;, who could look after him? Suddenly he stopped in his tracks, he put his hand to his throat, but there would be no one left, he thought, and surely he would die of starvation, or be eaten by the monsters. What would be worse, he asked himself, to be killed by a bomb, or eaten alive? Suddenly he felt sick.

He was only ten years old, he did not want his life to come to a sudden end; it all became too much for him, tears started to well up in his eyes. He reached the gates of the park, and quickly ran across to the drinking fountain. He began splashing; the cold water over his face, soon he started to calm down.

As he looked up, there stood Laura, smiling.
"Hello Harry are you alright? You look very hot."

He ran his fingers through his wet hair, pulling it off his face.
"I have been helping my Dad in the garden." There was no way he was going to admit that his mind was in turmoil over the threat of war.

As they walked across the park together, his thoughts began to lift. He pulled out half a bar of melted chocolate from his pocket and offered it to her.
She tried to pull the silver wrapper off, with a disgusted look on her face." This is horrible, it's all melted, where did this come from?"
He grinned with delight, "I pinched it this morning."
She started to giggle, "Each time I see you, you've pinched something."

He smiled shyly as they sat themselves down on the grass. They sat there, talking away for ages, he looked at her caringly; for some reason he felt safe when he was with her.

Later he lay in the big double bed, which felt empty without his brother and picked up his book from the chair beside him. He started to read, but the dim gaslight proved difficult tonight, his eyes were tired, and the day had seemed long. He closed his eyes, his thoughts were of his new friend Laura.

John woke early, he spent Sunday morning as usual, cooking the boys a breakfast and sending them out to play.
As he began to polish the oil lamp on the dresser, his attention was drawn to the wireless. It was the voice of Neville Chamberlain, strong and clear, in no uncertain terms he was declaring war on Germany. All sorts of emotions ran through his mind.
Then the boys came running in, looking bewildered.
"Dad, Dad, is it true, what people are saying out in the street, that there is going to be a war?"
He put his arms around them, "I'm afraid so."

THE CONVENT

Life soon became much different; shelters started to appear in public places. It was no longer as peaceful; the regular sound of sirens was the thing Harry hated most.

Throughout the war John hadn't got around to visiting Ruby at the convent in Watford, but after receiving a letter from her, inviting him and the boys to a special lunch, he knew he must go. She had informed him in the letter that she was now known as Sister Bernadette. He could hardly believe it, Little Ruby…
John called Harry from his bedroom, he looked at his son standing in front of him, feeling pleased that he was about to make him happy.

"Here you are Harry. I have saved this money and clothing coupons. I want you to go, to the In and Out shop, on the High Street, to get yourself a pair of long trousers. You are almost fourteen, and we are going to visit Ruby at the weekend, I want you and Patrick to look smart. We don't want to let her down, do we? It's a special family lunch, that's being given at the convent."

The delight on Harry's face was a picture. "Oh thanks Dad!"
At last, a pair of long trousers, this would surely impress Laura, he thought.
He made his way to the High Street, on his journey he stopped to think about some of the friends he had not seen for a long time, since the beginning of the war. He had watched them go off to the railway station to be evacuated, with their parcels, just a few belongings and gas masks. The sadness on their faces had never left him.

He walked towards the big store, there were two doors, marked above one was a sign which read 'In' and the other door was marked 'Out'. This was the first time he had been given money to buy his own clothing. Suddenly he felt grown up; after all he would be leaving school soon. He stood there, mesmerised at the well-stocked shop.

The shop was long and narrow, he looked up to the skylight in the roof; there was not a part of the store with any empty space. Hanging from racks, from wall to wall, were prams, toys, clothes household goods, everything you could possibly imagine.

He caught the attention of a grey haired shop assistant and waved his hand to draw her near.
He nervously asked, "Excuse me, can I have a pair of long grey trousers?"

She looked at him with a smile, and took out a tape measure from her pocket. "Come closer son, let me measure you."
He felt his cheeks turn hot, and he was hoping his embarrassment didn't show, as she put the tape measure along the inside of his leg. She told him to step behind the screen to try the trousers on.
He looked down at his long dangly legs, yes he felt good in them, he rubbed his hands together with delight.
He gave her his clothing coupons and money, and looked at her kind face as she replied, "I will get them wrapped for you."

He looked to his side; there stacked high was a pile of shoe boxes. If only he had enough money for new shoes he thought, they would really finish off his outfit.
Hurriedly he began lifting the lids off several boxes, finally came to size eights, and he quickly tried them on. They shone so much he could almost see his face in them.

Gingerly he looked along to the end of the shop; the lady was still busy wrapping his trousers. He watched her pull the crisp brown paper from the giant roll attached to the counter. Quickly he stuffed his old worn shoes under a pile of boxes, and put the new ones on, and then he nervously looked around to make sure no one saw what he had done.

As he approached his house he started to think of an excuse to give his father; he would certainly notice the new shoes he thought. Yes he would have to think of something quick.
He was about to get the key from inside the letterbox when he looked across the road to the house directly opposite, there sat Edie Wallace at her window. She sat there most days, watching the world go by. He gave her a wave as he often did, a smile came to his face, Oh yes that's it, he thought; he had now found his excuse.

John walked in, after a a long day at work. Harry eagerly showed him his new trousers, but he wasn't going to give his father chance to question him.

"Oh and guess what Dad, I was just coming in when Edie called me and gave me these shoes," he stared down at his feet.
"But they are new son," replied John, as he looked at the highly polished black shoes.
"I know Dad, she said they once belonged to her father, but he died, before he got to wear them."
"That was kind of her son; I must thank her when I see her next."
He kept his fingers crossed behind his back.
"No, no, she didn't want no thanks for them, she just said she was pleased they could do me a good turn."

Early on Saturday morning John shouted for the boys to get dressed, after the usual bickering between the two boys, Harry walked into the parlour. John looked at him with pride, this tall youth was his and Katy's son, how he wished she could see him now.

After getting to the train station, they looked around, at soldiers and sailors, standing about the dismal steamy station, most with rifles and kit bags.
As they wheedled their way through the mayhem and boarded the train, Harry looked out of the window, catching sight of the derelict and bombed buildings.
"Do you think people died there Dad?"
"Well if they didn't die, it's possible they were injured."
He didn't see the point of making excuses. The world was at war, nothing was going to change that for the time being.

Harry sat in silence for a while, thinking frightening thoughts of war. The thought of people, lying under piles of bricks, trapped, screaming out for help, and little helpless children, wanting their mums and dads, with no one coming to find them. He couldn't bear to think what it would be like.
Sweat started to run down his forehead, his hands became clammy, he jumped up, pulling down the window. He needed to breathe in air, the smell of the steam and soot from the engine made him feel faint.
Then suddenly he vomited onto the track. As he turned his head back into the train, he saw a blurred outline of his father.
He heard an echoing faint voice, "Are you alright Harry?"
"Yes Dad I came over very strange, it must be the jogging of the train."

Finally they arrived at Watford station, and departed from the train, John eventually got the attention of a porter. Eagerly he showed him the hand-drawn map that Ruby had sent him.
"Can you tell me how to get to Cherry Tree Passage?"
The porter took the map and studied it.

"Of course sir, when you, come out of the station, turn right, about ten yards down the road you will come to the White Horse Inn then you turn left into Cherry Tree Passage."
He thanked him then set about the last stage of the journey.

They turned into Cherry Tree Passage, and briskly walked along the long narrow road, the cherry trees on both sides were in full blossom, reaching across the passage making it almost impossible to see the sky. They came to the end of the passage; suddenly they were hit by bright daylight from the bold sunshine. Here they entered a small cobbled square, in front of them were two big wooden gates, with a wicket gate to let in visitors, either side was a high brick wall.
A big bell hung at the side of the gate, a sign read, 'Please ring for attention'.

John's breath was taken away by the beautiful scene that greeted them, as he looked across at a field of daffodils and irises. The only sound to be heard was the twittering of the birds, the instant calmness put him at peace.

He rang the bell, the small door opened; there stood an old nun with a sullen heavily-lined face.
"Good afternoon, are you here to visit?"
"Yes," replied John, "We have come to see Sister Bernadette Steele."
She beckoned them in, "Come follow me."
She opened the big oak door, and in front of them stretched a long panelled hallway, with a highly polished floor.

As they walked along the hallway Harry was aware that his new leather shoes were clicking loudly on the highly polished floor.
Then he caught sight of a picture that hung on the wall, it was of the Virgin Mary, her eyes appeared to be looking straight at him. He felt his body go rigid, he was transfixed, and it was as if his whole body had gone numb.

Oh no, he thought, as panic came over him, did she know he stole the shoes? His imagination, began to run riot as usual. What if all the nuns knew, what he'd been up to, and what if God had been watching over him? Surely he would be given some sort of punishment. Perhaps this was all meant to be; yes, he had committed a crime by stealing the shoes. As he looked up at the picture of the Virgin Mary, he looked into her eyes, silently begging forgiveness and promising himself that he would never steal again.

They had just entered the reception room when Ruby walked graciously in, she made her way straight to John, and looked at him lovingly.
"Oh Dad, how are you?" she whispered.
"I'm fine Ruby, just fine," he replied, as a lump appeared in his throat.

He really wanted to burst into tears, as he cast his eyes over her.
Her body was covered in the long black gown, this emphasised the beauty of her face, her pale skin looked fresh and he could see his Katy, that same beauty, now in her daughter.
He wanted the lump to leave his throat, he felt overwhelmed with emotion; he hadn't prepared himself for this.

A bell rang, Ruby informed them that it was calling them for lunch. They were about to walk into the dining hall when Ruby whispered in Harry's ear, "You look very smart, you must have been up all night polishing those shoes."
He felt a gush of panic come over him.
He looked across at the long table situated in the middle of the room, there sat a group of nuns. Ruby led them to a smaller table in the corner of the big room that was set aside for visitors. The crisp white tablecloth and highly polished cutlery looked perfect, in the middle stood a water jug.

Harry was feeling nervous, he wasn't sure how to conduct himself, Patrick sat with his head bowed, with the fear of looking up, and the big room frightened him. Ruby looked across at them, she wanted to put them at ease, so she put her hands together and smiled.
"We will say prayers, before we eat."
They all put their hands together, and remained silent as Ruby said the prayer, they were unsure what to do next. They waited for Ruby to lead the way, she looked across at the boys, with a glint in her eyes.

They had never sat at a table laid so perfect; it was all new to them.
Once the food was served, the conversion began to flow; John and Ruby spoke of the war, and Ruby's life in the convent. She asked Harry how he was getting on at school and when he told her that English was his favourite subject, she smiled.

"Well we have got something in common," she said happily. Very proudly she told them that she had passed her degree in English.
John felt a tear in his eye, somehow he didn't feel quite so bad about sending her away all those years ago, knowing that she had done well and was happy in her chosen path.

Patrick glanced over at Ruby, their eyes met, he was feeling irritated, no one seem to be taking any notice of him. Ruby sensed how he was feeling, she stretched across the table and touched his hand.
"And you little Patrick, what have you been doing with yourself?"
He looked at her shyly. "Well I like playing football, I don't like school, and I don't like the war."
She chuckled, "Well you know Patrick; you will have to pray each night, that we all come through the war safely."

After the meal, they went out for a walk in the beautiful gardens that surrounded the convent; they came to rest on a bench and reminisced of times gone by, then came an unexpected chime of a bell.
Ruby looked apologetic. "I'm sorry, it is time for prayers, in the chapel, I will have to say goodbye."

John felt the lump reappear in his throat as they each in turn said their goodbyes. John turned to watch Ruby walk back alone, into the big old house, thinking to himself he loved her like she was his own daughter. Katy's daughters had always been a reminder, of his beloved wife, and he knew it would be a long time, before they met again.

Spring was leading into summer; Harry knew the time was drawing near for him to leave school. His father thought he should start thinking about a career. He didn't want him to spend his life working on a building site as a carpenter like he had done all these years, he wanted more for him.

Bombs were raining down on England, causing death and fear, as people went about their daily lives. He could not even think about what he wanted to do with his life, he was only just fourteen, as far as he was concerned he might die tomorrow.

Harry woke to a hot July morning, knowing this would be his last day at school. He walked up the hill with his friend Jimmy, feeling uncertain about his future; he had no job to start, and his father hoped he would take a job as an office clerk. He knew this was not for him, but he also knew that he had to earn his keep, money was tight.

In school that day the feeling was lighthearted. It was the end of term for some, and others like Harry were about to go into the big wide world. He sat in his last English lesson, hoping to finish the book that Mr Hearn had given him to read; he was beginning to feel agitated for he had another twenty pages to go and he knew the bell would ring at any minute.

Feeling a presence at his side he looked up, there stood Mr Hearn looking down at him.
"Don't worry Harry, I was about to tell you to keep the book, it belongs to me, I would like you to have it as a leaving present. I know if anyone is going to cherish a book, it will be you."

Harry breathed a sigh of relief, he had loved this book from the very beginning, he remembered reading the first line: "A little boy David Scott Herries, lay in a huge canopied bed".

He stood up and thanked him, holding the green leather-covered book close to his heart. He slowly ran his fingers over it, he always loved to get the feel of a book, to him someone's mind was between the covers. With now a feeling of sadness in his heart, he shook Mr Hearn's hand and walked out of the classroom for the last time.

He walked home feeling deflated, his school days were now over, what would life have in store for him? Entering the empty house he went straight into the bedroom, putting the book on the chair at the side of his bed he pondered what to do next. He decided that he would read his book later, when he felt in a better frame of mind.

He walked into the scullery, and cut himself a slice of bread and dripping, opening the back door, the hot sun beckoned him outside. He sat on an upturned bucket and took off his shirt, the hot sun hit the back of his neck, closing his eyes.

He thought of Laura. She had been his friend for a long time, but lately his feelings were growing much stronger, in a different way. Her body was taking on a whole new shape, and when he stood close to her, he wanted to be even closer, his stomach churned, and there had been times when he wanted to put his hands on her breast.
Opening his eyes to the bright sun, he thought surely this could only be something that dreams were made of.

He started feeling bored with his own company and decided to go and knock up Jimmy. He was just about to knock, when Jimmy's sister Sally opened the door, she greeted him with a bright cheery voice, "Hold on Harry, I will give him a shout."
Jimmy appeared his usual ragged self, Harry leaned his tall slender body against the porch wall.

The two young boys walked up the hill heading towards the market-place. The streets were busy; the women were finishing their long day at the laundries. The smell of the soap suds were in the air, it was much

stronger on hot summers days; a smell that they had grown up with.
They walked along in the early evening sunshine, talking about the future. Jim, like Harry, was unsure what to with his life. He didn't have a bright brain like Harry; he knew he was limited, whereas Harry had a choice, he had always been the clever one at school.

He looked across at him, as he scratched his head. "How comes you know everything 'H'?"
Harry began to laugh, "I don't, I just read lots of books, who knows I might be a professor or a brain surgeon one day."

Heading back to South Acton, they walked along the lane, dusk was coming in. They were about to walk past the chocolate factory, Harry looked up at the dreary building.
He noticed the upstairs side window open slightly, grabbing Jims arm he pointed up. "Look Jim what do ya think, shall we go in?"
Not even bothering to answer him, Jim leaped over the wall, Harry followed with the same eagerness, trying to be as quiet as possible.

They then decided what their next move should be, Harry was first to climb onto a parked van, wedged close to the wall, and from there he leaped to the drainpipe. In seconds his long dangling legs had got him to the top window, he began to open it up a bit more and he swiftly got himself inside. Jim had one last look to make sure it was safe for him to make his move; he followed him up.

Once inside, they looked round the big room that appeared to be very dark. It took time to acclimatise, the sunset reflected in to the room, helping them to find their bearings. The long benches were stacked with cartons of chocolates, a conveyor belt was positioned to one side, this dominated the room.

Harry gingerly felt his way around, at first he thought he was seeing things, but no, he wasn't mistaken, there were mice running around everywhere.

He nudged Jims arm in panic, and blurted out, "Shit this place is alive with mice, for fuck's sake lets get out of here quick."
Jim began to laughed, "Surely you're not frightened of a few little mice? We'e got loads running around our house, they aint gonna hurt ya 'H'."

They carried on working their way around the building, tiptoeing so as not make a noise, they came to a dark stone staircase, as they spoke their voices echoed, and it was very dark. Slowly they made their way to a door on their right, turning the handle slowly, Jim lead the way in.

He started to open several cupboard doors, but found nothing of interest.

Harry walked over to a desk, pulling the draws open one by one, he was feeling agitated, as he got to the bottom drawer he put his hand on a small tin box.

He took it out shook it, there was definitely something inside, he called Jim to his side and shook the tin, "How can we open this?"

Jim went off in search of a tool to open it; he came across a cupboard with brooms and buckets inside. On a shelf above was a small tool box, he eventually found a screwdriver and went back to Harry. He waved it in front of him "Will this do?"

Harry showed signs of nervousness, "It better, it might make us rich."
He put the screwdriver into the small keyhole and began jiggling it around, finally the lock sprang open. He took the contents out, there were two keys, and some money. He felt like his heart racing, he couldn't believe what he was seeing.

"Look Jim, just look at all this money."
He counted it out on the desk, his hand started to shake with excitement.
"How much is there?" asked Jim.
"Eight pounds, five and six," he said excitedly.
Jim jumped up and down, "We are rich!"

Neither of them had ever seen so much money, and Harry swiftly put it in his pocket.
Harry tugged at Jim. "Let's get out of here."
Feeling more than happy with what they had got, they would share it out later. Jim pointed upwards. "Hold on, why don't we go back upstairs and take a couple of those big cartons of chocolates?"
"Don't be silly Jim, if we are seen with them, it will be obvious that we broke in here."

Jim walked towards the window, "Look 'H' we can go out the back way and get onto the railway embankment, we can run along there, and come off facing Stirling Road."
Harry appeared bewildered.
Jim began to explain, "Well it's like this 'H' my uncle takes all the stuff he nicks, to May King, she buys it from him and sells it at a profit."

They went back into the room full with chocolates and picked up a big box each. Then they made their way to the back of the building to search for a way out. The first door they came to was locked with a

padlock, they walked further along the dark corridor and found another door, this had two big rusty old bolts.
They struggled fiercely to undo them, and slowly it, then looking around them carefully making sure it was clear, they left the building, and ran up the railway embankment.

They darted across the road with the boxes and their heads bowed down. Eagerly they ran straight to May's door, giving it a loud knock.
A voice came from inside, "Who the bloody hell is knocking, at this time of night, its bleeding ten o'clock."

The door opened, in the dark passage stood a woman with white blond hair. "What do you two want, at this fucking time of night?"
Jim stepped forward. "We have got two cartons of chocolates, do ya want to buy them off us May?"
"Well how much do you want for them?"
Jim keen to get rid of them almost tossed the box in her face. "We'll take eight bob."

She stood firmly, with her hands on her hips.
"You must be kidding; I will give you four bob for them, and not a penny more."
"Wait there I will go and get your money for ya."
She then put the money into Jim's hand. Keep this quiet, I don't want no bloody coppers around ere, do ya understand?"
"Yeah, yeah we promise," they answered, and walked away sheepishly.

Harry and Jim made their way back home, the twilight evening was still very warm, and they walked along the back alleys. As they approached, the Victory Pub, the sound of the piano with voices singing war time songs echoed along the street. He pushed Jim playfully, "Come on, race ya home."

They headed into Park Road, and were still in a happy frame of mind. When they got to his house, Harry put his hand in his pocket and pulled out the notes.
"Here you are Jim." He handed him four pound notes, "We can sort out the rest tomorrow."
Jim took the money with delight, reminding him that they must keep their mouths shut; they didn't want to get in trouble with the coppers, or May, come to that.

DOWN SOUTH

Patrick lay sleeping soundly as Harry entered the hot stuffy room. He went to the window, opening it wide, and put his head out he looked up to the sky, there were thousands of stars. He remembered lying in bed, when he was a small boy, his father telling him that if ever you saw a shooting star to make a wish, oh how he wished to see a shooting star tonight.
He closed his eyes tight; his wish would be to kiss Laura; yes he must get to see her soon, he thought to himself.

He began take his off clothes, and looked at the book that Mr Hearn had given him earlier; he would finish reading it tomorrow. He reflected on the day, it had been his last day at school, and he had now done a burglary as well.
It was certainly something he didn't set out to do. His intentions had been to go for a walk, but he had no regrets, as he carefully counted the money one more time, it had all been worth it. He stuffed the money into his sock and then put the sock into his shoe.

John put his head around the bedroom door.
"Come on Harry, get yourself out of that bed, it's seven o'clock, you know you have got to get out and look for work."
"Alright Dad," he replied as he stifled a yawn.
He then heard the front door close, his father had left for work; he had no intention of going looking for a job, he had plenty of money, thanks to last nights burglary. As he pulled the bed covers over his head he felt snug and warm as he put his head deep into the pillow, and then dozed back off to sleep.

The midday sunshine was very hot. He took his book and went to sit in the back yard, determined to finish it, as he read on, he was living the part of David Harries, and his mind had been taken over completely. He finally reached the last page and he felt sad, as he always did, he could never understand why; he always became so attached to the books he read. Forcing himself out of his lazy mood, he thought he should at least make it look like he had left the house to look for work.

He turned into Park Road North, the street was busy, the young women were sitting on the outside wall of the laundry, it was tea break for them. He could hear their giggles, and felt himself tense up.

He never did like walking past them, for more often than not, they would shout out cheeky remarks as he passed.
His attention was then taken by Jim, frantically, waving from the other side of the street, he was sitting on the front wall outside his house, so he crossed the road, and walked towards him.
"What have you been up to?" asked Jim.
"Oh I felt a bit bored, I went for a walk, and then I ended up at the book shop, and got these books."
He was just about to take them out to show him, but Jim appeared disinterested.

Harry looked around sheepishly. "I have got the rest of your money here."
"How much is it?" Jim asked, already holding out his hand.
"Four and nine pence."
"Do you fancy doing it again some time?" said Jim as he stuck out his shoulders with bravado.
"Anytime you want, I'm always keen."

He eventually got a job as a laundry van boy; he didn't like it very much, with winter now upon them, getting up early on cold winter mornings was hard. He would often look at Patrick still snuggled up in bed, wishing it was him. He was now wishing he had listened to his father; the only bonus was that Laura worked in the laundry.
Sometimes he would catch a glimpse of her, in her white overall and hat; to him she looked beautiful in whatever she wore. He was almost sure that she had strong feelings for him; their friendship had lasted a long time; he could tell her anything, he trusted her with all his heart.

Throughout December it snowed almost every day. With only just over a week to Christmas, his dull job was brightened up by the amount of tips he was getting on his laundry round.
The big houses at Ealing Common were owned by very wealthy people. Even though he was grateful, it didn't compare to the money that Jim and himself got from the chocolate factory. He stood and looked at the big houses surrounding the snow-covered common, and assured himself that one day he would own a house like this. He found himself day-dreaming, then a growling voice shouted, "Move your bleeding arse, get in this soddin van, we've got work to do!"
He looked nervously at the old van driver, and detected a smile on his weather-beaten face.

Christmas morning, Patrick woke early, tugging the collar of Harry's pajamas. "Come on, get up lazy bones," he said cheerily.
Harry sat up rubbing his eyes. Patrick pulled a pair of socks wrapped in brown paper from under the bed. "Let's go and give them to Dad."

John had lit a roaring fire, Patrick walked over to him and handed him the present. "Here you are Dad. this is from me and Harry."
He smiled lovingly at his sons, and handed them each a gift.
"I hope you like them."
Harry smiled happily, he opened the small box, in it was a secondhand fountain pen, and he laid it in the palm of his hand to study it.
"Thanks Dad, it's just what I wanted."
It was the first time he had ever owned his own pen. Patrick hastily opened the tatty looking box, to his surprise, it was full of an assortment of meccano, and this was just what he wanted.

After breakfast John made himself busy, and went into the scullery to stuff the chicken, then he gave Harry the chore of peeling the vegetables. Christmas was now never treated with too much fuss.
He remembered back to the days when Katy was alive, when all the family sat round the big table, those were the days, he thought to himself. Katy and the elder girls would prepare the dinner, and the younger ones would play on the floor with their toys. Sadly he rubbed a tear from his eye. Oh they were lovely memories, he thought.

A gentle knock came on the parlour door, as he was laying the table; a voice came from the other side, "Mr Creedy it's me, Mrs Masters."
He opened the door, it was the first time he had seen her without her apron on, and she stood looking very smart in a plain navy dress.
"I have made you a Christmas pudding; I thought you and the boys might like it."
"Oh come in Mrs Masters, why don't you."

She stood there with a look of self satisfaction, as she looked down at the perfect-looking pudding.
"Mr Creedy, I'd like to wish Merry Christmas to you and your family."
He took the large pudding from her, delight showing in his face.
"Why don't you stay and have a small whisky with me Mrs Masters, you know you are most welcome."
She showed surprise, "Well thank you Mr Creedy, I don't mind if I do."
He went over to the dresser, taking a small bottle of whisky out, he poured one for himself and one Mrs Masters, as he handed it to her she smiled, "Do you know I have never had whisky before."
"Oh it will definitely warm you up Mrs Masters, you just wait and see, you will feel like you are on fire."

Harry looked across at his father, daring to ask, "Can I have one Dad?" He smiled, "Oh just a small one for you and Patrick, it is Christmas after all."

Mrs Masters sat facing the fire, her chubby cheeks started to look very flushed, as she sipped away steadily at her whisky. The alcohol seemed to be taking an affect on her; all of a sudden she didn't want to stop talking. It was like she had gained Dutch courage; John could hardly get a word in.

Then suddenly Patrick looked across at the door he couldn't believe his eyes, smoke was seeping through, quickly he jumped up, and shouted, "Fire, Fire!"
John ran to the door, to be greeted by a smoke-filled passageway. He waved his arms frantically, as if to edge it away.

A loud deep voice came howling down the stairs.
"Emily get yourself up here at once, the bleeding dinner is burnt to cinders, and Christmas is ruined for us. The one bloody day of the year when we get something decent to eat, and now it's ruined for us."
Mrs Masters jumped up in a panic.
"Oh dear oh dear, please excuse me, Mr Creedy, it seems there is a problem upstairs, I only have to turn my back for a minute, and something goes wrong."

She walked off disappearing through the black smoke. John hastily went to the front door to open it, letting the smoke out. He walked back into the room, Harry and Patrick were rolling around the floor laughing.
John gave a wink, as he thought, that was what Christmas was all about - a little bit of fun.

His father gave a loud snore, waking himself up. Patrick looked across at Harry imitating their father, they both laughed. John looked on, unaware what was going on around him, he appeared dazed, asked Patrick to go and make a cup of tea, and then glanced at the clock on the mantelpiece.
"Surely I haven't slept all that time?" he said with surprise.
He licked his dry lips; he knew he had drunk too much whisky at lunchtime.

Harry was feeling bored, and walked out to the front door to breathe in some fresh air. The bright moon shone on the frosted rooftops of the houses opposite. He looked up the hill, the thick ice on the road and pavement appeared like a giant wave about to roll down on him.

He rubbed his hands up and down his body, as he started to shiver, how cold he felt, then his attention was taken by the outline shadow in the upstairs window of Edie's house. He gazed across, there she was standing at the window, as she was every night of the year, just watching the world go by.

Christmas was now long forgotten; the thick January snow lay on the ground. Harry began to dislike his job even more; jumping in and out of a van, tramping through the thick snow, it all became to much to bear.

He left the house, he looked up at the sky, it was a glaze of red; he wondered if this was the affects of last night's bombing. In the air was a mist of dust; he ran his tongue along his lips, he felt he could almost bite the thick dust.

He walked into the laundry yard; the vans were lined up for a busy day's work, and his driver hadn't arrived yet; this gave him the chance to look for Laura. He walked into the warmth of the laundry. There she was standing at the press; he eventually got her attention and called her over, she ran towards him, looking flustered.

"What's up Harry? You'll get me the sack."
He had a shy smile on his face, he looked at her caringly and thought dare he ask her? Then he blurted it out. "Meet me tonight Laura."
In a hurry to get back she readily agreed. "Alright, what time?" she shouted out eagerly.
"Seven o'clock," he replied. "I will be waiting outside All Saints Church for ya."
With a beaming smile on her face, she ran back to her work.

He took special care with his wash and brush up, he was about to leave the house when John came through the door.
"Where are you off to son?"
"Oh Dad, I'm popping up to see Jim."
"Well wrap up warm, the snow is coming down heavy again."

The street lay covered by a thick blanket of snow, the sound of people's voices, still making their way home after work, gave life to the otherwise bleak surroundings. His stomach started to churn as he approached the church - there was no sign of Laura. Nervously he stood on the corner waiting, rubbing his hands together. He feet were turning numb; as he put his hand in his pocket he could only just feel the ten shilling note that he had took from the tin under his bed. Tonight he wanted to impress her; she might want to go to the pictures he thought.

Then he heard the sound of footsteps crunching in the crisp snow; it was Laura heading towards him. He could just about see her face; her beret was pulled down to protect her from the snow.
For some reason, tonight he felt edgy; he wasn't thinking of Laura as his childhood friend, she was now a girl, who he had completely different kinds of feelings for.

"Do ya wanna go to the pictures," he asked, wanting to please her.
She seemed uncomfortable, as if she didn't know how to reply.

He rested his arm gently on her shoulder, "Don't worry; if you don't want to, we can do whatever you want, I can afford it, I have still got money left from the burglary at the chocolate factory."
She laughed. "But that was ages ago."
"I know, but May told us not to draw attention to ourselves, so I tried not to splash it about."

She put her hand in his, "Let's just walk Harry."
They made their way up to the High Street as they laughed and joked, forgetting all about the bad weather. Before they knew it they were at Ealing Common. Laura let go of his hand and went running across the common, and then with an action as if she was about to take off and ski, she shouted, "Come on Harry lets have some fun!"

He rolled a giant snowball and threw it at her, running towards her, laughing, awkwardly he slipped.
She began to giggle, "You just wait," she said, with excitement in her voice.
She sat astride his back and rubbed his face in the snow. Their laughter echoed around the common, as he rolled on to his back pulling her towards him. He kissed her on the lips for the first time, she felt no surprise at this, she had been waiting for this kiss for a long, long, time.

In spite of the harsh cold weather, she felt her body take on a warm glow, finally they separated he pulled her on to her feet and was now beginning to feel, he had done wrong. He carried on walking in silence, as she glanced up at him.
What was it that made her like him so much? He wasn't what she called handsome, he was tall, perhaps a little too thin, and the spots on his face didn't do him justice, but nevertheless, she liked him, because he was different from the rest of the boys. He was daring and exciting.

She grabbed his hand. "Look at those lovely big houses Harry, I would love to go in one, just to see how the rich live."

"Come on then that's what we will do, " he said happily.
"Don't be silly, how are we going to do that?"
"Easy," he replied "just watch."

Because of the darkness of the war-time blackout, he didn't see this as a problem. She reassured herself, yes this is what she liked about him; he always wanted to please her.

Walking from the Common they headed towards a wide tree-lined street. He seemed to know exactly where they were going, he stopped suddenly, "Wait here I won't be a minute."

She began to feel a little scared, and begged him to be careful.

"Don't worry, this house is on my laundry round, I delivered here last week. The lady told me they were closing the house up for the rest of the winter; they were going away on business."

He walked up the stone steps to the front door, and then knocked on the door, to double-check the house was empty. Carefully he leaned over to look in the big bay window, as he peered in he could just about see the white sheets covering the furniture in the darkness.
He walked back to Laura. "Come on, we'll get in round the back."

Treading carefully around the side alleyway, she held onto his hand, feeling nervous and excited. Harry looked around; he found a small pile of house bricks poking out of the snow. As he picked one up; he gently put it through the small pane of glass near the back door handle. Slowly he put his hand through and lifted the latch on the inside.

Once in the house they found themselves in very dark surroundings. They moved slowly, she hung onto his jacket, as they made their way from the kitchen to the hallway. She took off her beret and banged it against the wall to shake off the snow.

"We will have to find a torch," Harry whispered, looking about. Finally he came to a cupboard under the stairs; he bent down and crawled in. Carefully feeling along the shelf, he touched different objects, but no torch.

He was about to give up, when he put his hand into a box, at last yes, he had found a torch and hoped it would work. He stretched his arms out, and accidentally put his hand on Laura's leg as he came out of cupboard. This sent a tingle over her body.

He touched her arm. "Look I found one."
Thank God, thought Laura, it was pitch black and unfamiliar; she felt very scared, as he took her hand.
"I will have to be careful, an air raid warden might go by, and if he sees the light of the torch we've had it."

Shining the torch downwards they moved along the passage, finally reaching a door, they slowly opened it. The creaking sound made them both jump; he poked his head around it, all he could see was the white sheets, covering the furniture.

"Let's go upstairs," said Laura, hesitantly.

They crept up the winding staircase; she was now feeling more confident. As she opened a door, the moon shone bright through the window, it gave enough light for them to find their bearings.
"Look Harry look, I have never seen such a big bedroom."

This room hadn't been covered with sheets; the big bed looked warm and cosy, sitting herself down on it she bounced up and down.
"They must be so rich."

He gazed at her lovingly. He walked over to the bed, and sat down. He pulled off his shoes, then taking off his damp socks he rubbed his feet to get some life back into them.

She began to giggle. "You're making yourself at home."
He smiled, "Well I'm going to have a house like this one day. You just wait and see."
She closed her eyes and secretly wished that if he did ever get a big house she would be sharing it with him.
"Why don't you take your coat off, and let it dry out a bit? You must be really wet from all that snow we got covered in."

As she hung her coat over a chair, she stood in front of the window. The light from the moon outlined her beautiful body, she turned to him. "Give me a cuddle Harry, I feel cold now."

He stretched his arms out and pulled her towards him, with the warmth of his body she snuggled in closer. Their cheeks met, he kissed her gently on the lips, his warm breath went deep inside her body. She felt like her stomach was doing flip flops, he slowly pushed her back laying himself on top of her. Kicking off her shoes she stretched out her legs.

She felt the hardness of his dick pressing against her. He struggled to undo her blouse, she made no attempt to stop him. He touched her small pert breast. He lowered his head to kiss her nipples. She put her hands behind her waist and unbuttoned her skirt, as she awkwardly wriggled out of it he pulled down her knickers and rubbed his hand over her pubic hair.

Moving his hand inbetween her legs, he felt how moist she was. He put his finger inside her, and she moved her body vigorously, not being able to hold on a moment longer. He put his dick inside her, as Laura cried out with pleasure he pulled away, her heart was still pounding as he kissed her gently.

"I'm sorry Laura."
"Don't be," she replied, "I knew it would happen one day."

She put her hand down to her legs and felt the warm thick liquid running down her thighs; she knew it shouldn't have happened but it did, and she didn't care one bit, she wanted to love him forever and ever, putting her head on his chest she felt very happy.

She suddenly became more aware of the fact that they had broken into the house. Laura began to giggle, "What if we had got caught, just then? It would have been a shock for the owners finding us in their bed."

This suddenly brought him to his senses. "Come on we had better get out of here."

Once they were dressed he pulled her close and gave her one more kiss, before they made their way down the stairs.
She stood there, not wanting to leave. "Oh Harry let's have one more look in the big room."

Ducking down with the torch they entered the room, slowly they lifted the sheets to see what was underneath. They started quickly opening the drawers of the big sideboard.
Frantically he began to search; he came across a silver cigarette box. He opened it, inside was full of cigarettes, and he sifted through, and came across a small jewellery box. Gradually a pile mounted up on the floor as Laura added some small ornaments.

"What we are going to do with all this?" she asked.
"We will take it to May; she will buy it off us."

He look across the room and spotted a violin case propped in the corner. He crawled along the floor, and took the violin out of the case. Laura began to load it with their stolen goods. Just then a beam of light appeared through the window.

"Quick get down out of sight! I think there is someone outside," warned Harry.

They crouched behind the sofa, a voice shouted out, "Is there anybody in there?"

Harry peeped over the top of the sofa, there was a man's face pressed firmly against the window. He grabbed Laura's arm.
 "We have got to get out quick; I think it's the air raid warden checking on the houses."

They made their way out through the back entrance, and slid the violin case along the floor behind them. They tried desperately hard not to make any noise. They crept along the side alley, gingerly looking around to the front of the house, saw the warden was still peering through the window.
He whispered in Laura's ear, "We will have to make a run for it."

Dragging the case as fast as they could behind them, they bolted past the warden. The warden turned around, just catching a glimpse of them, out of the corner of his eye.
He shouted loudly, "Come here you little bastards, you won't get far in this snow."

Harry turned to look back, just catching sight of the warden trying desperately to make chase, but slipping in the snow.
Laura held onto Harry, she turned, shouting back to him,
"Oh piss off, you old sod, you will never catch us."

As they ran across the common, the warden was still shouting in the distance. They began to laugh; he had no chance of catching them now. They headed towards Acton, their mood becoming more relaxed the further away they got.

Harry put his arm lovingly around her, as if to protect her.
"What a night, who would have thought it would end like this."
Laura smiled as she snuggled into him. "What's going to happen now?"
"I will take the case home for tonight, come on I will walk you to your street."

He kissed her on the lips, her cold nose pressed against him. He didn't want to leave her, but he knew he must get home quick, before he was stopped by the police. He watched her walk to her door, knowing she was now safe. The flurries of snow hit his face as he walked back along the dark silent streets.

He approached his house; he knew he had to find a way of sneaking past his father with the violin case; it wasn't going to be easy. Quietly he pulled the key from inside the letterbox, then from nowhere, a hand touched him on the shoulder; he felt his heart beat faster.

Then there was a deep voice saying, "What have we got here then?"

As he turned his head he was more than shocked to see a well-built policeman, standing only inches away from him. He found it difficult to make the words come out of his mouth, his legs began to tremble.

"It's a violin; I have been to practice at the town hall."
"Well it's cold out here son, you'd better invite me in to see how well you play it," said the policeman in a rather sarcastic tone of voice.

John woke from a deep sleep. Feeling cold he went to stoke the fire, he heard the sound of voices coming from outside, then a knock on the door.

"Who could that be, at this time of night?" he mumbled. Looking at the clock, it was half past ten, just gone, slowly he opened the door.
"Sorry to disturb you this time of night sir, I need to talk to this young man."
"Well you'd better come in, there's a draught coming through, with the door open."

Still not fully awake, he tried to make sense of seeing Harry with the violin case, and a policeman at his side.
"Well what's it all about?" asked John.
"There has been a burglary reported at Ealing Common tonight sir, the warden saw two young people run away from the scene."
"Oh, so what makes you think it's my boy?"
"Well sir, he reported seeing them dragging along something that looked like a violin case. What's your name son?"
"Harry."
"Well Harry, I think you had better show us what's inside that case."
Harry laid it on the floor and opened it up. John stood and looked on in disbelief.

"Well son," said the policeman with a smug look. "Where did you get this lot from?"

Trying to hide the guilt that he was feeling, Harry replied that he had found it near the railway station.
John butted in, "I think you're wasting your time here officer, my boy has never been in any trouble before."
"Well sir there is always a first time," said the policeman, determined to prove himself right.

Harry stared at the floor, afraid to look his father in the face.

"Answer me this son, who was the other person with you? The warden said he made chase across the Common and there were two sets of fresh footprints in the snow."

He stood there bewildered; there was no way he was going to bring Laura into this. He had to think quickly. He knew he wasn't going to get out of it.
Taking a deep breath, he blurted out, "Alright it was me, but I was by myself."
"Ha, now we are getting somewhere," said the policeman indignantly.

John stood silent, trying to come to terms with Harry's admission.

The policeman took out his pencil and notebook.
"Right son, I will just take your name and address for tonight. I must ask you to come to the police station, tomorrow morning at nine o'clock. I will take this lot with me so it can be used as evidence. Then eventually, returned to the rightful owner."

John, eager to see him leave, said, "I will show you to the door."
He walked back into the room; with anger showing in his face, he turned to Harry, in an abrupt voice he said, "How long has this been going on?"
Harry could see only too well how hurt his father was, "It's the first time Dad, honest."

TEENAGE YEARS

Harry walked into the station, nervously giving his name to the desk sergeant. He was then escorted into a room by a policeman with a weasel-looking face.

John was told to wait in the corridor. He looked up at the clock on the wall continually. It was all becoming too much to bear, and he began pacing up and down.
A feeling of anxiousness came over him as he walked back to the desk, and asked the sergeant what was happening to his son.
In an abrupt tone he replied, "We are trying to sort out a hearing at the Juvenile Court."

He felt his heart sink; never did he think the day would come when his boy would end up in court.

Harry finally reappeared, and John detected a tear running down his cheek. "Well son what is it, what's going to happen?"
"I have to appear in court on Friday morning at ten o'clock. Dad, you have to go in, they want to have a word with you, they want to know a bit more about me."

Trying to put on a brave front, inside John was feeling very edgy; he tried to condition himself to act as normal as possible. There was no getting away from it, yes he was angry with Harry about the whole sorry episode, but at the end of the day he was his son, and he was ready to stand by him.

He picked up a bag from the corner, and handed it to Harry, in it was a grey tweed jacket, waiting to see the expression on his face.
"I stopped off at the second-hand shop, you know the little one on the corner before the railway bridge? I hope it fits, it's good quality and I thought you could wear my new white shirt. You should look fine."
He smiled tenderly as he looked across at his son. "There is nothing like setting a good impression, well that's what my Father always told me."

Harry dragged in the old bath. Often an argument would break out on bath night, about who was going to get in first, but tonight he really couldn't be bothered, he would patiently wait his turn. Patrick helped him to fill the saucepans with water then carefully put them on the gas stove, before long the little scullery soon began to warm up.

John looked at the boys with a wide grin on his face, trying to bring a little bit of fun into the uneasy atmosphere.

"Right we will toss for it, heads or tails, who gets in that bath first."
As he flicked the penny into the air, Patrick shouted, "Heads!"
John looked at the coin on the back of his hand.
"Well it looks like you win, and I have no other takers."

Patrick hurriedly started throwing his clothes on the floor, as far as he was concerned to be first in was a great privilege, he jumped into the hot soapy bath, splashing water everywhere.

Harry sat on the small stool in the corner, looking forlorn.
"It's alright Dad, I will go in after you, I'm going to polish my shoes for tomorrow."

Eventually, it was his turn to get in the bath; he put his hand in the water it had almost gone cold so he boiled another saucepan of water and added it to the already dirty soap suds. He sat in the bath, his long legs dangling over the top, a relaxed feeling came over him and he closed his eyes, there were all sorts of thoughts going through his mind.

He had just about had enough of this week, what with all the lies he had told his Father about being at work, the last few days had been too much to bear; the least he could do was to put everything right, when he returned home tomorrow.

His thoughts were disturbed when his Father shouted, "We're off to bed now; don't fall asleep in that bath son." Then he heard a chuckle come down the passageway, "and scrub those ears, the judge will surely hang you if they're not clean."

His mind was preoccupied as he began to throw handfuls of water over his face; he liked the peace and warmth of this small room, and he listened to the rain hitting the window pane.

The winter had seemed long, he closed his eyes and thought of sunny, happy days, then a vision of Laura came to his mind; he needed to see her so much; there was a nagging worry, he hoped she wasn't avoiding him. The thing he wanted most was for her to be near him right now, as he lay there remembering that night when he fondly caressed her body and the feel of her smooth silky skin, the warmth of her mouth when she kissed him.

He felt himself becoming aroused, his dick felt hot, he watched it get bigger and harder, suddenly it appeared to stick up from the water, he ran his hand up and down it, his body began to tingle. How excited he felt, he wanted to shout out her name, his hand began to move faster and faster, then with a sudden jolt, the cum spurted out of him, his body went limp.
He uttered breathlessly, "Laura, Laura."

The water began to turn cold, he stretched out for the towel, wrapping it round his bottom half he began to bale out the water with a saucepan. He put on the kettle to make a cup of cocoa, he was now feeling refreshed after the bath and didn't feel the need for sleep.
Opening the back door he dragged the bath back outside, hanging it back on the nail. He suddenly realised it had stopped raining; the wet windy day had turned into a calm tranquil evening. He gazed up at the sky, it was full of stars, if only he could spot a shooting star to make a wish for tomorrow. Suddenly his thoughts were broken by the whistling of the kettle.

As he drank his cocoa, he knew he must force himself to sleep, tomorrow may be a day of uncertainty.

The next morning he crossed the road; there was Edie standing at her front gate; she smiled, "Good morning Harry, no work today?"
"Not today Edie," he replied reluctantly.

He wanted to carry on walking; he was in no mood for polite conversation but she wanted to continue. "What, are you not feeling well love?"

He knew he wasn't going to get any further unless he answered her question. "No I have got to go to the court this morning."

She tried to look surprised, but wasn't really.
"Oh, now you mention it, I seem to remember seeing the copper over your house the other night,
I wondered what that was all about."

He knew she liked to know everything that was going on. She took a step closer. "So what did you do that was so wrong then Love?"
He wasn't going to beat about the bush.

"A burglary," he said bluntly.
"Well Love, that's no way to go on in life is it now? What, are you are going to court on your own?"
"Yeah, my Dad has got to work."
She put her hands to her head, as to give the situation some thought.
"Hold on I will let my Mother know and I will come with you."
He tried to get her attention as she wondered off into her house, shouting after her, "No, it's alright Edie."

He didn't fancy walking along with Edie, he felt edgy, what would people think of him?
She returned with her handbag and what looked like her best coat.
"Now come on Love, I insist I come with ya, there is nothing like a bit of company in times of trouble."

Walking towards the court, Edie chatted on and on; it didn't give him much time to think about what lay in front of him and he didn't want to admit it, but he was now feeling pleased to have her company.

He began to walk up the stone steps heading towards the court doors; his stomach was turning over and over. Once they were in the big cold reception area he looked around him. The black and white tiled floor went on as far as his eye could see, and there were people walking about in different directions.
He listened to the sound of echoing voices; his nerves were getting the better of him, if it wasn't for the presence of Edie, he most certainly would have run off.

They sat on the bench, the clock chimed ten, and a man appeared a few feet away from him, dressed in a dark suit.
In a loud voice, he shouted, "Calling Henry John Creedy."
Harry stood up as if to stand to attention, in a quiet voice he replied, "That's me."
"Right, in this room please," said the man as he indicated to his left.

Edie followed behind him, with her nose up in the air, showing signs that she was pleased to be at his side.

"And who might you be?" he asked.
"I'm his auntie," she replied in no uncertain terms.

He then asked her to take a seat at the back of the room. He stood directly in front of them with his clipboard in his hand and told them the hearing would be starting shortly, and then pulling his glasses further down on his nose, he walked off abruptly.

Harry studied the room, it wasn't that big, this made him feel a little more secure. In front of him was a long table, where three men and one woman sat. He looked over his shoulder, the only other person left in the room was Edie; how pleased he was about that, her familiar face meant a lot to him right now. He gazed along at the people sitting behind the table, their stern looks made him feel like a dagger was being thrust into him.

The silence was broken when the man with a handlebar moustache said, "Please state your full name."
Harry answered in an unsteady voice, "Henry John Creedy."
The man introduced himself. "I am Judge Grudge, good morning to you."

Harry put his hand to his face, trying to contain his laughter; he couldn't believe what he was hearing, who could possibly be called Judge Grudge?

"Henry you are here today, because you have committed a crime."
"Yes sir," replied Harry.
"Sitting next to me I have Mrs Goodman and Mr Mansell, they are welfare officers, and Mr Jones is a probation officer."

He stood silent, as they whispered amongst themselves.

Judge Grudge then asked him, "Do you plead guilty to the burglary at Ealing Common?"
"Yes sir," he replied.
"Have you committed any other crimes? If so please tell us now, then from today you can start afresh."

Harry pondered, not knowing how to answer, shaking his head from side to side nervously. Then he replied quietly, "Yes I broke into the chocolate factory." He put his hand to his mouth, as if to stifle a cough, feeling nervous.

There were gasps from the welfare people as Judge Grudge conferred with them.
"Well Henry this is very serious, it sheds a different light on the matter."

He stood and watched, as they wrote on sheets of paper, praying for them to get it over and done with as quickly as possible.

The Judge rested his elbows firmly on the table in front of him.

"Well Henry, we have come to a decision, we have read the report about you, and studied it very carefully I might say. Because of the circumstances of your upbringing, with just one parent in the house, perhaps you have not always had the care and attention a young boy needed."

There was a long pause, and then came the dreaded words Harry didn't want to hear. "Therefore we are going to send you to an approved school for six months."

He felt his knees knock together; he stood silent, then a voice chirped up from the back of the room.
"You can't bloody do that; you can't send him away he's just a kid."
He looked around to Edie, and then came a stern voice.
"Sit down madam, or I will have you thrown out," said the Judge.
Edie did as she was told.

The Judge's face then softened slightly, almost breaking in to a smile. "Henry we are sending you to a place called Rowentree House, in a small village called Brambley, in Hampshire. You will board there and you may have visitors once a month. And when you return home to your Father, we hope you will have learned the error of your ways."

Harry looked up, feeling frightened and bewildered as he spoke quietly, "But who is going to tell my Dad?"
"Well your Auntie is here, she can inform him, also the welfare service will contact him, they are here for your best interest, you know. You can have five minutes with your Auntie, before the transport arrives to take you away."

He was left alone in the room with Edie; caringly she put her arm around him. She stroked his face gently, "I'm sorry Love." She tried to put on a brave face, to cheer him up. "The six months will fly by," she assured him.

He looked at Edie, she had a tear in her eye, at this moment in time he felt very close to her and wished she was his auntie.

A grey haired man popped his head around the door. "We are ready for you now Creedy."
Harry put his hand on Edie's shoulder. "Tell my Dad I'm sorry won't ya Edie?"
"I will Love, don't you worry about that," she replied. As she left the room he shouted after her, "Thanks a lot Edie."

He walked across the yard at the back of the court building, quickly taking in breaths of fresh air, in his mind there was the thought that he was never going to see daylight again, and he wanted to breathe all the air into his lungs that was possible.

Six months locked away, however was he going to get through it? He was escorted to a dark van; a uniformed man opened the back doors. He climbed in and sat down, sitting opposite him was a young boy about his age, with bright ginger hair, his face was covered in freckles and his left eye going into the corner. Harry nodded his head, to acknowledge him.

Glancing down to the floor he couldn't help but notice the boy's feet, his toes were gaping out of the hole in his plimsols. They sat with their heads bowed as they travelled in silence.

Then the van came to a sudden halt, throwing him onto the other boy.
"Hello, what's going on here?" asked the boy, who was looking bewildered.
A voice came from the front of the van, "It's alright no panic, a cow has walked across the lane."

This indicated that they were now in the countryside. Harry got himself together; he looked across at the boy as he tried to sit upright.
"Sorry about that, I didn't know where I was going."

"That's alright." said the boy, "I thought we was in a smash-up for a minute."
They both began to laugh.
"What is your name?" asked Harry.
"Its Jim-Bob, everybody calls me Little Jim-Bob," he replied with a cheeky smile on his face.

Harry liked him straight away; he hoped he would make Little Jim-Bob his friend, he certainly felt in need of one right now.
The van came to a halt, the uniformed man opened the van doors.
"Right, out you get."

Harry climbed out first, putting his hand over his eyes to shield then from the sudden light after the darkness of the van, slowly his vision became stronger as he looked up the long winding path.
In front of him was a big old house covered in ivy. They walked up the path, the wind and rain sent the branches of the many trees swirling overhead. He gazed up to the sky; a big black cloud was passing over, it gave him a feeling of depression.

They walked into the big tiled porch, the door suddenly opened, there stood a dark haired man with thick rimmed glasses, wearing a long black robe.

"Good afternoon, I am Brother Theodore; you must be Creedy and Smith."
He pointed his finger, to direct them. "This way to the study, there is some paper work to be done. Then I will explain what will be happening to you over the next six months."

Only the sound of their footsteps could be heard, as they walked along the creaky wooden floor boards, the big old house appeared to be in total silence.

The afternoon was spent being shown around the building; they were taken to the stores and issued with short grey trousers, blue shirts and grey socks, and a pair of striped pajamas.
Harry hated the fact that he would have to wear short trousers again, he felt humiliated.

The day dragged on and on, when finally a bell rang and a voice shouted, "Lights out."
He had never been so pleased to get into bed. As he cast his eyes around the big dormitory he counted eight beds; he felt pleased that he and Jim-bob had been given beds side-by-side.

The whispering of voices gradually stopped; he tried hard to sleep, but his thoughts were of his Father and Patrick; he knew his Father would be feeling deeply hurt, it was going to be a long time before he could tell him how truly sorry he was.

Tears began to well up in his eyes, before he knew it he was sobbing, he pulled the blanket over his face, to muffle out the sound, the last thing he wanted was to be a joke amongst the other boys.
Jim-Bob bent across and shook his shoulder.
"Are you alright there Harry?"
"Yeah, I'm just a bit restless," he said in a whisper.
He lay still and listened to the big clock ticking away on the wall.
Jim-Bob shook him again.
"You know Harry, I don't think I'm going to like this place one bit."

Harry felt pleased that he wasn't on his own about how he feeling at this moment.
"Hey Jim-Bob, how did you get a name like that?" he asked curiously.
He started to giggle, "Well it's like this, my Mum had six girls and when

I was born the family all went mad, a boy at last, both my grandfathers were round for Sunday dinner, when suddenly my mum was rushed upstairs to give birth to me. Auntie Violet shouted down. 'It's a boy.'" Well my grandfathers Jim and Bob started to argue over who I would be named after. And guess what? My Mum said they started fighting in the street, like cats and dogs. She still tells everyone the story to this day, so in the end they called me Little Jim-Bob."

As he listened to Little Jim-Bob talk of his Mum, he felt a little bit of envy, for that was the thing that he missed most, his own Mother, all he had was faded memories; it just wasn't enough for him.

Harry and Jim-Bob became good friends; a lot of their time was spent working on the farm; it was Jim-Bob, who had to drag Harry out of bed, at six in the morning to milk the cows.

Jim-Bob's life in the East End of London had left him uneducated; due to the continual bombing throughout the war; he had missed a lot of schooling, so it was left to Harry to write his letters home for him. With spring upon them he began to flourish, now eating three meals a day, his skinny body began to fill out, his spotty complexion disappeared, his skin had taken on a golden glow and he looked nothing like the undernourished boy that arrived months earlier.

It was a hot sunny day when Brother Daniel called Harry into the study; he leaned back firmly into his green leather padded chair.
"Well Harry I've called you in to tell you I will be taking you off of farm duties. This week you have proved how excellent you are with English verse. I have often heard you read poetry in class; it comes straight from your heart, and for a young boy such as yourself to read in such a beautiful way is most unusual. I know how you love books, so I'm going to make you Library Monitor."

Harry stood there feeling unsure, did he really want this? It meant being split from Jim-Bob, on the other hand he could think of nothing better than being surrounded by hundreds of books.
He looked at Brother Daniel sitting boldly in his chair and then in a grateful voice he said, "Thank you sir."

As he walked out of the study he heard voices and a scuffle going on in the passageway, as he looked across it was Jim-Bob fighting like mad with a boy twice his size. Frantically he tried to pull Jim-Bob off the boy, to avoid him getting into trouble. But Jim-Bob couldn't resist giving him one more punch, before running off along the passageway.

He then got hold of Jim-Bob, to try to calm him down.
"What was all that about?" he asked.
Jim-Bob rested his hands on his hips in an arrogant way.
"I don't believe it; he just called me a stupid fucking cockney."
Harry laughed, "I didn't know you could fight like that, Jim-Bob."
"Well it's like this Harry, when you're cross-eyed and ginger, you learn to look after yourself at a very early age."

Harry realised that he had grown to feel deep affection for the cheeky little ginger-haired boy standing in front of him, he definitely had guts, he would give him that.

It was a bright Monday morning; he had just left the dining hall after breakfast, with a feeling of uncertainty he walked into the library, bright rays of sun, came through the big windows showing the vast amounts of dust in the air.

Slowly he looked around at the high shelves stacked full of books, it appeared like they were almost closing in on him. He stood there for a while; he had never really noticed the amount of books in this room before, they were almost from floor to ceiling. Yes, if he was honest, he suddenly felt like this was a dream come true, it was almost like he was being rewarded instead of punished.

His thoughts were disturbed by Brother Michel.
"Good morning Creedy, I am told you are to help out in here."
"Yes sir," he replied.
Brother Michel's black gown flowed as he moved swiftly around the library, running his fingers across the top of books, checking for dust, then he turned sharply around to Harry.
"Right Creedy, you will have boys coming in here through the day looking for books, some needing certain books to help them out with their lessons, most are not as bright as you, so you are here to assist them. I will come back from time to time and check on you, at the end of each day the library must be left perfect."
He whacked his cane across a desk, as he looked into Harry's eyes.
"Do you understand that Creedy?"
"Yes sir," replied Harry nervously.

Throughout the afternoon the library was quiet; so Harry picked up a book and started to read it. It was the story of Mary Jones, a young woman of nineteen who lived in London who stole some cloth from a linen drapers in Ludgate Hill. Her husband was press ganged, leaving her alone, with a young baby to care for.

When she was spotted stealing the cloth she could do no more than offer to put it back, she didn't have the money to pay for it. But it was too late; the decision was made to hang her. The crowd watched as the young woman was about to be hung from a noose, with her small baby still sucking at her breast, then her baby was pulled away from her… He was so deeply engrossed in the book, as if he was actually at the scene, he couldn't bear to read on any further, it was all too much to contemplate. Forgetting where he was, he stood up and shouted at the top of his voice, "You fucking cruel bastards!"

A sudden whack hit his ear, it came from behind him so suddenly he felt like he was in some sort of trance. He couldn't think what was happening, the room was spinning, he felt dizzy; slowly his senses then came back to him.

He could see a blurred outline, then the objects around him got much clearer, he blinked his eyes, there stood Brother Michel, looking evil and angry.
"What do you think you are doing Creedy?"
"I was reading the story about poor Mary Jones sir."

Brother Michel screwed his face tight, this made him look even sterner, and he stamped his feet together making a loud noise on the wooden floorboards.
"Think of the Ten Commandments Creedy, thou shall not steal. Mary Jones did steal, and she was punished, and Creedy, that is why you are here, you too are being punished for stealing. Hold out your hand boy."

Brother Michel brought the cane firmly down on his hand six times. Harry closed his eyes and gritted his teeth, not wanting to show the pain he was feeling, then the whacks finally stopped. Slowly he opened his eyes and looked down at the balding little fat man, his instincts were to spit on his head, he felt an overwhelming hatred towards him, but no, he knew he must control his temper, or he might be punished even more.

Brother Michel rubbed his fingertips along the edge of the cane. As he spoke, his lips drooped downwards.
"I will allow you to stay in the library, purely because you are the right person to work in here, but I am warning you Creedy, oh yes boy, I am warning you, any more behaviour like today and I will send you to Father Dominic's study, where you will be severely reprimanded. Do you understand?"
"Yes sir," replied Harry.

Summer was here at last; he looked out of the window watching the boys plant the bedding plants in the big garden. In his mind he had a picture of when he was a small boy, helping his Father in their small garden at home. Now suddenly he began to feel homesick, for he hadn't received a letter from his Father for a couple of weeks.

Eventually a letter arrived from his Father, apologising that he had not written sooner, but the upheaval of the war had caused them to spend a lot of time back and forwards to the air raid shelters. He gave him the news that the top end of Stirling Road had been hit by a bomb, wiping out six houses, most were empty at the time, but as far as he knew there were four deaths.

Harry's heart sank, please God, he thought, no don't let it be Laura, that is where her house was situated. He felt sick as he was trying to make sense of what he was reading. The last thing he could cope with was for her to have been killed by a bomb.
No, it was no use, he must put it out of his mind straight away, or he would not get through the next few weeks, the thought of losing her was unbearable.

Harry and Jim-Bob got through the last weeks of their stay at Rowentree House, without too much difficulty. Jim-Bob managed to keep out of fights, and Harry kept his head down when Brother Michel entered a room.

Throughout the six months, the only real friend he had made was Jim-Bob, they were there for each other, come what may. So when the day finally had arrived when they were told they would be going home, there were mixed feelings.
They had grown to like the country way of life, and had become used to the smell of fresh air, the fresh vegetables and newly laid eggs straight from the farm, this was something they weren't getting back home in London.

They were ready to leave Rowentree House, fit and healthy young men.

After being given instructions for their journey home, and issued with their travel passes to get them home safely to London, the early morning was spent saying their goodbyes to everybody; it was now time to go back to the outside world once again. With their few belongings they headed down the winding lane to the bus stop. The hot sun shone down on them as they wandered along; at last they were feeling as free as birds.

Harry was highly delighted to be back in his long trousers, for the first time in six months. Then the heat became almost unbearable as they walked down the never ending lane; he took off his shirt and tied it around his waist, Jim-Bob turned and began to laugh at him.

"You know what it is Harry, working in that stupid library you have forgotten what its like to be outside in the sun." He pushed him playfully, "You just can't take the heat Harry boy, can ya?"

Their bus arrived on time, all eyes were on them, they got the feeling that the passengers on the bus knew they had just left the 'School for Naughty Boys', as the locals called it.

As the bus chugged along the county lanes, a feeling of happiness came over Harry at the thought of his newfound freedom.

Once at the railway station, their train arrived to take them to Richmond. As they headed nearer to their destination, the signs of bomb damage became noticeable.

Suddenly it was as if a dark cloud had formed over Harry, the thought of Laura's possible death was staring him in the face. He couldn't wait to find out what had happened to her. Finally the train pulled into Richmond Station – where Harry and Jim-Bob parted company.

The train arrived at South Acton station; Harry stepped out on to the platform. A gentle breeze brought to him the smell of the soapsuds from the laundries, yes there was no mistaking it, he knew he was back home. He walked across the familiar railway bridge; the first thing that caught his eye was the house where he was born.

He stood to gather his thoughts, was it what he had been told? Or could he truly remember the day his Mother's coffin was carried from there? A shiver went over his body.

He looked around him, the street was busy as usual at this time of the day, the hooters were sounding for the end of the working day. Suddenly he felt confused, with all the hustle and bustle going on around him, for the last six months he had only known the peacefulness of the library, or the country life working on the farm, with only the sound of the animals.

There had been no sound of air raid sirens to contend with, and there had been no fear of a bomb being dropped overhead; things were going to be different once again, he was back to the real fear of war.

He started to walk towards Park Road, and then turned swiftly. Thoughts were churning in his mind about Laura, no, he must go and look for her before anything else. He began to run like mad, dreading what might lie in front of him.

Taking a short cut through the alleyway, beads of sweat began to stream down his face, and he threw himself to his knees; he wanted to shout out for Laura, but there was no point; her house was now no more than a pile of rubble. Putting his hands to his face he mumbled, "Please, please Laura, be alive."

As he ran down the street, he began to feel like the pavement was coming up hitting him in the face. His whole body was trembling he began frantically asking people if they knew who was killed in the bombing, but nobody could help him.

He turned the corner into Park Road; the first person he saw was Alice Green. "Harry is that you?!" she screeched, looking surprised. "When did you get back?"
"Just now."
His throat was dry, he was finding it difficult to speak, he was still feeling bewildered.
"Your Dad's just gone indoors, I bet you can't wait to see him."
"Yeah, but Alice, I want to know what's happened to Laura?"

She looked at him very seriously; he was dreading what she was going to say then she smiled gently touching his hand.
"Didn't she write to you before she left?"
"She's left? When?" he asked, feeling relieved that she wasn't dead.
"I think it was just after you got sent away."
"Where's she gone Alice?"
"I'm not too sure but Jim told me they had gone back to her Mum's home town up north."
 He began to breathe more easily, "thanks Alice."

He put his hand inside the letterbox, pulling the key out on the bit of string he sighed with relief, he was home at last. He shouted along the passage, "Dad it's me, I'm back."

John and Patrick came rushing into the passage. Harry caringly put his arms around his Father's shoulders and touched his cheeks.
"It's good to be home Dad."
John looked at him longingly, "It's good to have you home son."
Patrick walked up to him to shake his hand, as he fondly hugged his brother, "You know we've missed you 'H'."

Harry noticed a much more relaxed atmosphere, his Father no longer seemed so uptight, but his grey hair had receded more, his face now was that of a gentle old man.

After a few days of being home he noticed nothing too much had changed. At breakfast the wireless went on as usual, the news was that the allied landings in Normandy, D-Day, had come at last.
It was the biggest gathering of men and war material ever massed together.
This lifted their hearts, with any luck this might bring the war to an end. There would be further bulletins throughout the day and it was promised that Mr Churchill would speak to the nation later.

VICTORY

The day finally came when Germany surrendered; the 8th of May 1945. The lights went on all over the country, and the church bells rang out joyously. Celebrations went on everywhere; people were dancing in the streets.

It had been a tough time, now after six long years of not knowing if you were going to live or die a great weight had been lifted. The young children that set off with their small packs of belongings who were evacuated to different parts of the country all that time ago, were returning, now in their teens.

The year after the war ended most people were still living in poverty. Serviceman gradually returned home to their love ones. When the prisoners of war returned home they were often a shadow of their former selves, the war had taken a dreadful toll on all of them.

Jimmy Downs knocked loudly on Harry's front door. Harry couldn't believe his eyes as he looked at him with shock; there he was, in a smart suit and his bryl-creamed hair swept back. He stood there with his arms folded in front of him, looking as bold as brass.

"Hello 'H' do ya fancy coming to Bernard's up the High Street? They got a dance going on there tonight."
Harry hesitated as he replied, "Don't be silly Jim, I'm skint."
Jim put his hand in his pocket and pulled out a roll of notes.
Harry's eyes lit up. "Where did you get that lot from?"

Putting his finger to his mouth, he whispered, "I done a job. Go on 'H' get yourself ready, I'll treat ya. Don't be too long, I'll sit on the wall and wait for ya."
They walked up the hill to the High Street; Harry couldn't help but feel a twinge of jealousy. There Jim was in smart suit, with plenty of money.

He couldn't help but to think he would have no chance; it would be Jim that all the girls would go for. Jim put his hand in his pocket and pulled out a five pound note, damping it down with his spittle he then stuck it on his forehead and made a funny face, he bent his head towards Harry. "Take it 'H' it's yours."

He had no intention of refusing, he playfully ruffled Jim's hair and thanked him, after all it wasn't every day someone handed over a fiver. "Oy watch it mate, I spent hours combing it like this, it's the latest fashion, don't ruin it 'H' mate."
Harry joked that it didn't look right anyway, as he looked at Jim's hair now standing up on end.

They walked into the big dancehall he looked straight at the stage; it looked like something out of a Hollywood film that he had seen at the pictures. Huge dark red velvet curtains hung at the sides of the stage, the band were dressed in tuxedos, and the glitter of the lights added to the atmosphere. The band was playing Glenn Miller music that he had often heard on the wireless.

Jim tugged his arm, "Let's get over there 'H' there are plenty of birds standing over near the bar."

Harry stood at the bar fascinated by what was going on around him. He looked across the dance floor towards the corner of the stage and spotted two girls looking over towards them. He stared long and hard finding it difficult to take his eyes off them.
They started to giggle, he grabbed Jim's arm for his attention.
"Look over there; I think we have got two admirers."

They were just about to head in the girl's direction, when Jim's younger sister Sal came up to them.
Jim looked her up and down. "What are you doing here?"
He tugged at her long hair playfully.
"I'm here with Marge, but I seem to have lost her."

Harry looked at her, "You look nice Sal, is that a new dress you're wearing?"
Sal smiled broadly, "Thanks Harry; Jim gave me the money for it."
Jim put his arm around her, "Well Sal, ya aint gonna get a better brother than me, but Sal we've had enough of your company, now push off."

The two girls had edged their way nearer to them. Jim turned to Harry, "Oh fuck it, I'm not going to mess about here, let's go and ask them for a dance."

"Hold on," said Harry, feeling a little uneasy, "Give it a while, don't be too eager."
"For fucks sake 'H' if we don't ask them now someone else will, they're the bee's knees, they really are."

Harry wasn't denying the fact they were lovely, but he wanted to take it slowly. It was alright for Jim, who all of a sudden had found a new gotten confidence with his pocket full of money, but he himself felt very nervous.

Jim walked over to them with a big grin on his face; he began to adjust his tie in a cocky fashion.
"Hello girls, what's your names then?"
They started to giggle. "I'm Dolly and this is my cousin Ellen."
"Well Dolly how would you like to come and have a dance with me, and I'll leave my friend Harry to look after Ellen."

Dolly walked onto the dance floor full of confidence, dressed in a royal blue dress nipped in tightly at the waist, her short dark curly hair showed the firm bone structure of her face. Jim pulled her close to him, putting his arm firmly around her small waist.

Jim took a roll of notes from his pocket, he wanted to impress them.
"What are you drinking girls?"
They both answered together, "Gin and orange."
"Right girls, two gin and oranges, it is."
He walked towards the bar swaying his shoulders.

Throughout all this Harry stood quietly, feeling like a fish out of water. Ellen couldn't help but feel sorry for the tall young man standing at her side; somehow he looked out of place.

He looked her up and down wondering how old she would be, he couldn't help but notice her beautiful green eyes; her low cut purple dress showed off her ample cleavage. He was taken in by her beauty; her chestnut hair hung loosely on her shoulders, her white wedge-heeled shoes emphasised her shapely legs. He began to feel uneasy, as if he shouldn't really be there, why would a beautiful girl like her want to know him? he asked himself.

Jim returned with the drinks. Harry knocked his straight back, hoping it would give him enough Dutch courage to ask Ellen for the next dance. The band started to play a ballad; he thought he could just about cope with that, it involved no jumping about.

The smoky atmosphere and the two brown ales he had drunk began to bring a more relaxed feeling to him.
"Come on Ellen, do you want to show me how it's done?"
She smiled, if only he knew it; she was feeling the same as him.
They waltzed clumsily around the dance floor, he tried hard to distract from his awkwardness, by firing questions at her. She suddenly started to show an irritation to what she took as prying.
"Why all the interest in me?"

He felt even more awkward he had upset her.
"I'm sorry Ellen I didn't mean to be nosey; I was really just trying to make conversation."
With that they both began to laugh.
They walked out into the warm August evening, the High Street was busy, people were leaving the nearby pubs, and groups of young people leaving the dance hall. Harry and Ellen led the way, with Jim and Dolly following in the distance. The smell of honeysuckle drifted towards them, as they made their way past the cottage gardens down the narrow streets.

Finally they arrived at Carton Road. He didn't want to leave her, he put his arm firmly around her waist and was determined to find out more about her.
"How come I haven't seen you before?"
She smiled gently, "Well this is where I live, and I work just around the corner at the Dolls Factory in Packs Road."

"Well I'm just around the corner in Park Road; it's strange we have never seen each other before."
Gently he pulled her towards him, before watching her head off in the darkness towards her house.

Back home he went into the bedroom, Patrick was sleeping soundly. In a melancholy mood he opened the window, and looked up to the sky, somehow he had never lost that old habit of looking up for a shooting star to wish upon. This was almost a ritual, especially when he really wanted something, and tonight the thing he wanted more than anything else was to win Ellen's affections.

He woke early on Sunday morning to the smell of fried bacon.
A shout came from the kitchen, "Breakfast up lads!"
He jumped out of bed and put on his trousers, then tried to flatten his wild hair, then shook Patrick to wake him.

"Come on, get up lazy bones, Dad's calling us for breakfast."
Harry always looked forward to weekends, to sit down around the table and eat one of his Dad's well cooked breakfasts.

John put down his newspaper, he took off his glasses; this usually meant that he had something serious to say.
"You know Harry I sat here last night thinking about you, you're eighteen years of age and you have been dismissed from National Service due to a slight ear defect, God only knows why, you have never complained about an ear problem before."

"Dad you can't blame me for that," Harry said in an irritated voice, "it's up to the doctor that examined me."
"Yes I know that son, but what are you going to do with your life? I know we have had this conversation many, many times, but you are missing out on the opportunity to make something of yourself."

Monday morning he set off to yet another new job, how long for he didn't know, this time it was in the Rag Shop, an outbuilding at the back of an old stable yard. His task was sorting through the rags, then putting them into different colours and bundles.
He considered himself lucky to get the job, to him this was a step up; his wage would be slightly better than anything he had earned before, and it would keep his father happy.

At half past five the whistle blew in the Rag Shop, he wiped the sweat from his brow as he walked through the old stable yard, the late afternoon sun was searing down on him.

Wearily he walked along Packs Road and looked across to a sign that read 'Carters Dolls Factory'. Curiously he looked up at the open windows, he could just about see the movement of people inside before someone started to close the sash windows.

A few seconds later, a group of women came out onto the street, his heart suddenly lifted; about to cross the road were Dolly and Ellen.
He heard a voice, shout, "Yoo-hoo, Harry."
He glanced across; there stood Ellen waving her hand beckoning him towards them.
He felt awkward, nervous, the other night was different, he had drunk two brown ales, that had given him confidence. He took a deep breath stuck out his shoulders and walked over to them.
Ellen appeared confident. "Where have you been then Harry?"
She wanted to show him interest; she liked him and wanted to get to know him more.

"I started a new job today, in the Rag Shop."
She looked surprised, "I thought you didn't like work, was it any good?" she asked cheerily?"
"Well not too bad, I've had worse."
She laughed, Dolly nudged her, "Come on Ell I got to get home."
"Go on then Doll, I will catch you up."
"Alright Ell, I've got to rush, see ya tomorrow, ta-ta Harry, see you soon."

He looked at her; she appeared different from Saturday night, his attention was drawn to her beautiful green eyes. Instantly he couldn't help but think how much younger she looked, her fresh clear skin without lipstick and rouge showed a kind of innocence.
There was no time to waste, he knew he must make a move on her now, or lose his chance altogether. She stood there, moving from foot to foot, as if she was uneasy with him.

He cleared his throat then nervously asked, "How do ya fancy coming to the pictures on Saturday night Ell?"
A coy look came on her face. "That sounds good, I just hope my Mum don't say I have to stay in for some reason or another."
He felt relieved, he now felt confident, yes, she must like him.
"Alright then Ell, I'll meet you outside All Saints' Church at seven o'clock."

The moment he said it he thought back to his meeting with Laura all that time ago; he instantly put it out of his mind.
She gazed up at him fondly, like she was pleased to be asked.
"I better be off then Harry, see you Saturday."

They parted company, he walked off feeling ten feet tall. As he turned into Park Road the first person he saw was Jim.
"You look pleased with yourself 'H'."
"Yeah well, I should be, I'm taking Ellen out on Saturday."
Jim playfully poked him. "It's alright for some, you lucky bastard, and guess what 'H', you aint fucking gonna believe this, I got my papers through today, giving the go ahead for my National Service."

All of a sudden the happiness left Harry, he was now feeling deflated, he was about to lose his best friend, things just wouldn't be the same without him.

Throughout the week Harry settled into his new job, and for once he liked it, but Saturday couldn't come soon enough; each day that passed he became more and more excited.

On Saturday morning he woke early and took the five pound note from the tin under his bed, he then decided to go to the In and out Shop to get himself a new shirt for his date with Ellen.
He walked up the steep hill whistling, once he arrived at the In and Out Shop he thought back to that day when he stole the shoes, a grin came on his face when he thought how nervous he was. Curiously he looked up at the skylight window in the roof, suddenly an idea came to him, he thought how easy it would be to get in there with the help of Jim.

He went down to the back end of the shop, he noticed the fire door and started to plan in his head the best way of going about it. They could come in through the skylight, that shouldn't be a problem, and then out through the fire doors.

He rubbed his finger up and down his chin and stood giving it serious consideration; he pondered for a while, yes, this could be a good place to burgle. Yes they could go for the smaller items like watches, lighters, pens and cufflinks, anything that was light in weight and small. Perhaps bring a couple of suit cases, fill them up and then take it all round to May's house.

His thoughts were interrupted…
"Can I help you sir?" a voice said.
He turned to the man in a smart suit. "Yeah, I'm looking for a blue shirt."
The man beckoned him to a glass cabinet of neatly folded shirts.
"I think we have just what you are looking for."

The man laid a pale blue shirt directly in front of him. Giving it a quick glimpse Harry said, "I'll take it." Then he handed the man the five pound note.

He stood outside All Saints Church; the church clock rang out seven chimes, the evening sky was turning to dusk; he looked down the road, there was no sign of Ellen. He was beginning to feel agitated then he thought what if she didn't turn up?

He felt himself begin to panic, he ran quickly across to the park and headed towards the drinking fountain, and gulped back a mouth full of water, splashing the remainder over his face to cool himself down; for some reason when he got nervous he always broke out in a hot sweat. It was no use, he knew he must calm himself down, or she would think he was some kind of idiot, he thought.

He crossed back over to the church, she was standing there, looking as nervous as he felt. He touched his damp forehead nervously, "Sorry Ell, I just ran over to get a drink of water."
"Sorry I'm late Harry, I had to wait for my Dad to go out before I could put my lipstick on."

He smiled, "You shouldn't worry about lipstick, you look nice anyway," he said and hoped that he was paying her a compliment.
"Shall we go to the Globe? Jim said they have got a good film on there this week."
"Yeah I'd like that," she replied.

As they walked she did most of the talking, this pleased him, he wasn't really sure what to say and didn't want to spoil anything by saying the wrong thing.
She was now showing signs of self confidence.

"How old are you then Harry?"
"I'm eighteen," he replied, in a confident voice
"How old you are Ell?"
"I'm fifteen," she said coyly.
"The other night Ell, when I met you at Bernard's, I thought you were much older."
"Well, I had to make myself look older or me and Doll wouldn't have got in."
He laughed. "Well it worked," he said admiring her cheek.

They finally reached the Globe Picture House, and joined the long queue.
"I think you are going to have to lie about your age again Ell, it's an 'A' film."
"That's alright," she said, full of confidence. "I do it all the time, a little lie here and there doesn't hurt anyone, does it?"

The more he got to know her the more he liked her; in a lot of ways she was like him. He pulled out a packet of cigarettes, tonight he was determined to be Jack the Lad
"Give me one then," she asked indignantly.

He started to chuckle, "Not only do you drink gin and orange, you smoke as well, it shouldn't be allowed at your age," he joked.
"Why not?" she said as a broad grin broke out on her face.
"I bet you do things you shouldn't."
He laughed, "Yeah all the time; if you done all the right things it would be a bit boring, wouldn't it?"

A feeling began to rise from the pit of his stomach; he was desperate to touch her; he pulled her to him, squeezing her waist tight. He gave her a light for her cigarette then watched her puff long and hard on it, blowing rings of smoke into the air. She certainly appeared more confident with the cigarette than he felt, he was finding it difficult to take his eyes off her.

The queue moved slowly, all he really wanted to do was to get in the darkness of the picture house to sit close and put his arm around her. When she had finally finished smoking, she flicked her cigarette end into the air.

He couldn't believe his eyes as he watched it land straight in the rim of the Trilbury hat worn by a man further along in the queue. He stood transfixed as smoke started to appear from his hat, then he began to panic. "Oh no, look Ell, for fuck's sake." He quickly put his hand to his mouth feeling awkward that he had swore in front of her, "Look what you've done, that bloke's hat's on fire."

She began to giggle loudly, finding it hard to believe what she had done. He turned to them angrily.
"I bet that was you two, you clever little bastards, I bet you couldn't do that again if you tried, how the fuck did that happen?"
He threw his hat onto the ground; then began to jump up and down on it trying to put out the smoke.

It all became too much for them, they tried desperately to keep a serious look on their faces, they gripped their stomachs, trying to suppress their laughter. The man walked off in a huff, he shouted back to them, "You horrible little fuckers you've spoilt my night."
Harry pulled Ellen tightly towards him; stroking her face as he laughed. "Oh well, that was a good start to the night wasn't it Ell?"

They sat in the darkness of the cinema, he put his arm around her shoulder, then he started to run his fingers through her hair, it was difficult for him to concentrate on the film. He began to feel aroused she put her head on his shoulder, he could feel the warmth of her body as if it was sending signals to him.
He kissed her gently on the cheek, it became difficult to control his hands; he wanted to move them over her breast, he had a warm feeling inside of him, it felt good he was so happy just to be this close to her. Suddenly the words 'The End' came on the screen.
This was to his relief for he could no longer trust his actions for he might have done something he would later regret. The lights came on and they made their way out onto the street amongst the crowd.

They chatted all the way down to Carton Road then she promptly stopped on the corner.
"I'm alright here Harry," she said hesitantly.
"No I will walk you to your door," he said protectively.
"No," she said about to stop him in his tracks.
"My Dad will go mad; he thinks I'm around Doll's house tonight."
He smiled, "I keep forgetting you're only fifteen." He gently pulled her to him. "Can I just kiss you goodnight Ell?"
She put her lips to his, the pleasure from the kiss forced their bodies into each other, quickly he pulled himself away, knowing he must not rush things.

He spent Sunday afternoon reading; every now and then he put his book down to think about Ellen, he really liked her.
A sudden shout came from his Father; "Harry, it's Jim is at the door for you."
Jim stood there looking irritated.

"Do ya, fancy coming out for a while 'H'? I can't stand being indoors a minute longer, my Mum and sister don't stop talking, yack, yack, yack, and they are sending me fucking mad."
"Hold on I will be right with ya, where do you want to go to, then Jim?"
"Well let's have a walk around to Carton Road I still fancy that Dolly, you never know we might see her and Ellen."
This made him happy. "Well what we waiting for Jim?" He swiftly shut the door behind him.

They walked along Stirling Road. Harry looked across at the empty space where Laura's house once stood, now it was just waste land. He felt a shiver go down his spine as he thought about the people that were killed there.

"Are you alright 'H'? You've gone a bit pale mate."
"Yeah, yeah, I was thinking about the day I thought Laura had been killed over there; it was one of the worst days of my life."
"You know mate she had a lucky escape moving away when she did."
"Yeah you're right."

He quickly put the thought out of his mind, they carried on walking through to Carton Road; there was no sign of Dolly or Ellen.
"Oh fuck it; I really am fed up now 'H'," Jim said in an angry voice.
"Let's do something else then Jim." Harry was trying to cheer him up.
"Like what?" asked Jim abruptly.

Harry rubbed his hands together; a feeling of excitement came over him.

"Lets go and screw the In and out Shop." Harry said, without a qualm.

"Are you fucking serious 'H'?"

"Yeah I'm fucking serious alright, what else have we got to do?"

"When are we going to do it then?"

"I thought as soon as it gets dark."

"Right, tell me the plan," said Jim, now looking a whole lot happier.

Harry was now feeling that the day at last had a bit of a spark after all.

"Come on Jim, come and sit on that wall over there and I will tell you how we can go about it."

"Well, its like this, I went in the In and out Shop, I had a good look round, the best way in is to go through the skylight in the roof, and then for a quick getaway, out through the fire doors at the back of the shop. We're gonna need a couple of torches, a lorry rope, and something like a suitcase to put the stuff into."

"Come on, let's go and get what we need, there are two torches in the cupboard under the stairs in my house, I'll creep in and get them," Harry said bossily.

"Alright when we've done that 'H' we will go to my house, I think my old man has got an old case in the garden shed."

They turned into Packs Road, they spotted a parked lorry; Jim looked up at the drop side lorry feeling pleased that their plans were falling into place.

"There ya are 'H' there's our lorry rope." He quickly pulled it off the back of the lorry; they walked away quickly, hoping that no one had seen them.

Walking towards Park Road it started to rain, Harry put his hands out as if to catch the rain.

"That's good, I'll tell my Dad I have come back for my jacket."

They walked to Jims house, the sky had got darker and darker, and the rain came down heavier.

"Come on 'H' don't make a nois,e we'll creep round the back."

Jim opened the door to the overcrowded dark shed.

"Lets wait in here, the rain might stop soon."

Harry pulled out the torch, "No, for fucks sake 'H' don't use that, my old man might look out of the window, and see a ray of light then he'd be straight out here; he's a grumpy old bastard, he might mistake us for burglars and try to fucking kill us or something."

They found an old battered suitcase and an army kit bag, now with all that they needed they were ready to go and rob the shop.

They walked with their heads bowed down, pleased with the early evening darkness due to the stormy weather, they hoped this would avoid them being recognised.
Harry led the way, along the side alley that ran to the back of the shop. They put the case and bag outside the back fire door, ready for their escape. The street was quiet; the only sound to be heard was that of rumbling thunder in the distance.

Jim scratched his head in anticipation, he looked up at the roof.
"Fucking hell 'H' how are we going to get up there without breaking our fucking necks?"
Harry looked up. "Shit it looks a lot higher out here than when you're standing inside the shop, and what with this fucking weather, it could be a bit slippery up there. I'll go first."

Winding the lorry rope around the top half of his body in case he should need it, he hesitantly climbed up a drainpipe, then he came to a narrow ledge that came out from the building. He stood on the ledge to get his breath before climbing the rest of the way up, he was just about to start climbing again when his foot slipped on the wet ledge, he held on to the drainpipe tightly, swinging from side to side. He felt his heart beat faster as he struggled to get his feet back on the ledge and finally regained his balance.

"Fuck it," he mumbled. He looked down at Jim, in a quiet voice he told him, "Be careful, I nearly had it then."
He carried on, finally getting to the top; he sat on the tiled roof as the rain came down in torrents, eagerly awaiting Jim. Then thankfully he saw Jim's hands gripping the edge of the roof, he breathed a sigh of relief, pulling him towards him.

Jim laid himself flat on the roof, trying to get his breath back, inbetween gasping for breath he swore frantically at Harry.
They lay there laughing uncontrollably on the wet tiles, waiting to go on with their next move.

With difficulty they crawled up to the skylight; a bright flash of lightning lit up the sky followed by a loud clap of thunder.
"This is all we fucking need," Harry said breathlessly.
"Well at least we' re going to get a bit of light to help us on our way," replied Jim.

The rain started to fall even heavier, they could hardly see as it hit their faces. Harry pulled at the skylight, it opened with no problem. He took his torch and shone it inside, with the aid of continual flashes of lightning he got a clear view of the inside of the building.

He turned to Jim. "It looks easy enough, the racks that are going across the building are quite clear. There's just a few prams hanging down on the racks at the other end; it's clear for us to drop ourselves down."

He took the rope and tied it onto a metal roof truss, he looked back at Jim. "It's only about a three-foot drop onto the first rack, and then about five feet to the one below that, then it's a bit of a drop to the ground, whatever you do Jim don't get on the rope before I hit the bottom."

"Fucking hell 'H' this is gonna be like swinging on a rope at the circus."

The lightning continued to light up the building, to their advantage. Harry hit the ground with a thud, his fall was broken as he landed in a pile of boxes, holding on to his torch he shone it up to Jim.

"Come on Jim," he said in a hasty voice. "Just let yourself go straight all the way down."

Jim came down the rope at full speed, his feet kicking Harry in the head as he landed; they both lay on the floor laughing amidst a pile of boxes. Jim sat himself up, shining his torch in Harry's face, "Do ya know 'H' that's the last time I'm listening to any more of your bright ideas.

Harry stood up and shone his torch around the building.
"You go one side Jim, and I'll do the other side, we will get out quicker that way," he said in a dominant voice. "Remember only go for things that will fit easily in the bags, all the stuff that's in here, we should find it easy to get rid of."

"Alright fucking bossy boots, don't you think we should see if there is any money lying about as well?"
"Yeah why not, we're here now, if there's money we'll have it."
Jim began to laugh. "And a couple of bikes for our getaway."
"Now you are taking the piss, we would probably get nicked for having no rear lights."
"But 'H' it's worth a try."

Harry shone his torch onto a glass cabinet it was full with lighters, cufflinks, and small ornaments; he picked up an empty box nearby.

Quickly he picked up a broom that was near at hand and then started to smash the glass with the broom handle. Then he began to grab whatever he could lay his hands on, throwing everything into the box.
He went along further and came to a shelf full of ladies' stockings, he threw them in, as he dragged the big box along to the back of the shop he came to a small office.

He flashed his torch at Jim, calling across to him, "How are you doing?"
"Yeah, alright, I've got a sack full of stuff here 'H' I don't think we won't be able to carry too much more."
"Alright Jim come over here."

The door of the office wasn't locked, they went in and began opening the drawers of a desk, inside was a cash box. Harry picked it up.
"Fuck me this feels heavy Jim, shall we open it here, or take it with us?" Harry asked, unsure of what to do.

"Hold on 'H' I'll go and find something to open it with."
"Hurry up then, I'm beginning to feel we've been in here too long."
Jim came back with a tool to prise it open, after a bit of a struggle the lock sprung open and he could feel his heart thumping with excitement.

"You know 'H' this reminds me of the night when we done the chocolate factory."
Jim opened the box; it was full of pound notes.
He laughed, "It looks like someone forgot to go to the bank before the weekend," he said happily.
Not bothering to count the money, he stuffed it in his pocket.

Harry opened the fire exit doors and pulled in the suitcase and kit bag, both bags were soaking wet from the continual rain. He started to pack all the stolen goods into them; he turned around, there was Jim with two bikes.

"Come on 'H' let's take these, its chucking it down out there."

They wheeled the bikes towards the narrow alleyway. Jim peered around the corner of the building and felt his heart jump up in his mouth, at the end of the alley stood a broad policeman, leaning against the wall smoking a cigarette.

He pushed Harry back, and put his hand over Harry's mouth to stop him talking; Harry instantly knew something was wrong. They both stood bolt upright against the fence, not murmuring a sound, the rain

continued to fall, soaking them to the skin. They heard a passerby shouting, "Goodnight constable."
The policeman replied, "Lovely weather for ducks. I'm off home now, it's the end of a long day."

Jim gave it a couple of minutes before poking his head back around the corner. He turned to Harry with relief on his face, in a calm voice he said, Thank fuck for that, he's gone."

They walked to the end of the alley to make sure the street was clear. He turned to Harry, "Thank God for the rain, it's kept everyone indoors tonight."

Then holding the wet heavy bags with one hand and steering the bikes with the other they set off to Sterling Road, in the hope that May would buy their stolen gear.

They cycled through the back streets, hoping not to be noticed and eventually got to the alley that led onto Carton Road, there they decided to abandon the bikes in the alley and go through to Sterling Road on foot.

They arrived at May's house feeling breathless, but at last pleased to be at their destination. Preparing for a ticking off for calling so late, Jim banged on the door, giving the knocker a hard slam. They both mimed May's words as if to know exactly what was coming, and then from behind the door came an angry voice, "Who the bloody hell is it, at this time of night?"
They both said together, "I told ya so."

The light went on in the passage. Jim shouted through the letterbox, "It's us, Jim and Harry."
May opened the door. "What is it with you two, do you think I stay up all fucking night or something?"

Jim pushed his way to the open door, "Sorry May, let us in we're soaking wet, we got something that might interest ya."
"I must be bleeding mad, go on take it into the back room."
They walked in to the dingy back room that smelt of damp.

"Right open the bags lets see what you got," she said in a matter-of-fact voice. She looked through the goods handling them roughly.
"Where's this lot come from?"
"The In and out Shop," replied Harry, wanting to take some part in the deal.

"Well you'll have to leave it with me and come back in a couple of days, I can't give ya a price right now."
"That's alright May, we'll come back on Wednesday."
"Please yourself, you'll just have to take the price I come up with, cause ya know, you two will find this lot hard to shift."
Jim stepped forward, "That's alright May, no rush."

After all they weren't that bothered, they still had a wad of notes to count.

When they left May's, they walked back through the alleyway to head home. The rain had now stopped, they dawdled along happily. The two bikes were still propped up against the post in the alley.

"What shall we do about them?" asked Jim
Harry felt in a good mood, they had done well tonight.
"Oh let's let some poor little fuckers think its Christmas when they see the bikes as they walk to school tomorrow; I can just imagine the look on their faces. There's plenty of kids around here with their arses hanging out of their trousers."

He liked the idea, little kids who had nothing finding brand new bikes, it would be a dream come true for them.

MOVING ON

Jim called on Harry on Wednesday when he had finished work for the day. The front door was open so he shouted down the passage, "'H' it's me."

Harry came out of the front room looking surprised to see Jim.
"Where have you been for the last couple of days?"
"Oh mate you won't believe it, I thought I was dying, it must have been because of the other night, we got soaked to the skin didn't we?"

He looked around him to make sure no one else was about and whispered, "Here's your money, 'H' from the In and out Shop, there's thirty five quid there."

Harry took the money, thinking, yes, we've cracked it again. His face broke into a broad smile; he put it quickly in his trouser pocket.
He then reminded Jim, "Don't forget, we have to go to May's tonight to collect some money from her."
"Do ya mind if I don't come 'H'? I still don't feel right."
"Alright," he replied, "I will go around there later."

He turned into Stirling Road, he was now beginning to feel hesitant about calling at May's, there was something about her that put him on tenterhooks. He put his hand on the knocker and took a deep breath, determined not to be trod down by her.

She appeared at the door, dressed in a navy and white printed dress, her blond hair set in tight curls. He could not help but notice her ample bosom, bulging over the low cut dress.
Smiling broadly she greeted him in a manner that he didn't expect.

"Come in Love," she said chirpily.
He now began to feel relaxed instantly.
"Come into the front room, I have got your money for ya."
She moved closer to him, "Why don't ya sit yourself down Love."
She went and stood near the fireplace. He found it hard to keep his eyes

off her shapely body, her small waist emphasised her extra large breasts. He wanted to take his eyes off them but was finding it increasingly difficult.

She smiled. "Would you like a little drop of gin with me Love? I'm fed up with me own company today."

He didn't quite know quite how to take her, but he decided yeah, she was alright, so he pushed himself further back onto the sofa, as if to make himself comfortable.

He readily accepted the drink and began to like her more by the minute. She stood at the sideboard, eagerly pouring herself another gin. He studied her face, how old would she be? Thirty or maybe a bit older? It had never occurred to him before, did she have a husband? If so, he was hoping that he wouldn't come bursting through the door at any minute.

She sat herself down beside him, "Here's your gin Love," she said as she forcefully put the glass in his hand. She looked into his eyes, he felt unsure why she was being so nice to him. Perhaps Jim was right after all, this might be her way of getting out of paying them their money.

Gulping her gin back quickly, she asked him if he would like another. He was now feeling slightly lightheaded after the first few gulps of gin. He readily agreed, for if he said no, she might take it as him being rude, and the last thing he wanted to do was upset her.

She started to ask him about himself, he readily told her all she wanted to know; in fact he was pleased she was showing him so much attention. As the evening went on, he plucked up courage to ask her a little about herself.

His first question was, "Do you have a husband?"
At this point a look of sadness came on her face.
"Yeah I did once, a right gent he was too. He comes from a right posh family. I'll be honest with ya Love, I never really knew what he saw in me."

She gave out a small chuckle, "Do ya know I loved him more than anything, but in the end, he just pissed off and left me for some rich widow, life can be a bastard, can't it Love? The only good thing is we never had any kids, that would have made it even harder to deal with. So I moved back here, to this house, it belonged to my mother, she died two years ago."

He looked at her; she was nothing like the hard-faced woman he met before. After several gins the ice was broken, they began to laugh. He felt he wanted to make her happy, to take away the sadness he saw in her eyes earlier.

The clock chimed ten; not wanting to outstay his welcome he rose to his feet, trying to regain his balance.
"I must be going May," he said in a somewhat slurred voice.
The effects of the gin seemed to be telling on him, and he fell straight back down onto the sofa.

She put her arm around him. "Oh are you alright Love?" showing concern.
"Yeah, yeah I'm alright May, I lost my balance somehow."
As he turned towards her, she pushed him further into the sofa and started to kiss him. The room felt like it was moving, almost like it was turning up side down, but whatever she was doing to him, he had no intentions of stopping it.

She took his arm, "Oh come on let's get you upstairs, you're in no fit state to walk home just yet."
He nodded his head in agreement, she was right he did feel dizzy. Once up the stairs, he was beginning to feel more composed.
"I will leave you here Love," she said in a caring voice.
He laid himself on the big bed.

Slowly, after a while his senses were coming back to him. He looked around the room; it was completely different from the rest of the house. The curtains gave an air of splendour, the tall mahogany headboard and thick cream eiderdown set off a room of warmth and elegance.

He studied the room, there was a hat stand in the corner, with silk scarves and underwear hanging from it, and a rich red velvet chair next to the bed. A picture in a rounded wooden frame, of a sailor standing boldly in his uniform, appeared to be staring straight at him; it made him feel uneasy as he wondered who could it be.

He never for one minute expected May to have a room anything like this, he read a book once about a French tart's boudoir and this is how he imagined the room to be.

He felt himself drifting back off to sleep, then his body felt hot, he didn't know if he was dreaming, then he was awake. He felt something moving over his body, and slowly opened his eyes.

There lay May next to him. He touched his body, a feeling of panic came over him, his clothes had gone. What could have happened? he asked himself, she must have pulled them off while he slept. He wanted to ask what was happening, but she was touching his dick, and it felt too good to distract her in any way.
She started to kiss him in a way that he had never been kissed before, and her experience showed. He lay there helplessly under the heavy eiderdown. She lay on top of him, and spread her legs across him, his hard dick went inside her instantly.

He wanted to shout out in ecstasy with this wonderful feeling inside his body. She gently went back and forth on top of him, he could hold out no longer, his heart was racing faster and faster, his cum shot out of him and his body shuddered vigorously. May stroked his face gently as he lay silent, not knowing what to say. She cuddled him tightly. He felt bewildered, how did all this come about? he asked himself.

The room started to show signs of dawn breaking; he slid out of the bed and began to gather his clothes, with the intention of getting home before his Father woke. May woke up, showing no signs of embarrassment. "Are you alright Love?" she asked as she stretched out to touch his leg.

He felt awkward, "Yeah I'd better be getting home though May."
"I'll see you to the door then Love, oh, and I wouldn't say anything about this if I were you. You know how people talk, and we wouldn't want that now." As they walked down the stairs he knew he now had to pluck up enough courage to ask for the money that he had come to collect last night.

She was about to open the door when he said nervously, "Oh May, the money, I nearly forgot it."
She looked surprised, "What money Love?"
"You know May, from the stuff we brought around the other evening."
"Oh, that money Love," she chuckled. "I think you have got to forget all about that. I mean Love, you've had more than your money's worth," she said assertively and began to giggle loudly.

He smiled shyly and walked out into the fresh morning air; his mind now in turmoil, how was he going to explain it all to Jim?

Over the next few days he managed to avoid Jim. Then on Saturday evening Jim tapped onto the front window of his house. This had been what he had been dreading most. He looked over the half nets, there

stood Jim looking forlorn, waving a piece of paper in his hand. Quickly he went outside. "What's up Jim?"
"What's up? I'll tell ya what's fucking up. I got this letter yesterday, it say's I start my National Service next week."

He felt like someone had struck him a severe blow; Jim was his best mate, without him nothing would be the same, and he knew it was coming, but he had put it out of his mind.
"Do ya fancy walking down to the Victory for a drink 'H'? I feel right fed up."
Wanting to please his mate, he said, "Yeah, why not."

This was Harry's first visit to the local pub, all of a sudden things were changing, what with the unmentionable incident with May earlier in the week, he was now feeling he was part of this man's world.

As they walked to the pub that early September evening, he knew he had to break the news to Jim about the money that he should have collected from May. There was nothing else for it, he could hang on no longer, he would have to tell him before he asked for the money, then in a sudden surge he blurted it out.
"You know, you were right Jim, May turned me over for the money."

Jim put his hands to his mouth, "Oh no mate, how come 'H'?"
"Well she gave me a few drinks, and to be honest there are parts I can't even remember."
He stammered as he spoke, his nerves were getting the better of him. Jim stopped in his tracks and leaned up against the wall. Panic came over Harry, he was now thinking Jim must be really angry with him. Then suddenly Jim slid down the wall, laughing like he'd never seen him laugh before. He could hardly speak, and then eventually, he composed himself.

"Oh this is just what I fucking needed," said Jim with tears rolling down his face.
Harry couldn't make out what was so funny, he grabbed Jim by the collar, he was now feeling confused.
"Well what is it?" he asked, feeling agitated.
"Oh mate you ain't fucking going to believe it."
Harry appeared bewildered.
"Oh 'H' mate, she done the same to me, when my uncle sent me around there to collect some money for him."
Harry saw the funny side of the situation, and began to laugh with him.
"Anyway 'H' what does it matter, we still got the money from the cash box aint we?"

He was now feeling much better; he wasn't the only one that had been taken for an idiot by May.
He turned to Jim, "You know what, you have got to say good luck to her, and she must be working at a hundred percent profit."
Jim started to laugh again, "Yeah thanks to silly horny bastards like us."
They stood at the bar and talked of their days growing up together. Then the piano started to play and all thoughts of National Service had left Jim.

On a cold winter's night, he put on his new suit and a Crombie overcoat. He looked in the mirror as he adjusted the new trilby hat that he had just bought himself. Yes he was feeling pleased with his appearance as he set off to Bernard's dance hall. He hadn't been there for a while, and as he walked in to the dance hall he felt all eyes upon him. He was now brimming with confidence and walked up to the bar and ordered himself a whisky.

He looked across to the door, there stood Ellen and Dolly. His heart started to jump, as they approached the bar near where he was standing. He was taken aback by how lovely Ellen looked in a grey tight-fitting dress that clung to her shapely figure. He walked towards her; those beautiful green eyes of hers appeared to jump out to him. He knew instantly, by the way she looked at him, she wanted him as much as he wanted her.
After their meeting at Bernard's, Harry and Ellen spent a lot of time together. In the year that followed, she began to understand him more: his love for poetry, and the darker side of his urge to steal.

They walked through the park on a summer's afternoon, and came to rest under a tree, and she laid herself on the grass. He stood against the trunk, looking lovingly down on her. He then wanted her more than anything in the world, but he knew he must wait, she was special and he didn't want to spoil it.
He started to recite Shakespeare, in a loud voice, full of fun, "How do I love thee? Let me count the ways. I love thee to the depth and breadth and height."

She looked at him and giggled, "Oh stop it Harry, you silly sod you know I don't understand any of that posh poetry."
He grabbed hold of her arm, "You don't have to understand it Ell," he said not wanting to put her down. "I'm just telling you Ell that I love thee."
She laughed, feeling slightly stupid as she said quietly, "I suppose I love thee as well."
Nothing could have made him happier, than to know she felt the same.

After leaving the pictures early on a Sunday evening, Harry and Ellen walked along the High Street, when he suddenly pulled her into the doorway of secondhand jewellery shop.
"Come on Ell give us a kiss," he said lovingly. They could hardly keep their hands off each other, and he rubbed her cheek. "Do you know Ell, it's two years since we first met?"
"I know I can't imagine ever being without ya now."

She turned to look in the shop window, "Oh look Harry, look at that ring, aint it beautiful?"
He looked into those green eyes of hers. "Do ya want it then Ell?"
She began to giggle. "But that's the sort of ring people wear when they get engaged, aint it?"
"Well let's get engaged," he said as he lifted her off her feet and pulled her towards him.
"But when?" she asked happily?
"Well how about right now Ell."

She looked at him mystified; he then looked down at the panel below the window of the shop. He felt around the edges it was held in by about six wood screws. Yes he'd made up his mind nothing was going to stop him now. Then quickly he fumbled in his pocket and pulled out a pen knife and started to unscrew them.
 She looked at him puzzled, "What ya going to do, you aint gonna break in there are ya?"
"Yeah," he said assertively, "I'm getting you that ring, all you have got to do is, just stand here and keep watch, and if you hear anyone coming just cough."

She readily agreed, for as much as he wanted to please her, she wanted to please him. After a little bit of tugging, he pulled off the panel, and wriggled his slender body through into the shop. Once he was in the darkness of the shop, he was now beginning to feel nervous.
He began to have second thoughts, what if somebody came by and caught them? It wasn't just him, he was also putting Ell at risk, but there was no going back now. He told her he would get her the ring and that's what he'd do.

After crawling around for a while he stretched his hand straight up to the shelf in the window and pulled the tray of rings towards him. He felt his heart beat with excitement, yes, yes, he had done it. It was hard to identify the one she had chosen in the dark shop, so he decided to take them all. He quickly put them in his pocket, and carefully poked his head back through the gap, he asked breathlessly, "Is it clear to come out Ell?"

"Yeah come on quick!" she said nervously. Finally he wriggled himself back through into the porch and pulled himself up. Eagerly he put his arm around her waist, asking her if she was alright. They locked arms and walked off along the street as if nothing had happened.

They made their way back through the marketplace, finally stopping at a street lamp. He showed her the hand full of rings, and smiled broadly.
"What one was it you liked Ell?"
She pointed to it; he put it on her finger and kissed her gently, "I told ya Ell, didn't I, we'd get engaged."
"Yeah," she giggled. "But I didn't think it would be that quick."
She held his hand tightly, "We will have to keep this to ourselves, if my Mum and Dad got to know they would go mad."
"Alright Ell I promise," he said tenderly. "It will be our secret."

He walked out of his house, there walking towards him was Ellen. He was pleased to see her. "Hello Ell where are you off to?"
"Nowhere in particular, I fancied a walk. Its so noisy in my house this morning, my Brother Ted was up early playing the piano and once he starts there is no stopping him, Bert and Henry are fighting over who's going to bath first, and my sisters are all going on about what clothes they are going to wear tonight. It's the same every Saturday."

He put his arm around her to comfort her. "Come on Ell cheer up, let's have a walk, let me and you have a wander to Gunners Park."
As they walked the gentle spring breeze began to lighten her mood. They sat by the lake for ages just talking, the swans were almost at their feet; how peaceful it was.
He pulled out a small red poetry book from his jacket pocket.
"You know Ell sometimes when I feel down, I get out this little book, and I read what someone wrote a hundred years ago, and I'm lost, I'm in a different world. You know, their beautiful thoughts that they have put to paper are with us forever."

They walked across the vast open space across the park to their favourite spot, and the cherry trees were in full bloom. There wasn't a soul to be seen. The sun shone bright; it was almost like summer. They decided to sit under the same tree that they always sat under. He stood up, taking out his pen knife from his pocket, and carefully carved 'H loves E'. Then he laid himself down beside her, and kissed her tenderly on the lips. Slowly and gently he caressed her shapely body. She began to respond to his gentle touch, she could not fight her feelings any longer, she loved him, and she wanted to show him just how much.
Today was to be the day that she finally gave herself to him.

THE FIFTIES

He combed his hair back into a neat quiff, and wiped the sweat from his brow, it had been hard going in the rag shop today, he looked up at the clock on the wall, thinking he knew better ways to earn a living. He walked out onto the cobbled courtyard, and glanced down to the arch gates the sun was blurring his vision a voice travelled towards him.
"Come on Creedy. Sprechen sie Deutsch mein herr?"
Putting his hand across the top of his eyes to shield his vision, he got closer, in an excited voice he shouted, "Jimmy! Is that you?"
Jimmy ran towards him, "Yeah it's me alright, who the fuck did you think it was?"

They embraced each other for the first time in two years. "Where did they send ya then Jim?" Harry asked hastily.
"First I went to Belford mate."
"Yeah I know that, your Sal told me, but where after that?"
"Oh mate, then they posted me off to Germany."
Harry squeezed his shoulder. "Oh mate it's good to have ya back."
"Yeah I tell you what though 'H' I've got to get some money together. I learned to drive when I was away; I've got the taste for it now. The first thing on the list is a new car." He smiled, "Well not brand new, second hand will do."
Harry grabbed his arm. "Come on mate let me buy you a pint, and bring you up-to-date with what's been going on around here," said Harry chirpily.

After a few weeks of Jim being back, Harry realised that he hadn't seen so much of Ellen, somehow they had lost touch. He decided he would walk along to the Dolls Factory at dinner time. He waited patiently outside, then he heard the sound of women's laughter spill onto the street; she was the last one to come out.
She was wearing a cream coloured turban around her head, and dark green overalls.
He called to her, "Ell over here."
She walked towards him. He stared at her for a while before speaking, her lovely clear complexion and green eyes always melted his heart.

"Hello Ell I was hoping I'd catch ya."
She looked at him surprised, "Oh I wondered what had happened to ya," she said with a sound of uncertainty in her voice. He put his arm around her. "Come on Ell let's walk." They made their way to the park near the church, where they met for their first date, and sat on the bench next to the drinking fountain
He put his arm around her; he wanted to look straight into her eyes, to tell her how much he really loved her. He looked around at the trees and the wild flowers and went silent for a while.

"Penny for ya thoughts," she said as she, nudged him.
"Sorry Ell I was thinking about when I was a kid, our air raid shelter was just over there, just near that acorn tree I can still remember how scared me and Pat were.
They stood up to walk; she put her arms around his waist and resting her head on his shoulder, he heard a whimpering sob.
"What is it Ell, what's up?"
The sobs became louder she could hardly speak. "Ell please tell me what it is."

She finally stopped herself from crying and looked up into his eyes, she wiped away her tears. "Harry I'm going to have a baby."
Instantly he felt himself wanting to pull away from her, he was lost for words, there was an awkward silence. His thoughts were yeah, he loved her but no, no, he couldn't love a baby, well not at this point in his life. Panic was rising in him, what could he say to comfort her?
Despair showed in her face, "Harry please tell me, what am I going to do?"

"I don't know Ell, I just don't know, let me think."
She began to feel angry; he wasn't showing her enough concern, she stamped her feet, she wanted reassurance. "Well I tell you what, when you've thought about it let me know."
Not being able to control her feelings any longer, she slapped him hard across the face, then went running from the park and off down the street. For the rest of the day the problem weighed heavily on his mind.

Ellen knew she couldn't hide her small bump any longer, she would choose today to wait for her Mum to come home from her work at the laundry. She braced herself as her Mother came bursting through the door. She walked over to the stove to put the kettle on and turned to Ellen sitting at the table.
"Where is everyone?" she asked
"Oh Dad and the boys are not home yet, and Vi and Lilly are doing overtime at work."

She smiled. "Well make yourself busy Ell and peel some potatoes, you know how hungry your Dad and the boys are when they finish at the coal yard."
Ellen stood near the sink attempting to peel the potatoes, suddenly tears flooded from her eyes, her sobs got louder, and louder. Ivy went over to her, "What is it Ell Love?"
She threw her arms around her Mum's neck. "Mum I'm sorry, but I'm going to have a baby."
Ivy quickly wrenched her arms away. "No you can't be, you stupid bloody little cow, what have you done? Please Ell, don't tell me that it's that Harry's."
"But Mum I didn't mean it to happen."

Ivy felt rage building up inside her she could think of nothing worse than one of her beloved daughters having a baby by that 'no good' everyone knew what he got up to - they would be the talk of the neighbourhood.
Ellen tried desperately to seek some understanding from her, and put her arms back around her. She sobbed, "I'm sorry Mum, I'm so sorry." Ivy pushed her away again, then began ripping Ellen's blouse from her in anger. She paced around the room, and put her hands to her face in despair. "How can a daughter of mine, cheapen herself like this?"
Ellen went down on her knees, and cried until her tears ran dry.

It wasn't long before Jim was talking Harry into doing another burglary; they were at the bar in the Victory pub, both feeling in a lighthearted mood.
"You know 'H' I've got to get some money together to get a car, once we've got transport we can get down to some serious business."
Harry paused for thought. "Well what ya got in mind then Jim?"
"How about James Watson's, the jewellers in the High Street?"

Harry banged his glass down hard. "You got to be fucking kidding; it's right next door to the police station."
"Exactly!" Jim said, feeling sure of himself. "They would never guess someone would do a robbery right under their nose, would they now?" Harry took a large gulp of his beer. "Alright when do ya want to do it?"
"How about tomorrow night" Jim said being as keen as ever.
They discussed their plans in great detail, Jim had already made himself busy, he'd been staking the shop out for a week.

The following night, putting the tools together in a hold all, came easy, Jim had planned exactly what they would need.
"Well what we're do 'H' is go down the alley at the back of the shop and we'll sling this lot over the wall, then go on to Bernard's to get our

alibi. We'll make sure we get noticed, then we can creep back to do the job about midnight."

The town hall clock chimed eleven as they took a slow walk to the other end of the High Street; they reached the back alley that ran along the back of the row of shops. Jim kept watch while Harry went down the alley to check all was clear, before they made their entrance. Harry gave a whistle; this meant it was alright for Jim to follow. Once they were in the small back yard, Jim took out the hacksaw and started to saw eagerly through the iron bars across the small window. Harry stood near the wall that backed on to the alley and listened carefully, to make sure the coast was clear.

Jim turned around to him, "For fuck sake 'H' my arms are killing me here, I'm never gonna get through these bleeding bars."
Harry walked over to him. "Give it here for fuck's sake. I'll have a go, you go and keep watch."
It wasn't long before he had sawn through, then wrenching back the bars, he then took off his jacket and wrapped it around his fist, he then smashed the window; quickly he threw in their bag of tools.
Jim climbed carefully through the window, trying to avoid the jagged bits of glass.

"Its so fucking dark in here, we ain't gonna be able to see anything 'H'."
Harry put his head through the window, then with one tug from Jim he was pulled inside. He pulled out a torch from inside his shirt, carefully shining it towards the ground and they began to feel their way about in the thick darkness.
They crawled along on their knees; they were now beginning to feel a little more confident; the shop didn't appear to be alarmed. They came to the glass cabinets, they were all locked securely.
"Oh for fuck's sake, this is not going as good as I thought it would be," said Jim impatiently.

Harry was now feeling angry, had it all been a wasted effort, but he had made up his mind no, he wasn't going to be outdone. He kicked the glass, it was tough and wouldn't break. Jim took a small hammer from his trouser pocket, and to their delight came the sound of the breaking glass, in this small dark shop the sound could only be compared to millions of nails dropping onto a tin roof.

A sudden flash of light came through the window. Harry looked up.
"Oh no, it's a fucking copper out there. Quick let's scarper."
They had no other choice, gathering their bag of tools they almost dived through the window that they had entered ten minutes earlier.

They hastily made their way through the dark alleys and back streets, running breathlessly back to South Acton, empty-handed.

After work on Monday, Harry decided he must see Ellen; he couldn't leave it any longer, so he waited outside the Dolls Factory, not knowing what he was going to say, or how she was going to react.
What he knew for sure was that he cared enough to know she would need him more than anything right now.
He waited patiently, his heart beating in anticipation, finally he caught sight of her, as she stood with her cardigan draped over her arm, in front of her stomach.

His heart went out to her, she appeared sad and alone, his immediate though, was that she was trying to hide her bump. He felt angry with himself, what had he done to her? This girl he loved so much. Or did he? Yes he did, today he would do the right thing by her, and ask her to marry him; he couldn't let her go all through this on her own.
She spotted him and walked over slowly towards him, and not a word was spoken. They gazed at each other lovingly.
He nervously touched her arm. "I've missed ya Ell." She smiled, but looked uncomfortable with the situation.

Then from nowhere came a police car, screeching to a halt, suddenly two coppers jumped out one of them grabbed him by the scruff of the neck.
"What's it all about?" asked Harry feeling bewildered. Ellen looked on at all the commotion, and panic was in her face.
In a sarcastic voice the younger one, of the two asked, "Do you like books Creedy?"
Trying to get his words out, in all the panic he replied, "Yeah why?"
"Well you aint going to like this one." He frantically waved a library ticket in front of him and smiled broadly.
"It's just got you nicked son, we found this ticket on the premises of James Watsons the jewellers."
There in very clear ink written on the ticket, was the name Harry Creedy. He looked at the crumbled ticket, in disbelief, how could he have been that stupid?
They pushed his head down and threw him forcefully into the car.
Ellen looked on bewildered as she stepped back from all the commotion going on around her.
He shouted through the open car window, "I love you Ell, you know that don't ya?"
As he was driven off, he looked out of the back window of the car as Ellen walked off into the distance with her head bowed down; he felt like his whole world had fallen apart.

After his court hearing, he was taken to Wandsworth Prison. On a hot summer's afternoon, as he was driven through the gates, he knew this was his home for next year and a half.

Issued with his prison uniform, he was taken to his cell. He looked around the small dingy space with two beds and a bucket. He punched the wall and shouted, "Bollocks!" over and over again, until finally he felt the anger leaving him.

It was pointless, he thought, there was no one there to care about how he was feeling.

He sat on the edge of the bed with his head in his hands, when in walked another prisoner. He looked up; there stood a tall man with dark cropped hair, his piercing blue eyes, stared straight at him, he held out his hand towards him and said, "Who might you be old chap?" His handsome face broke into a pleasant smile.

He stood up, "My name's Harry, I arrived a couple of hours ago."

"Oh, so you're my new cell mate, are you?"

"I suppose I am."

He was feeling a sense of relief, thinking it could have been much worse; he might have been put in a cell with some old down-and-out.

"My name is Edward, you can call me Eddie," he said in an upper class accent.

That night in the cell Eddie and Harry got to know a bit about each other. After asking Eddie what he was in for, his own small burglary in the jewellers hardly warranted time in the nick.

Eddie told of his life before crime, he joined the army when he was twenty and ended his career in the bomb disposal unit, this give him the knowledge that would later come in useful for his chosen profession as a safe-cracker.

After spending a few months in the prison, he had now come to terms with his life there.

He was missing Ellen more as the time went on, so he decided to take a chance and send her a visiting order, in his heart he thought it might be pointless, but he loved her and wanted to tell her so, he'd take a gamble, and hope for the best.

On Saturday afternoon, a prison officer came to his cell. "Creedy you have got a visitor; follow me to the visitor's room," said the stone faced prison officer.

Harry had never been so pleased to hear the clinking of those dreaded keys. He sat at a table, and gazed around the unwelcoming room, the only warmth was the heat that came from the other bodies in the room; his stomach started to jump as if doing summersaults.

He continually looked across to the door, waiting for her to appear, then suddenly he noticed her auburn hair, she had spotted him and walked across the room with a gentle smile on her face. He stood up and touched her hand and looked straight into her eyes, no there was no doubt about it he loved her, and her carrying his baby now meant the world to him.
It had taken a while, but he had now got used to the idea of a baby in his life. Her shapely figure had disappeared, but she still looked radiant, she seemed to be at ease carrying the baby. The troubled look she once had when she first got pregnant had now left her.

"Thanks for coming Ell, sit down." He couldn't help but notice her big bulge and wanted to put his hand on her stomach, and feel his baby kick. She sat down awkwardly.
"Did you come all this way on ya own Ell?"
"No Dolly's waiting out side for me."
He smiled, "She's a good friend to ya Ell."
"I know she's been by my side these last few months."
He clasped his hands over hers. "How is everything at home now?"
"Not too bad I think they are all gradually getting over the shock, they couldn't be treating me any better."
"Ell you know I love ya, don't ya?"
He was hoping to hear the word "Yes" but it went silent.
"Well Ell, when I get out of here we can sort things out. I know I've let ya down but honest Ell, I'm gonna make it all up to ya."

She looked straight into his eyes. Why? she asked herself, why oh why, didn't he show her this concern at the very beginning? It was all too late now. She touched his hand gently, "But Harry, the baby's due next month."
"Yeah I know Ell, but your family will help ya won't they? At least until I get out."
"I suppose so," she said, still feeling uncertain about the future.
"Do ya know Ell, that day the coppers nicked me, I was gonna ask ya to marry me."
She smiled; she would never know if that was the truth.
He asked her what had been happening on the outside.
"Not much really, I don't go anywhere much at the moment," she replied, perking up a little.
"Oh yeah, I saw Jimmy the other day, he said to be remembered to you, and don't forget to send him a visiting order; he said he's not forgot what you done for him,and you would know what he meant."
He smiled, "You know Ell; I can't wait to get out of this fucking hole, once I'm out I'm going to go straight, I'm gonna do that for you Ell. I mean why Ell, why? I just seem to get this urge to nick things."

She smiled. "I think that's what I always liked about you, it's because you never give a shit about anything."
For a second he saw a bit of the old Ellen coming back, that daring, vibrant, young girl he met at Bernard's Dance Hall, he leaned forward; and kissed her gently on the lips.
"Ell I don't expect you to come and visit any more, I just wanna ask ya one thing; promise you'll wait for me?"
She smiled, not uttering a word, then came the sound of the bell, it was the end of visiting time. He wanted to pull her close and give her one last passionate kiss, but she kissed him lightly on the cheek, turned and left the room.
He returned to his cell feeling deflated, the visit had not gone as well as he had hoped. It felt like she may have been holding her feelings back; he shook his head, no it was him who was at fault, he was an idiot, and she was slipping away from him. Not once did she say she loved him, a lump appeared in his throat as he asked himself, "What kind of bastard am I?"

It was a foggy morning, when he looked out through the bars of his small cell; a prison officer opened the door, calling "Creedy, come with me!"
They walked along the long corridor, there wasn't a soul about, it was almost like all the prisoners had absconded.
He told him, "We are going to get some wire from the centre, it's needed for a few odd jobs; it's a day's work for some of you prisoners." The store room lay under the centre, he was told to walk in front of the officer, he walked in silence along B wing then to wing B2.

He was just about to carry on up the stone steps when he heard a terrible scream; he looked up to the landing above him.
Behind the wire mesh stood a group of people; there was the Chief Prison Officer, a priest, and a young man with a prison officer on either side of him. Suddenly he began to kick at them, like mad a mad animal, he turned and punched the Chief Officer, sending him to the ground, he carried on kicking as he clung to the wire mesh screaming, "Mum, Dad, Mum, Dad, Mum, help me, I'm innocent, truly I'm innocent!"

The priest dropped his prayer book and began to prise the young man's fingers from the mesh. Then from around the corner of E wing walked the Prison Governor, dressed in a brown suit and brown hat, accompanied by another Chief Officer, walking a few steps behind him. He pointed to shouted, "Gag him, gag him, gag the bastard."
Harry looked on with fear, wondering what was going on. Then suddenly the other prisoner was grabbed from behind by his ankle, the prison officer dragged him back to the gate, at the bottom of B wing.

The screaming was still going on in the distance; it was a deathly sound, of a man fearing for his own life, fighting desperately to save his soul. He thought, perhaps this was an innocent man, pleading desperately for his life, and no one was listening.

Eddie lay on his bed. He passed him over a book. "Here you are Harry, perhaps you would like this to read."
He rubbed his hand over the red leather cover. "Thanks Eddie." He browsed through it. "It's Keats," he said happily.
"I didn't know you liked Keats, Eddie."
He smiled, "Oh yes; he's always been one of my best loved poets."
He got to know a bit more about Eddie; it pleased him even more that they both shared a love of poetry.

"It's strange," said Harry, "You have come from a well-to-do family, and where did you say you was educated, Oxford wasn't it?"
"Then take me, I grew up where all the kids had their arses hanging out of their trousers, half of them couldn't even read or write. And we've both ended up in here, life's strange aint it?"
Eddie broke into loud laughter. "I tell you what old chap, it didn't please my Mother and Father too much when they found out their only son had robbed a bank."

At the end of January, Harry was handed two envelopes, this always made him happy.
He opened the first one, that he knew to be from his Father, with the general news, he also wrote that he hadn't been feeling too well, but blamed this on the weather.
He put the letter back neatly in the envelope and felt sad; his Father had now turned seventy. He felt concerned about how lonely he must be; desperately he tried to put it out of his mind but it was no use he was angry with himself, all the worry that he had given him always getting in trouble with the law.

Then he studied the next envelope; he didn't recognise the handwriting. He held it in his hand for a while, this was something he liked, the thought of not knowing who it was from, once opened the surprise would be gone. His stomach began to churn, he felt jittery, and it was no use he could wait no longer, he opened it slowly and pulled out a card, on the front was a picture of a pale blue sky, with one lonely snowdrop on the green grass.

Carefully he opened the card and looked straight at the bottom; it was from Dolly, it read:

Dear Harry,

I hope you are well, I am writing to tell you that Ell had a little baby girl on the 6th January, she weighed 6 lbs 12oz, her name is Lena. They are both doing well. I see Jimmy, he sends his regards. I will keep in touch.
Take care

Love Dolly
xx

He stood alone in his cold depressing cell, thinking to himself it would be easier to fight ten men than it was to hold in the tears that were ready to spurt from his eyes. He was a father, and had a little daughter, but he couldn't see her and he couldn't touch her. Then to release his anger he kicked the wall in a fit of rage; he wanted to be with them; would it ever be possible? he asked himself.

Throughout the year that followed he now felt confident that prison had done him good. With the odd visit from Jim and Patrick to keep him going, he had now convinced himself that when he was released he would be staying on the straight and narrow.

Two days before Christmas 1950 he was given back his civilian clothes and let back out in to the world. He walked through the big gates and gazed back at the depressing prison building, he told himself, "Never again."

The snow lay thick on the ground, he looked up at the grey sky, as a flurry of snow flakes hit his face. He breathed in the fresh air, and patted his chest, feeling thankful to escape the smelly stuffy air of the prison, how good it felt.
Then in the distance, came a voice from an open car window, shouting, "Over here Creedy!"
He looked across, and there with that same broad grin on his face, sat Jim, in a dark blue Ford Pilot. Quickly he walked over to the car; in the back sat Dolly. Jim jumped out, opening the door on the passenger side, taking off his hat and bowing, he said, "Your carriage awaits you sir."
Harry shook his hand vigorously. "Well this is a nice surprise." He turned to Dolly. "It's good to see you Doll, thanks for keeping in touch."
As they made their way along the snow-covered streets, they chatted non-stop. Jim suddenly slammed on his brakes, and then in his normal chirpy manner he said. "Oh, this is just what we need."

He parked outside the big old rambling pub and they went in. It was noisy and crowded. Harry looked around and smiled as he thought how good it was to hear the laughter. It was full of the spirit of Christmas, the roaring fire sent out a warm cosiness. They stood at the bar; he couldn't help but notice the barmaid's curvy figure. Jim ordered two large brandies for them both, and a gin and tonic for Dolly, and pulled out a roll of notes.

"I see you're still doing well Jim," Harry said with a pleased feeling that his best mate hadn't changed.
"It can't be no other way mate, you know me, I hate to be skint."
They made themselves comfortable at a table close to the fire. Harry was now on his second brandy, a warm feeling began to take over, and he realised how good he was feeling inside. With prison now behind him, he was determined to live life to the full. He looked at Dolly and Jim and couldn't help wondering. where they together as a couple, or just friends? The brandy had now given him enough courage to ask about Ellen.

Jim went off to the toilet, now was his chance; he leaned across the table, in almost a whisper, he asked, "How's my little girl Doll?"
Dolly's eyes lit up, "She's beautiful; Ells Mum and Dad think the world of her, they treat the baby as if she were their own."
"How about Ell, how is she?" Dolly went silent.
"What is it Doll?"
Jim returned, he had picked up on the tension, Dolly still could not answer him, and Jim butted in.
"'H' you aint gonna like it mate, but your gonna find out sooner or later, she's married mate."

Harry stood up, he hadn't bargained on hearing this, he felt as if someone had just stuck a knife in him. He walked out of the pub, needing time to think, he felt angry, how she could do this to him?

The snow was now falling heavier, he started to tremble, and lit a cigarette and puffed on it hard. His mind was now feeling very confused, "No, no, she can't be married." He went back inside, with anger boiling up inside him.
"Doll tell me when all this happened, when did she get married?"
She looked at him; he looked like a child who had been punished. "It was back in the summer, she married Jack Bunter; he's always liked her. Look Harry, at one time she loved you more than anything, but in the end, she couldn't see any future for you and her. Jack was there for her when she needed somebody; they are living at her Mum and Dad's house.

Harry you've got to understand what it was like for her, she couldn't cope with everyone talking about her having a baby out of wedlock; in spite of her happy-go-lucky ways, this all proved too much for her."
He sat there trying to make sense of it all. "But Doll my baby must have been just a few months old when she got married, she could have at least waited until I got out, we might have been alright, if she had just given me the chance."
All he could think of was his daughter, she was his, he didn't want any other man to take her on.

They turned into Park Road, the snow was still falling, Jim stopped the car. "Home at last 'H'. Harry was about to get out of the car, when Jim put a handful of notes in his hand.
"Here, take this 'H' it was good you taking the rap, not bringing me into it, I know it's all been hard for ya mate."
Not giving it another thought, Harry stuffed the money in his pocket as he waved them off. For the first time in a long time, he put his hand inside the letterbox, there the key was still hanging on the bit of string; he smiled to himself, thinking some things never change; it had hung there since he was a small boy.

The passage was in darkness; he called out, "Dad it's me."
A frail voice came back to him, "I'm in here son." He walked into the small front room, the instant heat from the fire hit him. There sitting in the armchair was his Father, with a blanket wrapped around him. He went over to him; and put his arms around his shoulders.
"It's good to be home Dad."
He looked up at him feebly, a tear ran down his cheek. "It's good to have you back son."
He took a step back. "What is it Dad? You don't look well."
"Oh it's this cold weather, it don't help my chest none," He broke into a coughing fit. Harry looked on helplessly and then ran to get him a drink of water. He was feeling sad to see his Father sitting all alone and sick. Wanting to make up for lost time, he tried to make his Father as comfortable as possible.

That night he had the big double bed all to himself, after the uncomfortable bunk he had in his prison cell it was pure luxury. The next morning he woke and pulled back the curtain; the snow lay thick on the ground, it was Christmas Eve; and he was determined to make this a good Chistmas for his Father. Childhood memories came flooding back to him. He looked across the room thinking to himself that Pat must have got snowed in somewhere.

He counted the pound notes Jim had given him, twenty six crisp notes, and put them neatly in his pocket, feeling happy that this would keep him going for a while. He put on his overcoat and hat to set off to the shops; he trudged along in the thick snow; he was still savouring the feeling of freedom. The shops were alive with people doing their Christmas shopping. He stood patiently in the queue at the grocers, after all he had all the time in the world to do what he wanted to do, he was a free man. The woman in front of him, turned around, to his surprise it was Ellen's mum, and he braced himself, waiting for her to say something. This was the closest he had ever been to her, they had never spoken, he had only ever seen her from a distance; she didn't say a word.

He touched her gently on the shoulder, in a nervous voice he asked, "Mrs Keller can I have a word with you?"
She herself looked nervous. "Alright," she replied. "Come outside I don't want everyone knowing my business."
They stood in the shops porch, "Well what is it you want?" she asked as if she had no time to spare him.
He bowed his head as he spoke. "How's my little girl Mrs Keller, is she alright?"
She studied him; she could see he was hurting inside; a gentle smile came on her face. "She doing well, we'll make sure of that."
He looked down at the ground, finding it hard to look her in the eyes. "I just want to say I'm sorry Mrs Keller."

"Well she' married now, its all in the past, you should have done something about it at the time, and you would have had your little girl with you now. You know my Ellen's been through a lot of heartache."
He looked at her showing concern, "Once again, I'm sorry."
Hoping that he had made some amends to the situation, he then walked back in the shop.

The harsh wind was blowing the large snow flakes directly into his face. He had been in almost every shop; his arms were laden with bags. He was about to cross the road when he saw Mrs Keller, she was about to turn the corner. He hastened his step to catch her up; he pulled out a box of chocolates from one of his carrier bags.
He called her, she turned towards him, and he put the box in her hand and wished her, "A Merry Christmas." She smiled as she looked at the picture of a thatched cottage on the chocolate box.
"And Merry Christmas to you Harry."
He headed off home, feeling that things might get better, and that he may get to see his daughter after all.

John was sitting in the armchair when he walked into the warm cosy room. "What have you got there son?"
"Just you wait and see Dad," he said excitedly, as he started to take the shopping from the bags, John looked on in amazement. There was a chicken, fruit and vegetables, a bottle of whisky, and a Christmas cake. He looked at his father hesitantly, "Don't worry Dad; Jim gave me some money yesterday."

He touched his heart as if he could feel happiness pumping from it, thinking how good it was to have his son back home.
Harry glanced up at the mantelpiece, and picked up the one and only Christmas card. It was hand-made by Ruby, on the front was a picture of an angel; it felt as if, her eyes were looking deep in to his soul. He held the card close to him, and thought of Ruby, he had never really understood to this day, how she could spend her life in a convent.
Suddenly he heard voices, he went to the front door, and there stood a group of young children, warmly wrapped in their thick winter clothes. He looked at their bright faces, their rosy red cheeks were glistening, and one of them rattled a tin in front of him as they sang 'Silent Night'. He kept the door open wide to make sure his Father could hear the carol, he had always liked it since he was a young boy at school.
Then he watched them walk away in the crisp snow, he shouted after them, "Have a Merry Christmas."
He went back in to the room with a tear in his eye, John was stoking the fire he turned to him. "You know son, I think I'm going to enjoy this Christmas after all."

Harry took two glasses from the sideboard and poured them each a whisky, and put it into his Father's shaking hand. The sound of the front door opening drew their attention, in walked Patrick covered in snow, his red nose just showing above the scarf wrapped around him. He walked over to hug his younger brother.
"Oh it's good to see ya Pat, it really is."
Patrick was still recovering from his long journey; his hands were purple with the cold as he tried to unbutton his coat.
"Do you know, I didn't think I was going to make it home for Christmas. Doreen's dad has just driven me all the way from Harefield. There were no buses or trains, because of the bad weather, we almost crawled along, and the roads are turning to ice."
He walked over to the fire and held his hands close to the flames, to put back some warmth into his body. Harry poured a whiskey and handed it to him. He put his arm around his younger brother. "Get this down you Pat; it will warm you up in no time."
John sat, feeling the most contented he had felt in a long time, with both his sons at his side.

Suddenly the door of their front room burst open, they all looked up and to their surprise, there stood Dickie Masters, their upstairs neighbour. He looked around the room with a flustered look, realising he had entered the wrong door, he appeared startled.
"Oh I'm sorry Mr Creedy; I stopped at the pub on my way home from work to celebrate Christmas, I think I might have had one too many," he said in a slurred voice, as he swayed from side to side.
John looked at him amused. "That's alright, while you're here, you might as well have a glass of whisky with me and my boys."
With a big grin on his usually serious face, feeling highly delighted at the invite, Dickie sat himself down.

As the evening went on the laughter got louder and louder, then a knock came on the door of the front room. A voice shouted from the other side of the door, "Mr Creedy, it's Mrs Masters, do you think you could keep the noise down a bit? My husband is in bed with the flu."
Patrick opened the door, she glanced in, and a look of shock came on her face. "Dickie, what the bloody hell are you doing here?"
Before he could answer, Patrick pulled her into the room, "Sit yourself down Mrs Masters, have a Christmas drink with us."
She gazed around the cosy room that looked very inviting, as she sat herself on the sofa she replied, "Well, thank you very much, I don't mind if I do."
Harry looked across at her, he wanted to laugh, the vision came back to him, the last time she had a Christmas drink with them the house nearly went up in flames.
The drinks were flowing when John asked Patrick to go to his bedroom and bring the small case from under the bed. Doing as he was told, he returned with the dusty case. John put his hand straight to the bottom of the case and pulled out his mouth organ.
Harry began to laugh. "You know Dad, I don't think you have got the breath to blow that these days."
John got out of his chair, after a couple of blows, to get himself in tune, he started to play 'I'll take you home again Kathleen.'
Patrick and Harry listened to the harmonious music. Harry felt the tears run down his cheek, his Father had once told them this was the song he liked to play, to their Mother.
Mrs Masters interrupted. "Mr Creedy, I don't suppose you can play 'When Irish eyes are smiling', it's always been a favourite of mine, ya know." She tapped her chubby knees and gave out a loud chuckle.
He went straight into it, as she sang along like a nightingale.
The clock struck twelve, Mrs Masters in panic pulled Dickie up onto his unsteady feet.
"Come on, we had better get up those stairs." After some banging and crashing, the house went silent, and the lights went off.

WINE AND ROSES

In the New Year, John's health was still poorly, there was Harry still with no work so things didn't look too bright, but at least he was there to look after his father. John survived on his small pension, and Harry still had some of the money left that Jim given him on his release from prison but he knew this wouldn't last for ever. Wistfully he gazed out of the front room window; the snow had nearly all gone. He turned to his father. "I think I had better get out and find some work, Dad." John smiled weakly.

He stopped to get a newspaper and cigarettes, before setting off to look for work. He walked along the street, browsing through the paper and looked up to the top of the page, there in bold print was the date, 6th January 1951; he stopped in his tracks, it was his little girl's birthday, she would be one year old today. Suddenly he felt angry; he asked himself, "Why, oh why?" There was no answer, it was all down to him, he had let it all happen. He stood against a lamp post and tore the date off of every page in the paper, he tore it in shreds and threw it up into the air like confetti; anger was sieving up inside him, and he couldn't stand to be reminded of what might have been.
Now he had now lost all interest in finding work, he roamed the streets feeling melancholy, eventually he found himself in the High Street; he felt sad and alone.

His attention was taken by a toy train whizzing around in a shop window, he became mesmerised and he looked further along the display, there propped up on the shelf, was a big brown teddy bear. He put his hand in his pocket, took a ten shilling note and decided to buy it. Now feeling in a slightly happier frame of mind he headed towards Carton Road with the teddy in his arms. He knew he could not give it to Ellen in person but he would leave the teddy on the doorstep for his little girl's birthday present and hope that Ell would guess who it was from, he thought, surely this was allowed. He placed it carefully on the doorstep and was about to walk away from the house, when he heard the clinking of milk bottles being put on the door step. He looked behind him and there stood Ell at the door.

She looked good, her figure had now returned to its shapely curves. She picked up the teddy and glanced over towards him.
He stood there for what felt like forever, their eyes met but not a word was spoken, and she gently closed the door. He walked off feeling he had lost the most precious two people in his life, Ell and his daughter; his heart was aching and he just wanted the pain to leave him.

With the summer now upon him, he began to feel happier with life, he still hadn't found work but he found it very easy to walk into a shop and take whatever caught his eye, well, within reason.
Harry and Jim were having their usual Saturday night at Bernard's, they stood at the bar chatting, when Sal walked in with her friend Marge, he studied Sal carefully, she had definitely lost her little girl look.
In a tight white dress and high heeled shoes, she looked quite attractive.
He turned to Jim, "I tell you what Jim; your Sal looks good tonight."
"I don't know about that mate, but I don't half fucking fancy that Marge."

He went over to Sal. "How do ya fancy dancing with ya brother's best mate then Sal?"
She smiled, as if her prayer had been answered. He had found something about her that he liked, and he sensed she was more than pleased at his attention.
He spotted Jim happily shuffling Marge around the dance floor and knew he wouldn't be having much contact with him for the rest of the evening. Immediately he grabbed Sal's arm, for some reason he really fancied her tonight.
"Jim's a bit busy with your friend, why don't I walk you home Sal?"

She picked up her bag and readily put her arm into his, they were about to leave Bernard's when he noticed Dolly and Twinkle standing near the stage.
He told Sal to hang on and walked over to have a word with Dolly; he touched her gently on the shoulder and pulled her to one side.
"Doll, do ya think you could do me a big favour? It's something that's been on my mind for a while."
She looked surprised. "What is it Harry?"
He spoke quietly. "Do ya think you could bring my little girl to see me without Ell knowing?"

She didn't know what to say, she appeared puzzled as he put his hands together, as if to pray.
"Harry I want to help you, I know it must be horrible for you, but Ell's my cousin, and best friend, she would go mad if she thought I betrayed her."

"But Doll please, just this once, I promise you I will never ask you again, I know it's time to get on with my life, but if I could only hold her in my arms just once."
Dolly listened to his heart-rendering plea. "Well I tell you what I will do, I'm taking my baby sister Belinda to Gunners Park tomorrow, I'll ask Ell if I can take Lena as well, but I can't promise anything."

He pulled her to him and give her a big kiss on the cheek; she walked towards Twinkle, shouting back to him, "I'll see ya at eleven o'clock tomorrow near the boating lake."
His heart felt lighter as he joined Sal, he picked her up and playfully threw her across his shoulder. "Let's get you home Sally Downs."

Sal laughed all the way home, thinking at last she had got the man of her dreams, she leaned against the porch wall; she was longing for him to kiss her, but he kept at a distance, after all she was Jim's sister. He had known her since she was a little girl, but tonight he found himself fighting with his feelings.
He felt a warm tingling feeling in his dick, it had gone hard; he put his hands in front of himself trying to hide the bulge sticking out from his trousers. It was hard to keep his eyes off her shapely figure in the tight white dress, and with her hair dyed blond it had changed her appearance completely. He did want her, he wanted her right then, he felt like he was going to explode and just wanted to put his dick inside her.

She stepped towards him and kissed him, putting her tongue gently in his mouth; he put his hand inside her low cut dress and fondled her breast, quickly she began to respond and started to breath heavy. He pushed himself against her, but really wanting to fight it, her body felt warm, he could hold on no longer.
Then he grabbed hold of her roughly and pulled her around to the side of the house, where they could not be seen by passersby. Quickly he pulled up her dress as she undid his fly.
She began to rub his dick; there was no awkwardness about her, she seemed to know exactly what she was doing. Not being able to wait a minute longer he pulled down her knickers and put his dick inside her, it was too late to stop now, then she kissed him passionately as she whispered, "I love you Harry, I always have."

His breathing became heavier and heavier, his heart was thumping like mad, as he came quickly he pulled away, kissing her on the cheek. He leaned back on the fence opposite her, desperately, trying to regain his breath. He stared across as he watched her tidy herself up, his mind was in turmoil as he questioned himself, thinking, for fuck's sake, what have I done?

He was now feeling it should never have happened, in the short space of about ten minutes he felt he had made a big, big mistake.
He couldn't think of one word that he thought might please her as she started to giggle and threw her arms around him.
"Well I never expected that to happen," she said in a happy voice.
The suddenly there was the sound of footsteps coming along the pavement, they were getting closer, he was praying that it wasn't Jim, but they gradually disappeared into the distance, as he breathed a sigh of relief.
He kissed her once more on the cheek, then said in a matter-of-fact way, "Oh well Sal, I'll see ya soon."

She flung her arms around him again, not wanting to let him go.
"How about tomorrow?" she asked sharply. He clasped her hand in his.
"I'm sorry I can't tomorrow Sal," he said, feeling guilty after what had just happened between them.
She looked at him like he had let her down. He began to feel uneasy, now wanting to get away from the situation, he detected a touch of anger in her face.
"What is it, are you taking that Dolly Todd out?"
"No I'm not she's a friend." But if he was honest; there had been times lately when he wished Dolly was his girlfriend. He felt irritated, he didn't feel that he needed to explain his whereabouts to her.
"Anyway look Sal, I better be going, I will be in touch."
She put the key in the front door, feeling confused and unsure as to what lay in store for them.

He sat on the bench opposite the boating lake; the summer sun was already beating down on him as he watched the young mothers walking by with their children. There was no sign of Dolly so he carried on reading his newspaper, trying not to look up every time he heard footsteps.
Then he was distracted by the sound of a young child crying, slowly he peered up and there stood Dolly dressed in a pale blue dress, she was pushing a dark blue pram. He stood up, and looked caringly at her then smiled. "You look nice Doll, thanks for coming."
At one end of the pram sat Belinda, and at the other end sat Lena.
He laughed. "Which one's mine then Doll?"
She picked a child up, and handed him his daughter. He felt uncomfortable, not being familiar with little children.
"It's alright Harry, you can put her down, she has just started walking. But he didn't want to put her down, the thing he wanted to do most was to hold her close to him forever. As they walked they talked non-top, they felt good in each other's company.
"So this is the youngest one of your family, is it Doll?"

"Yeah my mum said this is definitely her last."
"Well do ya think my little girl looks like me Doll?" he asked wanting reassurance. Dolly smiled and thought to herself how he must be feeling at this moment.
"Yeah she does, she's got your eyes."
He smiled appreciatively.
"You know Harry I don't want to hurry you, but I can't stay that long, I have to get back and help my mum."

He felt his heart sink; he promised her last night that he wouldn't ever ask her to betray Ell again, it was no use he would have to let her go.
"Alright Doll can I walk part of the way with ya?"
Dolly wanted to cry for him, she could see the heartache in his face as they walked on to the main road after leaving the park.
She smiled, "I think I had better go the rest of the way on my own Harry; someone might see me with you and tell Ell."

He understood and cuddled his daughter tightly, he rubbed his fingers through her fine curly hair, and there was nothing else for it, he handed her back to Dolly. He kissed Dolly on the cheek, somehow he felt he wanted to give her a long lingering kiss on the lips, she had always been good to him and he felt a closeness to her, for a brief moment he wished it had been Dolly and not Ellen that he fallen in love with. Not being able to speak a word, he then turned and walked away, thinking to himself he could never see his daughter again.

Harry sat in the back yard reading, every now and then he put the book down, he felt unhappy; there was no real reason, he couldn't pin point what it was. Then he heard the sound, of his father coughing loudly, this was nothing new, he had good days and bad days; his health had started to show signs for concern. He tried to read his book again, then the sound coming from his father disturbed him.

It began to get worse, and then came the sound of an uneasy groaning, he ran inside and John lay on the floor, fighting for his breath. Harry rubbed his hands across his forehead in panic, trying to think what to do. He leaned across him cradling his head in his arms and gently touched his father's cheek.
"What is it Dad, what's happened?"
He could not answer him, he just shook his head, and quickly he ran into the bedroom to get him a pillow and rested his father's head on it. He whispered in his ear, "I won't be long Dad; I'm going to the phone box to ring for a doctor." John blinked his eyes as if to say he understood.

That night he sat at his father's bedside, hoping that Pat would arrive home soon. He sat on a chair at the side of the bed resting his head on his father's chest, in the silence of the room the only sound he heard was the ticking of the clock. He flittered in and out of sleep; he was woken by the bird song.
He gently touched him, asking, "Are you alright Dad?"
There was no response; resting his head to his chest he could still hear a faint heartbeat.

Wearily he went in to the kitchen to make a cup of tea then he heard the sound of Pat come whistling through the front door. Quickly he ran to meet him, he felt angry, how he had got through the last few hours alone he didn't know, angrily he tugged at Pat's arm in panic. "Where the fucking hell do you think you've been all night?" He had to take his panic out on someone, it was hard to cope, not knowing if their father was going to live or die
Pat looked at him puzzled. "Alright, hold your horses, Dad knows I can't always get back, Doreen's Mum and Dad always let me stay on the sofa, if I miss the last bus home. Has something happened?" asked Pat, he was now looking fearful.
"Yeah it's Dad, he's had a stroke."

Pat rushed into the bedroom and sat on the bed and wept like he hadn't done since he was a young boy. Harry put his arm around his young brother to comfort him, then an idea suddenly came to him, he bent down to get the old case.
He opened the case and took out the picture of their mother and father on their wedding day and studied it closely, thinking to himself what a beautiful looking woman their mother was. Gently he put it in his Fathers hand.
His eyes flickered, and then came a long drawn out groan followed by a sudden gurgling sound.
Harry leaned close to him and then looked up at Pat, with tears running down his face. "I think we've lost our Dad."

He walked quickly to the phone box to ring the convent, he was feeling shaken inside, the last thing he was expecting was for his father to die. As he dialled the number his hand shook vigorously, he took a deep breath and then asked to speak to Sister Bernadette telling the person, "It is a matter of great urgency." He was told to hold the line, and then a gentle voice came to the phone.
"Good afternoon, Sister Bernadette speaking."
He took another deep breath, "Ruby it's me Harry."
Her voice brightened up. "But Harry what do you want; I thought you would be on your way here by now, the fete has already started."

There was silence. "Is something the matter Harry?"
He tried to speak but the words wouldn't come out.
"Harry, Harry, are you still there?"
He then blurted out, "Ruby, it's Dad, he died early this morning,"
There was a long period of silence then came a clunking sound, he waited, had she dropped the receiver?
Then she spoke, "I'm so sorry Harry, it's something I never expected to hear." She then asked how it all came about.
"Will you ring me and let me know about the funeral, I'm now going in to the chapel to pray. Harry God bless you and Patrick."
Then the phone went dead.

On the day of the funeral there was a small gathering Harry, Patrick, Ruby and Sister Marie, a nun from the convent who had accompanied her on her journey. Jim turned up at the last minute to give his best friend support.
Back at Park Road, Mrs Masters, being the ever good neighbour, made them tea and sandwiches. Harry heart felt lighter, the worst was out of the way, he had been dreading the funeral. The very thought of his Father's body being put into the ground, and covered with earth, had all been too much for him to bear.

He pulled Jim to one side, "Do ya think ya can take my sister back to the station?"
Jim tried to stifle, his laughter. "What's so funny?" asked Harry feeling bewildered.
Jim leaned across to him, in a quiet voice he said for fuck's sake 'H' what will people think seeing me drive along the road with two nuns in me motor?"
Harry asked eagerly, "Will ya do it if I come with ya?"
He laughed even louder, "Oh fucking hell 'H' it will look like we're out on a foursome."
Anxiously he squeezed his arm. "Keep your voice down and show a bit of respect, it's me Dad's funeral after all."
Jim put his hand to his mouth. "I'm sorry 'H' I forgot where I was for a minute."

Patrick had now left home and married Doreen, in a quiet ceremony, and went off to live in Harefield.
There was rent to be paid, and still with no proper job, Harry had no other choice but to carry on doing robberies with Jim, but now he had the space to store the stolen goods. No one to answer to now, with his Father gone, and the money was coming in fast. It wasn't long before he had his own car and all the local girls regarded him as a good catch, but as far as Sal was concerned, nobody was going to have him but her.

She knew exactly what Harry wanted, a strong woman to stand by him in times of trouble. The way she saw it she could do this better than most, after all she was familiar with the police calling at all hours, looking for Jim.

In 1952 Sal realised she was going to have a baby, and she knew only too well she would be frowned upon, but what did she care. People would soon forget, and she was almost certain that Harry would marry her. After all the business with Ellen having a baby, then marrying someone else, it was unlikel; that he would want to go all through that again, it broke his heart.

Harry sat in the front room that was once his Father's old-fashioned parlour; he was counting money from a robbery that had taken place the previous evening.
When Sal had let herself in with the key hanging from the string, his concentration was broken by the sound of footsteps; he jumped up stuffing the money down his trousers, the door opened.
"Whoops sorry Harry," said Sal with a giggle.
There was a slight detection of anger in his face. "Oh for fuck sake Sal, don't you ever think about knocking."
"Well fuck you too," she said angrily, not wanting to be put down by him.

He smiled, his bottom lip dropping slightly, as it sometimes did when he felt shy or awkward. Quickly he wanted to make amends he grabbed hold of her arm.
"I'm sorry Sal but for all ya know, that could have been the coppers walking in on me."
"I've got to talk to you Harry."
He laughed, "But Sal you never ever stop talking."
"No this is serious," she said harshly.
He looked worried. "There's nothing wrong with Jim is there?" He stepped back if; it wasn't Jim, what else could it be that would concern him.
"Come on Sal, spit it out what's the matter?" She sat down next to him and looked him straight in the eye.
"I'm going to have a baby."
He went silent, and then he couldn't get the words out, fast enough.
"Well it doesn't mean it's mine Sal."
She stood up and slapped his face, screeching in a loud voice.
"Who the fuck do ya think got me like this, if you're saying its not you? I thought you might have learnt your lesson from the last time with Ellen."
She couldn't bear his attitude a minute longer and ran out of the house, leaving him feeling bewildered.

He sat in silence, staring into space, with a feeling of despair looming deeply over him, yeah he liked her, he always had done, but to spend the rest of his life with her, well that was a different matter.
In all this there was Jim to think about, his best mate, how would he take it if he let her down? The answer that came to his mind was not too good.
He stood up and threw the handful of money in to the air; oh what the fuck he thought, what had he to lose? So he made up his mind there and then, yes he would ask Sal to marry him.

He hastily married Sally with just a small quiet ceremony, he stood on the steps of the Town Hall, Registrar Office, and looked ten yards down the road to the Juvenile Court House where he was sent away, as a young boy; he sighed to himself as he thought, this is probably another major cock-up.
Sally now felt content; she had got her man at last. She got him to leave the small flat at 120 Park Road, and move into the ground floor flat of her parent's house. Now with her brother Jim, Mum, Dad and new husband, Sal couldn't have been happier.

In the early hours of a cold March morning, Harry and Jim returned from a robbery empty handed, but were greeted by the cry of a new born baby coming from the downstairs front bedroom. Sal's Mum Nell, known to everyone as Ma, walked into the dimly lit passage to greet them.

"Where do you think you two bastards have been? There's my daughter in there giving birth and her husband nowhere to be seen."
Harry took off his hat, and held it to his chest. "I'm sorry Ma." Never for one minute did he underestimate her. There stood this little chubby lady, with her long grey hair tied firmly in a bun, he had known her since he was a small boy. There had been many a time he had seen her set about Jim; he was determined to keep on the right side of her.
He looked at her puzzled then asked, "But the baby wasn't due for another month, why has she had it so early?"
She shrugged her shoulders, "Oh I don't know, I've delivered a few in my time, some come early some come late, these things sometimes happen, anyway your little boy looks fit and healthy."

"Did you say little boy Ma?"
"Yeah that's right," she said directly. He pulled her to him and kissed her on the forehead, now feeling full of excitement.
"Did you hear that Jim? I've got a little boy"
Jim, unperturbed by the whole thing said, "Good luck to ya mate, I'm off to bed," and wearily walked up the stairs.

Ma straightened her apron, trying to get herself together, it had been a hard night watching her own daughter go through child birth. Then her face softened.
"I tell you what go, and make me a nice cup of tea, while I get them cleaned up, and then you can go in and see them both."

He went in to the small bedroom, Sal sat up in bed. Her blond hair was clipped back at the sides and he looked pale and tired as she held the little bundle closely to her chest. He stood over them mesmerised, feeling overwhelmed with emotion, tears ran down his face as she held the baby out to him. "Here give him a cuddle Harry."
Nervously taking the baby in his arms he felt an instant love for him, but he wanted the nagging doubt to leave him, was this beautiful little thing really his?
"What we going to call him Sal?"
"Why don't we call him, George ?"
He smiled, "Yeah that's nice Sal."
As he climbed into bed, nothing prepared him for a broken night's sleep with a new born baby crying.

It was a hot summer's night when Jim and Harry decided to break into a jewellers' shop, in Richmond. They had been going to Richmond for a few weeks to assess the best way of going about it. They sat in the Tudor-style pub opposite the shop, which was situated in narrow cobbled road; the street was busy with people walking about enjoying the balmy evening.

They had worked out that if they got up on to the flat roof it would be easy to go in from the upstairs window. After watching carefully throughout the week they had noticed that no lights ever came on in the building at night, so therefore it must be empty.
Harry parked his car in a quiet little street around the corner from the pub and they sat in the small rustic bar until closing time, slowly sipping their beer, knowing too well how important it was to keep a clear head. Eventually they made their way back to the car and sat patiently waiting for the streets to be free of people.
Then taking their tools from the boot, discreetly they made their way to the back entrance of the jewellers. The continual sound of a dog barking put them ill at ease, as they climbed the unsteady wooden fence Harry turned to Jim. "You know I got my fucking doubts about this."
"Oh for fuck sake 'H' we're here now there's no fucking turning back."
They carefully made it onto the flat roof, edging their way to the building; Harry smashed one panel of the sash window, praying that no one was inside, and then he felt gingerly around for the lock, to pull the window open.

Jim quickly put on his gloves, "You know what 'H', what if it's alarmed? Most of these places are now, you know."
Harry turned to him; his face broke into a nervous smile, "It is alarmed mate."
"How do you know, that then 'H'
"I came over here last week at closing time I watched the old boy lock up, I was just pretending to look in the window; the alarm is in a small cupboard near the door."
"Well you kept that fucking quiet 'H'." Jim was showing a slight sign of anger.
"Well look at it this way mate if I'd told ya, you probably would have backed out. All we've got to do is hope that it's only the shop that's alarmed, and that we aint going to find out until we're in there. Don't panic Jim once we get down the stairs, I'm going straight to the cupboard and smash the glass door, then I'm going to cut the wires, and if it still goes off, just run straight back up here."

Harry led the way in to the dark room, he shone his torch; there was a desk in the corner, with some books on top, it looked like it was used as some kind of office.
Slowly he turned the knob on the door, it was locked, taking the jemmy out of the hold all, Jim struggled to prise the door open, he breathed a sigh of relief. Once they were on the dark landing they crept along very quietly. They could still hear the dog barking outside; they hoped it wouldn't draw attention.
They shone their torches in the direction of the stairs, the humid heat added to their nervousness. Harry put his foot on the first step, the loud creek almost made him leap in the air, at the bottom of the stairs there was another solid wooden door, firmly locked.

Again Jim put the jemmy to the door, after great difficult, with beads of sweat pouring down his face, it finally opened.
Harry turned to Jim, whispering, "Wait here." WIth a hammer and a pair of pliers, he crawled along the floor; suddenly he leapt up, and quickly started to smash the glass cupboard door vigorously.
The sound of a bell went twice as he quickly cut the wires, and then came a welcome silence. He peeped out of the shop window; the street was empty, as far as he could see, and he then went back to the bottom of the stairs where Jim was standing.

"Let's give it five minutes, and pray no one heard that bell."
There was an uncomfortable silence in the dark and stuffy shop, Harry put his hand to his chest, he could feel his heart pumping. They gradually began to feel their way about, trying not to use the torches, for fear of drawing attention from passersby.

Harry crawled along; behind the counter his hand touched the cold metal of a safe. He whispered across to Jim to come over to him. Moving his hand slowly across the safe he tried turning the dial, he was just hoping that it might open.

Jim's nerves began to get the better of him. "Oh fuck it 'H' just leave it, we're never going to get that open, unless we knew how to blow it open."

Harry took two hammers from the hold all. "Alright, let's just smash those glass cabinets and take what's in them."

The long slivers of glass crunched under their feet, it was all around them. Within minutes they were loading the trays of rings and watches into the bag.

"You know I bet this lot's worth fuck all, I reckon all the best gear is in that fucking safe," said Harry, feeling they could have got more."

A sudden sound of someone coughing came from the shop doorway, the side profile showed a man lighting a cigarette.

"That's it, I'm fucking out of here," said Jim nervously, as he made his way back to the stairs. Harry crawled along with the hold all laden with jewels.

Jim took the other bag, that was almost empty, apart from a few tools. They ran up the stairs breathlessly, and stood in the room that they had first entered. They sat on the floor to get their breath back.

Harry peeped out of the window, the big moon shone down; he felt his shirt, it was covered in perspiration. He started to unbutton it before climbing out onto the flat roof, the air was hot and stuffy, the only sound was that of the dog still barking.

He looked along the row of flat roofs; there were still a couple of lights on in the upstairs windows of the other buildings, he beckoned Jim out on to the roof, telling him to lie flat.

Then dragging themselves to the end of the flat roof, they took a rope from the hold all. Quickly they tied the two bags together and lowered them to the ground. Jim was first to lower himself on to the drainpipe, gripping it tightly he swiftly reached the bottom. Harry followed, immediately losing his grip he fell the last few feet, falling into a pile of rubbish. He got up from the ground, only to be greeted by the bright eyes of a cat peering at him from the edge of a wall. His heart was racing like mad as he tried to wipe away the smelly debris that he fell in. They made their way into the narrow street, he began to feel calmer. Jim stood behind a hedge, as Harry checked it was safe to carry on walking, suddenly the sound of footsteps appeared to be getting closer.

A deep voice came from across the street, shouting, "Hold on a minute you two, what have you got in those bags?"

Harry turned to look he couldn't believe what he was seeing; he dragged Jim by the collar of his shirt.
"Quick it's a fucking copper."
They began to run as fast as they could down the street, the clicking of the heels of their shoes echoed, as they ran along the cobbled road to where they had parked the car. The frightening sound of the policeman's whistle was getting louder and louder.
Once they were safely in the car, Harry frantically pulled the starter.
"Oh fucking hell what's happening?" He got a dull thudding sound.
"Oh mate, you have got petrol, aint ya?"
"Of course I fucking have." Angrily Harry gave it another pull.

As the policeman's hand touched the car door, the engine roared loudly, he breathed a sigh of relief as he put his foot down firmly on the accelerator and sped around the corner. Harry looked in the mirror as they came to the main road.
"Oh no I don't believe it, there's a copper's car coming behind us."
The sound of the bell ringing from the car appeared to be getting closer; Jim leaned across to switch the car lights off.
Harry pushed his hand away. "What the fuck are you doing."
Jim retaliated, "Well mate with no rear lights, they won't be able to see your number plates, will they?"

He put his foot down full throttle; they appeared to be getting further away from the police car. They carried on driving; Jim looked up at the sign post which read Chertsey. The feeling of panic began to ease. Jim turned to him, "I think we're alright 'H' but just keep going, we don't want to lose what we've got, I think we've had a good night's work."

They kept on going down the long winding lanes, the bright light of the moon shone directly down on them; the still almost humid heat was taking its toll on them. Suddenly he noticed a field and turned his steering wheel sharply; then drove straight across it. The solid dry ground caused the car to veer from side to side.

"Hold on mate, stop let's think what we're going to do," said Jim feeling flustered.
"I already have," Harry replied as he got out of the car.
He stood in the middle of the dark field; there was nothing in sight, only the sound of the crickets. Jim got out and handed him a cigarette, they sat on the grass propped up against the car.
"I tell you what Jim; it's no good going any further with those bags or this car."
"Alright mate what have you got in mind?"

"Well I think we should hide the bags, and come back for them tomorrow; we might be seen with them."
"No don't be silly 'H' who's going to see them in the car?"
"No Jim I'm not taking the car, I'm going to set fire to it."
Jim gasped, "Are you fucking mad or something?"
"Look, for all you know, that first copper might already have the licence plate number. This way I can tell them, that is if we come a cropper of course, that I sold the car a few weeks ago. What happens to it after I sold it, is nothing to do with me, is it?"
"Ha got ya," said Jim, now understanding him fully.

They walked across to the very edge of the field, where they came to some derelict gravel pit workings. Here they found an old shed that looked like it was about to fall down at any moment. Jim went in first, wiping away the cobwebs that had covered his body.
He shone the torch to the ground, there was a pile of sacks and some old boots and tools scattered about.
He passed the torch to Harry; then took the bags and hid them underneath the sacks, he looked up at Harry. "We will just have to hope no one finds them before we get back for them."

As they walked back across the field cautiously towards the car, Jim nudged his arm. "Are you sure about this mate?"
"Yeah I can always get a new one; it's not the end of the world, is it?"
He went to the glove compartment, to take out his personal belongings. Then he went to the boot, and took out a can of petrol and turned to Jim, "Right, when I throw this match be ready to run for your life."
Nervously he threw several lighted matches, and then quickly the flames took hold. As they ran into the distance, they could hear the frightening sounds of the car being blown apart.

They ran along the ditch at the side of the long lane, they ran and ran until their legs gave up on them. It was no use they could go no further; finally they rested behind a bus shelter keeping out of sight of the road. After regaining their energy, they walked discreetly through the night.

Harry walked into the front bedroom and looked down at little George sleeping soundly in his cot. Sal lay there awake; she threw the bed covers back, jumping out of bed in a rage.
"Where do ya think ya been all night, out with some tart? It's bleeding half past six in the morning."
He rested his arms on her shoulders. "Alright Sal calm down, I've been out on a bit of work, with ya brother and it all went fucking wrong."
Her face softened, "Well did you get anything?"
"Yeah, Yeah, it's a long story," she began to take off his shirt.

"Come on Harry Creedy, get in this bed and give ya wife a cuddle."
He pushed her back playfully, "Oh anything to keep ya happy Sal."
He thought a lot of Sal, he liked her free spirit and her attitude to life was "Fuck everyone" as long as she and her family were alright. Sometimes he thought he loved her, but sometimes, just wasn't enough.

Jim walked in to their small kitchen he was wearing a white shirt and black trousers, looking very tanned and handsome. Happily he bent over little Georges pram, and gave him a kiss, asking, "How's my favourite little boy?" George waved his rattle at the unexpected attention.

Harry and Jim set off for Chertsey, to regain their stolen jewels. As they drove through Ashford, they decided to stop at the Star and Garter pub, here they made their plans, why waiting for dark to fall.
Jim sat behind the wheel, feeling edgy, they had got this far, he didn't want anything to go wrong now. Finally they came to a little dirt track leading to the disused gravel workings. He turned the lights off the car to ensure they went undetected.
Harry looked across the field to see if he could see the remains of his car, there wasn't a thing to be seen through the pitch blackness. The only sign of light was the fading embers of the cigarette hanging from his mouth.
They pulled as close as possible to the shed where the stolen jewels were hidden. Their hearts were thumping, praying that no one had been there before them.
Harry shone his torch, then bending his slender body into the shed; his heart began racing faster and faster. He kicked the sacks away; praying that all was well, he breathed a sigh or relief. Still there were the two bags; he picked them up, throwing them to Jim who put them in the boot of the car, carefully covering them with the spare wheel.

At just gone midnight, they returned home, he put the bags in the coal cellar under the stairs, and bid Jim goodnight. Now they were feeling happy, they had retrieved the jewels which they now regarded as theirs.

The morning sun shone through the gap in the closed curtains, he smiled to himself, yes he felt good inside. He went to the cupboard under the stairs, and took out the bags to examine the jewels closely, for the first time. With a feeling of great pleasure he let a necklaces drape over his fingers, and stared at it, finding it hard to believe their luck. Sal woke suddenly, her eyes opened wide as she look at the mound of gold and diamonds.
"For fuck sake Harry, how much do ya think that lots worth?"
"I don't know," he said calmly.

She picked up a small box and opened it.
"Look Harry, diamond earrings, I have never seen anything like it in all my life."
"Take em, they're yours," he said casually.
She quickly put them in her ears, tucking her hair back behind her ears to show them off. He peered at the diamonds, "Yeah they look good Sal, it's gonna be wine and roses from now on for us, you know."
He went over to the window to pull back the curtains, he wanted to let the sun into the room, thinking to himself, it's good to be alive. Then he took a step back almost losing his balance, and put his hand to his head, showing signs of despair.

"No, no, fucking hell we're surrounded by coppers, do something with this lot Sal, and do it quick."
She rushed into the passage, to little George's pram, lifted up the base panel, went back in to the bedroom to get the jewels and began wrapping them in the cover from the bed. She quickly rushed back to the passage and then laid them in the base of the pram. Then she quickly put the mattress back on top and then proudly sat little George in the pram, where he sat unperturbed by all the activity going on around him.

A sudden bang came on the door, followed, by a loud shout, "Open up it's the police!"
Sal pulled her hair back over her ears to hide her diamonds, then went confidently to the door. She looked out into the street; there were three police cars and a group of policeman surrounding the house. She was confronted by a short stocky, plain clothes detective.
"Good morning madam, we're here regarding a break in, at a jewellers in Richmond."

"Oh yeah," said Sal brashly, "what's that got to do with us?
"Well madam I believe that Jimmy Downs and Harry Creedy live here."
"Yeah that's right; they are in bed at the moment."
"Well in that case madam, you won't mind if we come in?"
He held a search warrant up to her face. Harry, hearing the conversation jumped back in the bed pretending to be asleep.
The policeman hailed his men to follow him, before long the whole house was full of police running up the stairs, and in the back garden. They frantically searched everywhere, almost pulling the house apart. Then the detective put his head around the door, with a sly grin on his face. "Alright Creedy we've got nothing on ya at the moment, but that don't mean it's the end of it."
Harry stood up not saying a word, but inwardly feeling very relieved. The policeman walked past little George's pram, he ruffled his hair, unaware that he was within inches from the stolen jewels.

He turned to Harry, "I tell you what Creedy, you aint going to be around long enough to see this little one grow up." Then he went out slamming the door.

Later that day with the help of Jim's uncle, arrangements were made to take the jewels to a buyer.
Harry and Jim left the house dressed in their smart suits. They drove through the leafy suburbs, heading towards Gerard's Cross, to make their meet with Maurie Cohen.
Following the plan to detail, they parked Jim's car, at the back of the row of houses. Harry adjusted his tie to ensure he looked the part of a confident jewel thief. Jim looked at his watch, it was exactly half past nine, darkness had fallen, and the street was quiet. They walked up the pathway to the immaculate nineteen thirties detached house.

Harry pressed his finger firmly on the doorbell, and waited in anticipation until the door was opened by a small man with a pigeon chest; he had thick grey hair and was wearing black horn rimmed glasses.
He took his pocket watch from his waistcoat, checking the time. Then he looked over the top of his glasses and glanced down at the bag; he wrung his hands around each other under his chin.

"What can I do for ya boys?"
Jim stepped forward feeling slightly on edge, "Are you Maurie? Me uncle called ya earlier."
"Oh right, right boys, come on in, I see you are on time." He led them into the large ornate room, with paintings covering most of the walls, their feet sank in to the thick red and gold carpet.
"Well boys show uncle Maurie what you have got for him."
Harry slowly unzipped the bag, and then looked across at him trying to weigh Maurie up.
"Well lay it out on the table son; let me see what you've got there."

He took his magnifying glass from a small wooden box, taking off his glasses, as he carefully put the magnifying glass to his eye.
He waved his hand, to them, "Make yourselves comfortable; sit yourselves down boys why I look."
He picked up each piece, as he mumbled, over and over. "Yes very nice, very nice."
They sat there in silence, waiting to be acknowledged.
 He looked up, "Well boys it's worth about two and half thousand."
Harry swallowed hard, thinking at last they had cracked it. Maurie wrung his hands again, under his chin.
"Well boys I'll take it off of ya for eight hundred pounds, and not a penny more, do ya understand?"

Harry felt deflated, that was a big drop from two and half thousand. He looked across at Jim for reassurance and Jim nodded his head in agreement. He stood up, taking Maurie's hand and shaking it firmly. "Alright Maurie it looks like ya got yourself a deal."
He looked at his pocket watch, "Well boys, I think we all deserve a drink." He opened the door, in a domineering voice, he shouted, "Miriam I'm sending the boys through for a drink."
He indicated to the room opposite, were they were greeted by his wife. This was Maurie's way of being left alone to sort out the money. In the privacy of his room, he slid a picture along the wall, to get to his safe. Then he made sure no one was going to know where he kept his money but him. As he slid the picture back across the wall, he looked across the hallway. There from the half opened door, he spotted Harry's eyes peering at him, from the opposite room.

He counted the money very carefully then walked into the room, where they were waiting for him. Carefully he picked up the large whisky that Miriam had poured him.
He glanced across at her, she sat on the sofa her grey hair, looked like she had just left the hairdressers. She began turning her head, from right to left, as she waited for the next move from the three men.
Her pearl earrings were dazzling in the light reflected from the large chandelier. Maurie looked across at her, not saying a word, but indicating for her to leave the room.

He held his whisky glass to eye level, pointing at Harry.
He smiled slyly, "You know boys, if I thought word ever got out, about the deals that go on in my house, or even more so, about where I keep my money, you know what would happen to whoever who let it slip."
His grin became wider, "Well do you want to know what I'd do to him, well I'll tell you this, I'd cut his fucking cock off."
He took a gulp of his whisky. "Yes that's exactly what I'd do, so there!"

Harry stood with his legs astride, with his hands covering his manhood. He could almost feel the pain panic took over, he had to think quickly. He knew this remark was aimed at him.
"But Maurie, for all you know there might be no cock to cut off, the person you have in mind may be a hermaphrodite."
Jim put his hands to ears, mumbling, "Oh no for fuck sake 'H' you're going to far this time."

Maurie stepped back away from him, with fear in his eyes, thoughts were running riot in his head. "No surely not a hermaphrodite, in his house, what would people think?" He had only ever heard talk of people such as this. He didn't really know too much about them.

He had heard something once; they could be a bit of both, man or women, but no, no, there was no way; he was going to deal with one. Throwing the money on the table, he said, "Take your fucking money and go." He scratched his head in disbelief and mumbled under his breath, "For fuck sake, have I got two nancy boys here or something?"

Once outside the house, they roared with laughter, as Jim rammed the money in his inside pocket.
"You know 'H' his face was a fucking picture."
Harry pointed down to his manhood. "Do ya know mate, I'd say anything rather than get me fucking cock cut off."

RUNNING WITH THE BIG BOYS

It was a sad journey after a fond farewell to Ruby at the convent, and he knew it would be a long time before he would see her again. She was leaving England to go and teach English in Italy. It had been the first time he had seen her since the death of his father. Whenever he was with her for some reason he always felt an inner peace, was it because her life was so right? he asked himself. He knew that she was aware of his criminal activities, after all his father had to confide in someone, but she never tried to preach to him. Her final goodbye to him was, "God bless you Harry, I will pray for you."

He drove into the sunset with times gone by on his mind. He stopped the car at Ealing Common; and got out to stretch his legs. The birds were still singing, as the early evening sun glistened through the trees. Wistfully he looked across the common thinking back to himself and Laura, rolling around in the snow all those years ago. He could almost hear her voice shouting, "Come on Harry let's have some fun."
A smile came to him, as he wondered what had happened to her, she was probably married with children of her own. He lit a cigarette, shaking his head, to bring himself back to the present.

Suddenly he felt sad and was about to get back in the car, when his eye caught a glimpse of the quaint little pub on the corner. He looked at his watch, it was half past six, and found himself walking in that direction, the doors were open.
Entering the pub he could smell the beer and smoke drifting towards him. As he walked into the cosy bar; taking in the jovial atmosphere he ordered himself a pint of bitter, then he heard a familiar voice come from the other end of the bar.
"Harry you felonious fellow, how are you, old chap?"
He couldn't believe his eyes, there dressed in a pale blue shirt and Prince of Wales check suit, stood Eddie.
"Well I say Harry what a pleasant surprise, it must be four years since we last met, are you still in the same line of business, old chap?"
He raised his glass, "Yeah I suppose I am how about you Eddie, what have you been up to?"

"Oh I've popped one or two, here and there matey."
He knew instantly what he meant, Eddie had cracked a few safes.
"I had full intentions of becoming an honest man, but found it so very bloody dull; you know what I mean Harry." Eddie turned to the two people with him.
"Oh how bloody rude of me, let me introduce you. Harry, this is my friend Graham, and his charming wife Josie."
Harry shook their hands, unbeknown to them; his eyes had been fixed firmly on Josie, since he first entered the pub. He pulled a wad of notes from his pocket.
"Eddie let me buy you and your friends a drink."
"Well that's very decent of you old chum"

One drink led to another, and he was now finding it very hard to keep his eyes off of Josie. Her husky voice came across as well spoken, but every now and then, she let slip and he detected a slight East End accent.
She lifted her glass; he could not help but notice the diamonds on her fingers. Her clothes were plain, but had class, with her auburn hair, and blue eyes, this all added to a look of pure elegance.
Graham was a man in his early thirties, with blond curly hair slightly receding. His eyes were firmly fixed on his wife, his body language stated that she was his and his only.
Harry knew that people like them had firm rules; you didn't mess with someone else's wife. He smiled to himself, as he thought, yeah but rules are made to be broken.

Eddie and Harry spent the next couple of hours catching up on the past then Eddie pulled him to one side.
"You know old chap, I've rented a flat across the common there, and I never stay in one place too long. Graham and I are planning something you might be interested in."
"What is it?" He showed surprise at being asked.
"It's a jewellers, we need a third man, and perhaps I can teach you the skills of blowing a safe."
He shook Eddie's hand.
"Well I think I might be the man you're looking for Eddie."
"Well here's my address old son, do pay me a visit tomorrow night."
He gave Harry a wink as he clinked his glass on Harry's glass.
He looked at his watch it was ten o'clock, he was beginning to feel fidgety; he'd told Sal he would only be a couple of hours. He turned to make his apologies, telling them he must leave. He shook Eddie's and Graham's hands, then bent towards Josie and kissed her on the cheek, whispering quietly in her ear, "Perhaps, one day."
She smiled, "It's been nice to meet you Harry."

Sal was in bed when he finally arrived home, he was about to get undressed, when she began ranting at him, "Where the fuck do ya think you've been?"
He tried to reason with her, "Come on Sal I told ya I was going to the convent to see Ruby, didn't I?"
"Yeah but that was fucking hours ago, are you sure you aint been with some tart somewhere?"
"Give it a rest Sal, why is it every time I leave the house, you think I'm with another woman? If you really want to know, I met up with me old cell mate Eddie, he's going to put a bit of business my way."
She suddenly perked up; her eyes now saw pound signs.

After making plans at Eddie's flat, they went on a trial-run to Brighton. Graham was the getaway driver. He was chosen by Eddie, because of his fantastic skills as an ex-racing driver. They drove along the winding lanes, in a black Humber Snipe; here the three men got to know each other on a more personal level.
They would often stake out a jewellers and return the following week to do the necessary work. Eddie had made a golden rule that they would never work close to home.

The next job they had planned was slightly different, this time they had chosen a bank in the Sussex town of Worthing, with the help of inside information, they were ready to pounce.
They sat in the car, a few streets away from the bank.
All three men were going in to the bank tonight. On some occasions, Graham would wait in the car, ready for a quick get away, but tonight he was needed inside.
With the help of their inside information, they were told to break into the furniture shop, next door to the bank. The inside man assured them that this would be a doddle.
The bank was situated at the far end of the sea-side town next to a railway bridge. This had been specially chosen, to their advantage, with the hope that the sound of the goods trains going through the night would drown out any noise that they might make.
Graham dropped Harry and Eddie off at the back entrance to the furniture shop. Armed with the many tools required for their night's work, he then drove off to a nearby street, to park the car, out of sight.

The furniture shop proved no problem to enter, with the aid of the jemmy and their own strength, they were inside in no time. The shop appeared overcrowded with furniture; in the darkness he was difficult to find their bearings. After a search crawling flat across the floor with their torches, they were more than pleased to find no alarms.

They settled themselves in a small untidy office, at the back of the building, carefully planning their next move.
Graham couldn't resist exploring what was inside the cupboard next to him, and came across a bottle of whisky. It was as if he had just found gold, he held it up in the air, turning to his partners in crime.
"I say old chaps, anyone for a small tipple?"

Harry searched around and came across some old stained cups on a cluttered table and passed them to him hesitantly.
"Here you are Graham, we'd better make them small ones, we've got to keep clear heads. If we have too much of that stuff we'll be laying on one of those beds out there still fast asleep when they turn up to open the shop in the morning."
Graham laughed, "That would give them a bit of a shock, three drunken bank robbers, laying there pissed out of their minds."

The more time he spent with Graham and Eddie, the more Harry began to like them. Graham's cheeky grin often reminded him of his best mate, Jim.
They were like chalk and cheese: there was Graham with his upper class accent, and expensive clothes, and Jim, who swore like a trooper. Eventually they decided to get to work; they rolled up their sleeves, it could be hard going, robbing a bank wouldn't be easy.

Eddie drilled four holes through the wall, to make a small opening for them to get through to the bank; he filled them with gelignite, and lit a match to it. Then he tried to muffle the sound with a mattress that just happened to be near at hand. They covered their ears, praying the explosion wouldn't be too loud, after all this was still at an early stage, for something to go wrong now would mean disaster.
The bricks crumbled instantly, the room soon filled with thick brick dust, causing them to cough and splutter. Then Eddie carefully made himself busy and pulled away parts with his bare hands, to give them a clear entrance.

Eddie went in first sliding along the floor slowly on his stomach, then he felt his way along, rubbing his hand along the mahogany panelled wall. His inside help had told him exactly where the alarm system was placed; his heart beat fast, with the fear of activating it.
After minutes, thanks to his skilful training, the alarm was no longer a problem to them; he then gave a whistle, this was their all clear signal. Once through the hole, Harry and Graham, then reached with difficulty, for the mattress, from the other side, this was used to slide over the hole in the wall, to drowned out any noise from the explosive that they were about to use.

Eventually they came to the big old safe, there was no feeling of fear now, just overwhelming excitement over how much loot was in there, and they knew the job must be done quick and accurately.
After drilling some small holes in to the safe, Harry then packed the gelignite firmly into them. Then he put the detonators to the door, and sat patiently why they rehearsed the getaway for the final time.
The three men's eyes met in the dark hot room. Sweat started to run down Harry's forehead as he continually wiped the drips from the bridge of his nose; he felt like his heart was pumping out of his ears.

Then he edged his way forward, rubbing his hand together as if to pray; he looked around at the others, "Fuck it, I'm going for it now," he said.
Eddie quickly started to edge away. In a cool calm voice, as he pointed his finger to Harry he said, "Fire away old son, just fire away."
Then a succession of loud thuds echoed out, in the midst of the smoke from the gelignite, they gingerly went back over to the safe.

The door was hanging to one side, Eddie shone his torch inside and turned to them and winked, with a big smile on his face, "We've had an excellent night old chums, bloody marvelous."
Harry shone his torch on his watch, "For fuck sake let's work fast, and get out of here."
Eddie started to pack the notes into the big hold all, amidst the smoke and dust.
Following their plans to the last detail, Harry and Graham made their way quickly back into the furniture shop, climbing back through the hole in the wall.

With great caution, Eddie continued stacking the money, while Harry stood near the back entrance of the shop, with all their tools gathered at his side ready to go. Graham had discreetly left the building, to go and get the car.
All three men were checking their watches at regular intervals, everything had to be timed to precision, one little slip and that could be the end for them. Then came the sound of Eddie's footsteps approaching him. Harry checked his watch one more time; it was one minute to two.

Then came the sound of car wheels along the gravel narrow road to the back entrance, this meant all was well, Graham had returned safely with the car. With the greatest feeling of elation, they sped along the dark narrow lanes, with heavy rain hitting the windscreen.
Eddie and Graham sat at the front of the car, feeling ecstatic with the way things had gone. They were humming the odd tune as they drove through the night.

Harry lay stretched out on the back seat, using the hold all full of money as his pillow. They breathed a sigh of relief, when the car finally pulled up at Park Road.
Harry stepped out of the car taking the hold all with him.
Eddie wound down the window; and flicked the ash from his thick cigar, as he smiled at him.
"It's been an excellent night's work old chap; if we just carry on as planned there should be no problem."

Harry bid them goodnight and the car drove off into the darkness.
As he looked up to the top of the house, there was Jim, leaning out of the window giving him thumbs up sign.
He put his key in the door, creeping in quietly, not wanting to wake Sal.
Jim was standing bare-chested, at the bottom of the stairs, waiting in anticipation. Without saying a word he indicated for Jim to follow him to the back kitchen. As he sat down; he suddenly felt his legs begin to tremble.

Jim looked at him curiously. "Well, did it go alright mate?"
He sat there unable to answer.
"'H' mate are you all right? you've gone a bit pale."
It was no use he couldn't just sit there; he stood up and gripped the mantelpiece, hoping this would make his body go rigid; he was finding it difficult to stop his legs from trembling.
He turned to Jim, "You know what, it's just hit me mate, I can't fucking believe it; I've just robbed a fucking bank."
Jim rubbed his head in his dead pan way and smiled as he lit a cigarette.

"Yeah it's a bit different from robbing the fucking chocolate factory, aint it? You got any booze in here mate?" Jim asked, feeling they should celebrate.
"Yeah it's in that cupboard over there."
The two cups that were going to be used for tea were now being filled to the brim with whisky.
Wearily Harry looked at the clock, it was half past four; suddenly he began to feel calmer, and then he began to unzip the hold all.
"Oh well I suppose we had better sort this lot out straight away."
Jim put his hand inside the hold all; and grinned like a Cheshire cat, "Fucking hell, what a lovely, lovely feeling."
"Oh yeah," Harry beamed with delight, "we are running with the big boys now Jimmy boy."
He started to take some of the bundles out; and counted three thousand pounds, in fives, ones, and ten shilling notes.
Jim looked on in disbelief, "There must be fucking twenty grand there 'H'."

He looked up and winked at him. "Yeah and Eddie said he left a few quid in the safe."
"Fucking hell" H" lets hope you've got away with it."
"That's why I brought its here and didn't leave it with Eddie, the police are bound to pay him a visit; he's done time for it before."
"The plan is to keep it hidden for about three months, but to share out this three grand now, just to tie us over, ya know what I mean? But here, take this couple of hundred for your part Jim, then I will see ya alright when the big share out comes."
"Remember Jim, not one fucking word to Sal, the only people that know are the inside man, Eddie, Graham, me and you, and that's the way it's got to stay."
Jim zipped the hold all up, "You can trust me with your life mate, and you know that, don't ya?"
He pulled Jim towards him and hugged him; "I know that, you're the best mate anyone could have. Right I'll leave it with ya Jim; I've got to get some kip, goodnight mate."

Jim opened the back door quietly as possible, the cold air hit him as he crept across to his Dad's old garden shed. He had spent time earlier that evening taking up the wooden floor, and digging a deep hole, it had been a hard night's work in the pitch darkness. He was now ready for his next task, very carefully he lay out the roofing he had found propped up in the corner. It had been left over when his Dad had fixed the shed roof earlier in the year.
Then he put the hold all down on top of it and then wrapped it around the bag, and tied it firmly with string. As he concentrated carefully on what he was doing, there came a sudden noise of banging and crashing, from outside. It felt as if his heart was going to stop, this was the last thing he needed, was for people to be woken up, and start looking out of their windows.

"Fuck it," he murmured over and over again.
He peeped out of the small shed window and breathed a sigh of relief; the culprit was a cat sitting on a dustbin lid.
He wiped the sweat from his face, knowing now that he wanted to get out of there as quick as possible, tiredness was setting in and he knew if he was caught there was no way he could explain himself.

Quickly he covered the hole with earth. Finally he then began to put the floor base back carefully. He was finding it difficult, working in the dark, but there was nothing else for it, Harry had given him the job and it had to be done. Quickly he went all around the shed; to check that everything was back in place and then double-checked everything once more to make sure he had left no clues.

Everything had to be just perfect, for he knew if he left just one thing out of place, his Dad would pick up on it. He closed the door firmly behind him, feeling more than pleased with himself. Then the thought went through his mind, who the fuck, would ever guess that there was money from a bank robbery, under his old man's garden shed? He smiled, as he reassured himself, "Fucking no one."

Harry lay sleeping, Sal was busy in the kitchen, giving little George his breakfast, when came the sound of the ringing of their newly-acquired telephone.
She ran into the passage, and eagerly picked up the receiver, and began to speak in her posh telephone voice.
The voice on the other end was a well-spoken man, asking for Harry. She tried hard not to let her voice slip; she asked if he would be so kind to hold the line, she was just about to lay the receiver on the table, when he said, "You must be Harry's charming wife Sally?"
A smile came to her face.
"Well dear Sally, I've heard so much about you, let's hope we can meet soon."

As she listened intently, she was trying to picture his face, who could he be she thought? She went into the bedroom, nudging Harry to wake him.
"What is it Sal?"
"Quick wake up, there's this really posh bloke on the phone."
He rubbed his eyes and yawned, "Oh that must be Eddie."
Promptly he went to the phone; and was greeted by a cheerful voice.
"Old chap good morning; I hope I didn't wake you?"
"No, no that's alright Eddie."
"Well did everything go OK old son?"
He turned around; Sal was still at his side, and he gave her a wink, as he put his hand over to cover the receiver, "Sal aint you got things to do?"
She glared at him, and then mimed for him to "fuck off."
"Yeah, yeah it's all done and dusted.

He walked in to the kitchen. Sal stood indignant, "What did he want ya for?"
"I was with him last night doing a bit of work." He didn't want her to know too much.
"What was it then?" She was determined to find out; she never liked to be left out of any of his business.
"Oh Sal for fuck sake, it was a little shop over Epsom, nothing much, we got a hundred and fifty quid between us."
She began to soften, "Well that's not bad is it for a nights work, is it?"
She walked over to kiss him, and he felt himself wanting her.

"How do ya fancy coming back to bed?" he asked, as he put his hand in between her legs.
She fondly rubbed her head into his chest.
"Ya know I do love ya Harry, don't ya?" He caressed her tenderly, as he ran his fingers over her body, she opened her legs wide, welcoming his dick, inside her. This was the first time she had felt truly wanted by him for a long time.

A little later Harry walked in to the pub; and hung his rain mac on the coat stand. Voices were echoing out all around him, he looked across the smoky haze for Eddie. Suddenly he heard his laughter as he made his way through a group of people. There he was leaning with his back against the bar, and he walked towards Harry, his gushing voice greeting him. "Harry chummy, what can I get you?"
He was about to answer when Eddie held a pound note up in the air, calling to the barman.
"Give me a large whisky, the best in the house young man, and of course one for your good self."

Standing at his side were two young women, neither of them very attractive, their dress sense showed no signs of class.
Playfully he nudged Harry's arm. "Oh Harry I'd like you to meet, yes I'd like you to meet.." He glanced at them both in turn with a puzzled look on his face.
"What did you say your names were again?"
They started to giggle, then the one with bright red hair replied, "I'm Stella, and her name is Babs."
He eyed them up and down. He had expected to meet Eddie on his own. Eddie handed him a cigar.

"Harry, shall we have a word in private old son?"
They made their way into the gents; he glanced around the drab cold toilets to make sure they were alone, before he pulled out the money.
"Here you are Eddie, that's yours and Graham's, and you did say you were going to sort out the inside man didn't you? The rest is done, it's all safe until we do the big share-out."
Eddie put it straight in to his inside pocket, patting his jacket, he then shook his hand, "Excellent really excellent, chummy."
His deep blue eyes sparkled, like a young boy who had just been given a new toy.

They were about to return to the bar when Harry asked, "Anyway Eddie, who are those two women you're with at the bar?"
Eddie laughed his hearty laugh, as he replied, "Fuck knows old chap; they were here when I arrived. They seemed to latch on to me for some

reason or another, they may do us for the night though; we could take them back to my flat later."

Harry smiled, "Well put it this way, I won't be fighting you over either of them."

The evening wore on, the drinks flowed, the bell rang out for last orders, a belting voice echoed from behind the bar,

"Drink up, let's be having your glasses please."

He started to put his rain mac on when Eddie said in a slurred voice, "Chummy don't leave us, come back for a drink, the night is still young."

Harry looked at the three of them waiting for his agreement; his shy smile appeared on his face. "Alright I'll have just one."

He followed Eddie's Humber Snipe car en route to Ealing. Eddie had chosen the redhead, as his passenger, and left him with the slightly timid fair haired girl. They walked to his car, he noticed her swaying as she walked, caringly he put his arm around her, "Hold on, are you alright Love?"

She looked up at him and started to giggle uncontrollably.

"No I'm not alright, I think I'm drunk you know, and I've never enjoyed myself so much, I don't usually drink."

Her legs were about to give way on her as he got her into the car, the remainder of the journey was silent. When they arrived at Eddie's, he steadied her on her feet, she started to giggle again.

Fuck it, he thought to himself, what have I got myself into?

"Would you like me to take you home Love?" he asked, as he wanted to show her some concern.

"No, no, no I never want to go home, I want to be with you," she said drunkenly.

He murmured to himself, "There's not much chance of that."

Once inside, Eddie poured the drinks and put on the music, with the table lamp giving out a soft glow, the room appeared inviting.

Eddie and Stella began to smooch around the room, as he craftily edged her towards the bedroom.

Harry now began to feel awkward, sitting in the big room, next to a woman he didn't find at all attractive. He sat with his head bowed down; he didn't want to make eye contact with her; he looked out of the corner of his eye at her, she seemed to be sobering up slightly. He began to feel sorry for her; she looked at a loss as to what should happen next.

As he looked across the room at the clock, it reminded him that he shouldn't be there. What should he do? he asked himself, she was

probably feeling unimportant, so he put his arm around her shoulder. As he told himself, oh fuck it why not? he started to kiss her and her response was good, a lot better than what he thought it might be.
His cock began to throb, he was beginning to feel excited. Suddenly they fell from the sofa onto the heavily patterned green carpet.

Quickly he began to take off her clothes and she readily helped him. She panted heavily as she frantically undid his belt, and tugged at his trousers desperately; she put her hand on his cock, and opened her legs wide. He thrashed his hot cock inside her; yes he had under estimated her. She kissed every part of his body, and there was nothing else for it but to respond as eagerly to her passion. They rolled across from one end of the carpet to the other, holding on to each other tightly, for fear of letting go and losing the wonderful feeling that they were both sharing. She screeched out in pleasure, until finally he came, his body trembling in ecstasy. He lay there feeling his blood had been drained from him, but yes it had all been worth it he thought.

He woke to an empty room, there were empty bottles and glasses left scattered about from last night. They were there to remind him immediately that he had a hangover, a bad one at that, desperately he tried to lift his head, it was painful.
Then he heard a tenor voice singing loudly; it was coming from the direction of the kitchen. This was the last thing he needed; slowly he rose to his feet.
"Is that you Eddie?"
Eddie popped his head around the door, a big grin on his face.
"Good morning old son, a good night had by all, what!"

Harry felt forlorn; and started to button up his shirt, "Oh fucking hell Eddie, I've got to go home and explain this lot."
Eddie stepped towards him, "Old chap take it easy."
"For fuck sake Eddie, you wouldn't be saying that if you were in my shoes, Sal can be a right cow."
"Really is that so? You do surprise me; she came across as a sweetie on the telephone."
He laughed, "I think you might change your mind when you meet her."
"Oh by the way, old chap, the girls left early, they had to get to work or something silly like that, but said they hoped to do it again some time."

As he drove down the narrow road that ran along side of the common, he couldn't help but notice the carpet of beautiful red and gold autumn leaves. He stopped the car; he got out and looked across the common. Yes he had a great affinity for it, whatever season of the year, it always looked beautiful.

He lit a cigarette, and leaned against the car, he knew he must go and face Sal, but the damage was done, whether he went home now or in an hours time, it would make no difference.
He paused to think about the previous evening and questioned himself why he did what he did. The young girl came into his mind, had he been unfair, she was only an ordinary young girl, nothing special in the way she looked.

Yes now he remembered asking where she worked, was it Lyons Tea House or something? he could barely remember.
He felt guilty all of a sudden, as if he taken advantage of her; she would probably be standing by some tea urn, pouring tea all day, feeling angry with herself for giving in so freely to him, but no it wasn't his fault. He began to console himself; she thought she was on to a good thing when the drinks were flowing, and he was not responsible for her actions.
No he would put it out of his mind and go home to face the music.

Nervously he walked in to the hot steamy kitchen there sat Sal and Ma, neither of them acknowledged him.
 He felt the tea pot, it was still warm, and poured himself a cup of tea, then waited patiently for one of them to fly into their usual rage, he thought it would be best to get it over and done with straight away. Still feeling anxious he turned to look out of the back window on to the garden, and then suddenly came an almighty crash, it was a plate or something narrowly missing his head, and it went flying through the glass window, followed by a string of abuse.

Sal started to shake him, "You fucking no-good bastard!" then Ma stepped in, resting her hands on her bulging hips.
"Do you know Sally; I don't know why you don't send him packing, he's always been a no good; I told ya that at the very beginning, didn't I now Sally?"
He stood there rigid; he smiled shyly, his bottom lip slightly dropping, "Oh come on Ma, Sal, let me explain."
Sal stamped her feet in a rage, "What's it gonna be, another lot of lies? you know Harry, your imagination really does run riot."

Yes she was right, it always had done, since he was a little boy, he thought.
"Look Sal I went to meet Eddie last night. I had a few drinks, and I knocked a drink over some bloke, well you would have thought war had broken out, before long, I had a mob of them jump on me. Then some one called the police, I have been locked up in a cell all night, you can imagine what that was like can't ya? Fucking hell Sal have a little bit of feeling, for me."

He waited for her response, hoping he had given her a sad enough story. It went silent, and then an idea came into his mind that would surely do the trick.
"Here you are Sal, take this, take Ma out shopping with ya, and treat yourselves to something nice."
Swiftly he put a roll of notes in her hand, knowing this would win her over if nothing else would.
 She put her arms up around his neck, "I'm sorry Harry, when I worry it always brings out the worst in me, you know that better than anyone."
"That's alright Sal I forgive ya, I just need to get a bit of kip, I lay in that dingy cell tossing and turning all night."
He breathed a sigh of relief, thank God for that, he thought to himself, if she knew the truth she would certainly kill him.

It was a cold December day in 1954, when Sal went to answer a knock on the door; there in front of her stood a stranger.
"Good afternoon young lady, is it possible to speak to Harry?"
She looked at the handsome man and she seemed to know the voice, but hesitated, not knowing what to say next, for all she knew, he could be a copper. One wrong word and she could drop Harry right in it, for one burglary or another.
"No I'm sorry he's not here at the moment, was he expecting you?"
"No not really, I just turned up, on the off chance, hoping to catch him at home."
"Well who shall I say called?"
"Oh dear lady tell him it was Eddie."

She suddenly felt herself brighten up, "Oh come in, he might not be too long."
She offered him a chair in the back kitchen, finding it difficult to keep her eyes off him, he was the most handsome man she had ever met. As she stood at the stove waiting for the kettle to boil, she could feel his eyes fixed firmly on her. There was a feeling of excitement building up inside of her, it was the sort of feeling that made her body feel as if was tingling all over. As she handed him his cup of tea, she purposely bent towards him, showing off her cleavage, in her low cut tightly fitting sweater.

"I must say dear lady; Harry has often spoke of you, no wonder he keeps you safely tucked up indoors, I shudder to think of all the admirers you must have after you."
She giggled, thinking how nice it was to be getting all the attention. Suddenly their conversation came to a halt; they were interrupted by the ring of the telephone.

She walked into the passage. "Good afternoon," she said in her best speaking voice, and then came the sound of laughter.
"It's alright Sal, no need for your posh voice, it's only me, I'm just off to see an estate agent, I've just seen a lovely house for sale, and I think it's about time we moved on. I'm going to be a good while yet," he said caringly.
Showing excitement in her voice, she told him to take his time, not mentioning that Eddie was waiting for him.

Happily she asked Eddie if he would like another cup of tea, she glanced towards him.
"Oh by the way, that was Harry, he's been delayed."
"Oh not to worry my Love, I will drink my tea and catch up with him another time."
"Would you like a small whisky in your tea? It will keep you warm once you go back out into the bitter cold."
"Oh how very kind of you Sally."
She looked into his eyes, yes, he was a charmer alright, but she couldn't help herself being drawn towards him. The afternoon wore on; Eddie had now taken to drinking straight whiskies.

She went to take a look at little George, he slept soundly, so she decided to join Eddie in a drink. The laughter got louder, as he told her one hilarious incident after another, about his his road to crime.
She had made up her mind she liked him, in fact she liked him a lot, and then hesitated, before asking, "Have you got a wife then Eddie?" praying the answer would be no.
"Oh my dear, dear girl, if only life had been kind to me, and I could have met someone like you. No when I was younger, I was busy being educated at one boarding school or another. Then I went on to join the army, and then of course after that came my life of crime. There has never been time for a serious relationship."

He studied her, he liked her, she didn't have much class but she was fun, yes he could easily see what Harry saw in her. The affects of the alcohol were now taking affect on him, there was a warm snug feeling welling up inside of him. He glanced at his watch.
"Oh well dear Sally, as hard as it is for me to leave you, I must be off."
She felt saddened; she didn't want him to leave, for she had more fun in one afternoon with him, than she had in a long time with Harry.
As she led him along the dark passageway to the door, she began to help him on with his overcoat; suddenly he leaned forward to give her a goodbye kiss on the cheek, the kiss lingered for a while.
It was no use she could not resist any longer; and turned towards him, and kissed him fully on the lips. He responded by putting his tongue

deep in to her mouth. There was no stopping him; his hands were touching every part of her body. She could feel him becoming more and more aroused, every so often a thought came into her mind of Harry coming through the door, but it was too late, she was enjoying the attention. She couldn't stop now even if she wanted to, and she began to take his coat.

"Dear Sally, what are you doing to me?" he asked breathlessly.
She pulled him in to the front bedroom; and he quickly pulled off her sweater, and pushed her back on to the bed. He began to unzip his trousers, he put his warm cock in to her hand, slowly he ran his fingers gently up her leg, he continued to undress her, and she put his cock inside her, she hadn't felt this much excitement and pleasure in a long time. Gently he cupped her breast in his hands then began to kiss her nipples, she groaned at the pleasure he was giving her. It was almost becoming painful as he thrashed up and down on top of her, but it was a pain she never wanted to stop.

They both groaned with ecstasy, all thoughts of Harry had now left her. She prayed that nothing was going to spoil the moment, then the telephone started to ring, "Fuck it," she groaned, as his cum spurted inside her.

She tried to get her breath back, and quickly put on some clothes on, then went rushing into the passage; she tried to compose herself before picking up the receiver.
Hello?" she said breathlessly.
"Are you alright Sal?" You sound a bit breathless."
"Is that you Harry? Yeah I just been playing with little George."
"Yeah? I've been to look at the house, it looks promising, I will be home soon Sal."

She put the receiver down and she went back in to the bedroom to Eddie, who was hurriedly getting dressed.
"That was Harry, he's on his way."
Eddie pulled her towards him; there was no sign of guilt on his face.
"We must do this again sometime Sally darling."
She kissed him passionately on the lips, "I can hardly wait," she said pushing herself back into him.
He put his finger to her lips, "Sally my darling this must be our little secret, we don't want to spoil things, do we?"

As he headed back to Ealing Common, Eddie prayed that Sally would never let slip what had happened between them, after all the money from the bank robbery was still buried in their back garden.

He was almost certain that if Harry found out about what had just taken place, he wouldn't give him his share of the money, well why should he thought? he'd just fucked his wife.
Yes he would have to let Sally think that he had fallen madly in love with her, at least until the money was sorted out.

Harry walked through the door calling, "Sal!"
She walked into the passageway to meet him; she was now feeling slightly guilty.
Harry looked happy, he put his arm around her, "It looks good Sal; I have to go back within the next few days to leave a deposit on the house, come with me tomorrow to view it?"
She tried to smile, but was finding it difficult, her mind was elsewhere. "Oh by the way Eddie called to see you."
He looked surprised, "Why didn't he wait?"
"I don't know he was in hurry or something."
He knew instantly what he was there for, the time had come to sort out the money.

It was the week running up to Christmas; Harry and Jim went into the garden shed and worked through the early hours, taking up the base floor. The howling wind made the atmosphere tense; every sound set their hearts racing.
Jim turned to him, "What the fuck you gonna do with all this lot?"
"Well mate I'm gonna buy that house I was telling ya about and I'm gonna give you a chunk of it. Then I'll give the others their share, and I'm gonna hide the rest of mine away again. It's not good to be seen throwing money about, I'd soon have the coppers on my back, wouldn't I?"

Once they had recovered the money from the ground, there was an instant feeling of relief. Harry opened up the bag.
"Do ya know Jim, just looking at this lot, I'm breaking out in a hot sweat, just thinking about it."
Jim laid his hand over the top layer of money, and rolled his tongue along his lips as if to savour the feeling.

"Fucking hell 'H' I never ever thought I would see anything like it, in my whole life."
Harry put his hand inside and pulled out a bundle, without counting it and handed it to Jim.
"Here you are mate, take it, it's yours."
"I don't fucking believe this 'H' your gonna give me this lot?"
"Yeah enjoy it, that's what it's for, aint it."

They put the floor back in place, and set about tidying the shed, careful not to leave any clues, then carefully brushed the dried damp earth from their clothes.
"Right I'm going to leave this under the bed for tonight, then get it over to Eddie's tomorrow."
"Yeah but what about Sal 'H', what if she sees it?"
"It don't matter now, time has elapsed, there is less chance of getting caught now, and some how I don't think she's gonna turn her nose up at it, do you?"
"Not fucking likely mate, money's her God."
They bid each other "Goodnight."
Jim merrily leapt up the stairs, with his pocket bulging with money.
Harry crept in the bedroom, trying not to wake Sal or little George, and started to undress, when Sal opened her eyes, "Where ya been Harry?"
She looked at the hold all, "What ya got there then?"
"Go back to sleep Sal, I'll tell ya in the morning."
She sat herself up, "No come on Harry, ya know what I'm like, no way will I sleep until ya tell me."

Slowly he began to undo the zip, a nervous smile began to break out on his face, and then he tipped the hold all up, emptying the contents all over her.
Her eyes almost bolted out of her head, as she giggled uncontrollably, she put her hands to the sides of her head, and looked on in disbelief. Excitedly she began to rub her hands over it; she looked up at him, and shouted, "Fuck me Harry."
He bent across and kissed her on the lips, then smiled as he replied, "I will when I have counted it."
She giggled at the double implication.
"Well tell me all about it?"

"Well Sal I robbed a bank with Eddie and Graham, a while back."
"What and you kept it to ya self? You rotten bastard."
"You know me Sal; I just didn't want to worry ya."
He picked up a bundle and waved it through the air, "Look Sal this is for our new house. I will take Eddie's and Graham's money over to them tomorrow."

The mention of Eddie's name brought a more serious look to her face, she felt angry. He had gone out and robbed a bank with her husband, had sex with her, she began to wonder now, had he intentionally used her? Was he about to blackmail her, if thing went wrong over the money? Perhaps he was worried Harry wouldn't come across with his money from the robbery.

Then she thought, Eddie could hold it over her, about what happened between them that afternoon in the bedroom. It might be his way of making sure he got the money, was she just being silly, or was she just letting the whole thing, get the better of her?

Harry clicked his fingers in front of her eyes, "Come on dolly day-dream, what are you thinking of?"
"Oh nothing I'm in shock, I've never seen so much money."
She hoped she was wrong, and that Eddie really had true feelings for her, alright yes she loved Harry, but in her heart she had always felt second best to Ellen. Here she was now, hopefully with two men in her life, and both with money.
He pulled her towards him, "Make yourself useful Sal, and help me divide this lot up."

The next morning he arrived early at Eddie's flat, Eddie opened the door in just his underpants.
Harry looked him up and down, "I'm sorry Eddie not a bad time is it?"
"Well chummy I've got a beautiful young thing waiting in my bed for me, but this is much more important, come on in old son."
They stood in the kitchen talking quietly, as to not be overheard by Eddie's visitor. Discreetly Harry opened the hold all, "Check it if ya want mate."
"No, no, there's no need I trust you implicitly old chap."
"Well I've paid Jim off so what you got there should be right for you, Graham and the middle man."

Eddie cast his eyes swiftly over it, "Would you be wanting coffee, chummy?"
Harry grinned, "Come off it Eddie, I'm sure you don't want me hanging about, when you've got a woman waiting in the bedroom."
"No perhaps not, oh and by the way, how's that charming wife of yours? She really is a cutie."
Harry smiled as he turned to leave.
"Oh by the way old chap I may be going away for a while, you know lay low and all that."
He walked back to Eddie and shook his hand and tilted his hat slightly.
"It's been good doing business with ya."

Harry and Sal walked into the estate agents with a brown carrier bag full of notes. A slim grey haired man called them into the small office littered with paper.
"Oh Mr and Mrs Creedy, good day to you both, how nice it is to see you, there are a few documents for you to sign, and then the house situated just off the common will be yours."

Harry handed him the carrier bag. "Here you are Mr Herbert; I think you will find it all in there for you, you have already got my deposit, this is the balance."

Mr Herbert looked down his nose, as he took off his glasses; a smile appeared on his somewhat serious face. It appeared that he had never seen anyone before walk in with a carrier bag full of notes to pay for a house outright.

The documents were finally signed; he counted out the notes and began to put them in the safe.

Harry looked on, wistfully thinking to himself it may be a challenge to come back later and blow the safe open and regain his money back.

Mr Herbert looked across at him, as if to read his mind, and coughed nervously, "We don't usually keep this much money on the premises, I'll get my brother to take it to the bank later, we've had a very busy day you know."

Harry adjusted his tie, "Oh yes Mr Herbert, and you can't be to careful, can you?"

Sal squeezed his arm and mumbled quietly, "No it's not always safe in the bank either."

Finally after everything was dealt with he handed them the key to their new home. Then he broke into a false chuckle appearing happy that the deal had been done. He gripped Harry's hand firmly.

"Well I do hope you will both be very happy; it really is a lovely house you know."

"Well thank you Mr Herbert, I'm sure we will be. It would never have been possible if it wasn't for the sad death of my uncle, who was kind enough to leave me a tidy sum."

Mr Herbert broke out into loud laughter. "Oh I see, that explains everything, I wondered how a young man had accumulated so much money. Well goodbye to you both, and good luck in your new house."

Once in the new house in the tree-lined street that conveniently led on to the common, Harry felt he had achieved his goal. This was something he had always wanted.

On a bright morning, they sat in their large dining room, drinking coffee, when Sal decided to broach the subject.

"What happened to your friend Eddie, don't he live around here somewhere?"

"Yeah he did Sal, but he said something about lying low for a while. I think he's still got the flat, but you know what he's like, when I went there with his money, he had some woman there with him.

He's probably took her on some exotic holiday, or something, he's a right womaniser."
Sal felt anger rise up in her as she put her cup down heavily on to the saucer. Her thoughts drifted to Eddie, it seems she was just one of many, she could kick herself, that she had been taken in by his goods. He stood up and put his arms around her, "Are you alright Sal?"
"Yeah, yeah."

With a feeling of overwhelming sadness she glanced around the big room, taking in the number of books that he had on the shelves. Some days he would disappear in here and she wouldn't see him all day. She thought about him, no he wasn't as handsome as Eddie, well not in a prince charming kind of way, but he was tall and good looking, there was definitely something about him. His golden hair had started to recede slightly, this seem to emphasise his big blue eyes, she often watched them flitter about, they reminded her of a big blue waves dancing on the sea. She smiled to herself; yes they were busy eyes, always wanting to take in everything around him.

It wasn't long before Jim had got the bug to go on another job. They sat in the Victory Pub, the sound of the piano made it easy for Jim to put his plans forward to Harry.
"Come on 'H' just one more time, you've always been up for it."
"Yeah I know, but I don't need to at the moment, not since the bank job."
"Well make this your last time "H."
He gulped his whisky. "Well I must admit I do like the thrill of it, go on then Jim tell me what ya got in mind."
"Right I've been seeing this girl; she's a right looker as well. The other night she was telling me she works in the office at the dairy down the lane, and she deals with the wages. The way she was talking, that safe is sometimes full to the brim."
Harry carefully listened to Jim's every word, and felt himself becoming interested.
"Alright Jim, when do we do it?"
"Thursday night mate," he replied with a smile, as he rubbed his hands with delight after winning his mate over.

It was a cold night, the wind was blowing fiercely, and they parked the car around the corner from the dairy.
They took their bag of tools from the boot, over the years they had now served many purposes and been used for many a job.
As they walked across the railway crossing, they looked all around them, the street was empty, it had just gone midnight when they approached the dairy.

They could hear the clanking of bottles; it was the night workers, loading the milk crates for the morning delivery.
They made their way to the little man-made road that ran at the side of the dairy, carefully edging their way down to the big old house at the back that was used as the dairy office.
They hid behind a row of bushes, and peered across at the night watchman, sitting in an old run down cabin. The bitter wind hit their bodies causing them to shiver profusely. They could just about see inside the cabin, the light was very dim, but he seemed to be moving from window to window, checking that all was well.
Harry blew into his hands to warm them up, before putting his gloves on.

"You know Jim this is not gonna be easy, it looks like that old boy takes his job very seriously, let's make our way up there now."
"We'll crawl along behind these bushes," said Jim, determined not to give up.
They finally reached the building and went around to the back, the complete darkness made it difficult to find their way about.
Jim went to put his torch on, as Harry grabbed it out of his hand.
"Fucking hell Jim, don't put that on; the slightest little ray of light could draw attention, don't forget there are people still working over there."
Suddenly he put his hand across to bars that were placed in front of a French window to stop people like them getting inside.

"This will do," said Harry, "We'll saw through this."
Jim took the saw from the bag and got to work immediately. Harry was now growing impatient. "Here Jim give it to me mate, let's have a go." He wiped his brow as he sawed through the bars, stopped to rest and turned to Jim, "Well this has warmed me up."
Jim tugged at the bars, them came apart, rubbing his gloved hands together, he turned to him. "That's it 'H' I'll just take this pane of glass out, and we're in."
Harry leaned against the wall and watched Jim finish it off. "Let's hope it's not alarmed."
Jim looked across to him. "No, no, it won't be that's why they got that old codger, keeping watch at the end of the road."

They were soon inside, Harry searched around the room, and finally came across the safe. Telling Jim to keep watch at the window he began to take his tools and the gelignite from the bag. Then a flash of light went across the room, he threw himself down on the floor.
"Fucking hell Jim what was that?"
"Relax 'H' it's only a milk lorry going by."
"Well you could have fucking warned me."

Suddenly another stream of light came across the room. "Alright 'H' it's another lorry."
Abruptly he threw his tools down on the floor, he was feeling angry. "It's no good Jim, my heart's not in this, it's too risky."
Jim sat himself down on the floor beside him, "Alright mate, if you aint happy with it we'll leave it."
Jim started to rummage through the drawers, suddenly his voice showed signs of delight.
"Oh what have we got here for fuck sake?"

As he pulled out a tin cash box, he didn't bother trying to open it; he thought they could do that later. Harry was now feeling deflated after getting this far as he started to gather up the tools. He gazed out of the window, the trees at the side of the road were blowing fiercely, the sound of the wind whistling gave an eerie feeling. Heavy rain started to hit the window pane; he watched the raindrops running down, all he could see was misery. He began to question himself, why had he bothered to put himself in this situation, when he had money safely tucked away at home?

Carefully he pushed open the French window. "It's alright Jim, it looks safe out there, and sorry we didn't pull it off mate."
Jim grabbed Harry's hat, pulling it down over his face as he often jokingly did.
They crept back along behind the bushes, he nervously grabbed Jim's arm, "What the fuck's that? I just heard voices."
"It could be the workers in the dairy 'H' they might be changing shifts or something."
Then they heard the piercing sound of a police whistle, and then the sound of heavy footsteps heading towards them. They froze in panic, keeping themselves down as low as possible, as they made their way to the end of the man-made road.

Harry glanced through the bushes; "I think we might be alright Jim. They are running up towards the office, if we can get on to the street quickly, we can run for the car."
"No, no, 'H' I don't fucking believe it, the crossing gates are down."
They were briefly deafened by the sound of a goods train roaring through. Hastily he grabbed Jim's collar, "Quick don't fucking hang about, let's go over the bridge."
Once they were on the bridge, they were cocooned in steam from the train; they could hardly see a thing. Harry instinctively threw the bag of tools over the bridge; they landed on the wagon of the train as it went through. Jim then threw the cash box over, now they hoping there was no evidence on them of ever being in the dairy.

They ran down the steps of the bridge gasping for breath, only to be greeted by six burly policemen waiting for them.

As the steam cleared, reality was staring them in the face; they had been caught. It was no use trying to put up a struggle; they were done for good and proper. As the cufflinks were being put on them, a belting voice came from out of the darkness.

"Hold on minute Sarge, I think I might have some vital evidence here, I just found it at the side of the track, it's a cash box, and if I'm right, it looks like a label on it, which states it belongs to the Express Dairy."

He smugly handed it over to the sergeant.

Jim and Harry were then pushed into the back of the police car.

In the early hours of the morning, feeling tired and deflated by the whole episode, they were dragged into the police station.

There they both stood in front of a desk in a small office that smelt of stale smoke. Harry peered down to a bald-headed plain-clothes policeman, sitting with a look of distain on his face. He appeared busy with paper work.

Harry turned to Jim. "It fucking stinks in here, don't it mate?"

The policeman looked up from his desk. "Well, well, if it aint you Creedy. I told you didn't I, you wouldn't see that kid of yours grow up. Oh and by the way if you think it stinks in here, just wait until you go down in the cell. Unfortunately we've had a couple of drunks in there earlier, I've been told one of them had a bit of an accident and unfortunately, there's no one to clear it up at the moment."

He turned to Jim, "And you Jim Downs, I knew we would get you sooner or later."

They both remained silent as the policeman let out a hearty laugh.

Sal woke to the sound of the phone ringing; she turned to Harry's side of the bed, it was empty. The sound of little George crying from the next room, began to fluster her. She ran downstairs to answer the phone, shouting "Won't be a minute George, Mummy won't be long." She picked up the phone breathlessly, without saying a word.

Harry was first to speak, "Sal it's me, we've been nicked."

"Who's we?"

"Me and your Jim."

She ran her fingers through her hair, as she often did when things went wrong, clutching the phone tightly, she blurted out, "You stupid fucking bastard."

He distanced the phone from his ear. "Hold on a minute Sal you could show a bit of compassion, anyway I aint got time to argue with ya, we're in court this morning at ten o'clock."

Her knees started to tremble, "Alright I'll try and get there," she answered in panic.

Sal ran up the stone steps and entered the corridor, she looked around; there were people going in different directions, she finally found a court usher.

"Excuse me, could you tell me what room Henry Creedy and Jim Downs are in?"

He indicated to a board, on the wall opposite where they were standing. "That should give you the information you want."

He put his nose up in the air and walked away abruptly.

As she tried to make sense of what was written on the board, he turned back to her and said, "The case as probably started by now."

She ran further along the corridor, she was just about to put her hand on the door handle, when a barrister came out.

"I'm sorry madam you can't go in there, the case has just been summed up."

"What happened?" she asked, concerned, "It's my husband and brother."

"Oh I see, they are remanded in custody, they will be going to Wormwood Scrubs to await another hearing."

"Is there any chance of me seeing them?"

"I wouldn't think so madam, they are sure to be on their way as we speak."

After two months of waiting, they were finally found guilty; Jim was given a three and a half-year sentence and sent off to Wandsworth prison. Harry was given a four-year sentence and sent off to Dartmoor.

ON THE MOOR

Throughout the long tiring journey Harry drifted in and out of an unsettled sleep. He had been transferred from van to train, and once at Taunton station, back to the remainder of his journey in the prison van. He didn't regard this as the best way to travel, handcuffed to a prison guard, and he wanted desperately to put out of his mind what lay in store for him. This had been something he wasn't expecting, four fucking long years on the moor.

He felt someone tug at his shoulder as he stepped out of the prison van.
"Come on Creedy, wake up, you are at your new home."
Even though it was late afternoon on a spring day, all he could see was a thick hazy mist. His eyes felt as if they were stuck, and he rubbed them to familiarise himself with what greeted him. He felt his heart sink deeper into despair, as he took in the uninviting look of the grey dreary Napoleonic building. He looked up to the building all he could see were lines and lines of small windows.
He put his hand to his throat, it felt tight as if he couldn't swallow, and he felt the need to gasp for air. His body felt rigid as he looked at the granite rock wall that surrounded the prison. His mind flashed back to a book he had once read as a young boy, about this building being built for the Napoleon prisoners of war, never in his wildest dreams, did he think he would actually be held prisoner here himself.

After taking off his civilian clothes and being handed his prison uniform, he knew life was going to tough from now on.
He lay in his cell on his first night, completely alone, with no cell mate, this he was more than pleased about, after all this was no place to make pleasant conversation. He looked around the small cell, there was a bucket, a bowl, a chair and a table, he looked at the narrow bunk beds, his thoughts turned to all the other men that had been there before him, wondering had they felt the same despair he was feeling right now, he rested his hand on his heart, thinking at least they were free now, he sighed, at least his turn would come one day. What he had seen so far, he could only describe as a hell hole, his body shivered with fear.

A small ray of light shone through the bars of his cell window, he heard footsteps, then came the sound of clanking keys entering the lock, on his cell door, this brought him to reality.
Had he been dreaming? He was somewhere on horseback, galloping across a field, with the sun beating down heavily on his back, and he could see Ellen in the distance leaning on a gate, with that beautiful smile showing boldly on her face, as he got nearer, he was just about to reach out and touch her, when he awoke.

He shook his head and began to shudder as he sat himself up; the last thing he remembered was bringing a rough blanket up around his shoulders to keep warm, it was difficult to believe he had slept the whole night through. He gazed around the brick cell that had been painted over in cream, the frame around the barred windows were painted dark green, he could smell, the paint as if it had been painted within, the last few days, probably a job to keep the prisoners busy, he thought to himself.

As the cell door opened, he was surprised to be greeted by a prison officer with a fresh face that looked even younger than him, instantly he wondered why someone so young and clean cut would want to spend their time working in this depressing place.
"Right come on Creedy, empty your slops, then get in the queue for breakfast, and make it fast" said the prison officer, as he stood with his legs astride, swinging a chain heavily laden with keys.
Yes Harry had already summed him up, the reason he had chose to work there was to have power over others, he had met his type before, and he was one of those who wanted to rule with a rod of iron. Somehow they seem to get enjoyment from it, in the outside world they would just be one of many, here they could be top dogs; he looked at the sneer on his face, and he didn't like him.

He stood on the prison landing as if in a trance, when a firm hand gripped his shoulder
"I told you Creedy, make it fast," said the prison officer in a strong Devonshire accent.
He looked along the orderly formed queue, and studied each man individually, all he could see was fear, shame, and despair in their eyes, he clenched his fist tightly, thinking, "Fuck you Jim, I've no need to be here."

The days rolled by, he had not spoken a word to a soul, except when he had to answer a prison officer and this he done with great difficulty, all he really wanted was to be left alone. He lay on his bunk, and tried to read but his heart wasn't in it, his thoughts drifted to Sal, to the day she

visited him in the Wormwood Scrubs, with the news that she was going to have another baby.
He sighed heavily, why did he always have this nagging feeling that Sal was never completely honest with him? Her mood was certainly edgy on that day she visited.
Yet, that same nagging thought wouldn't go away, was the baby his? Well alright he knew she had gone off dancing, a few times, but there were no real clues that she was seeing someone else.

His mind always went back to how easy she came across, the first night he took her home from Bernard's Dance Hall he didn't have to push her into anything, and she was more than willing. No he wouldn't want to change anything about little George, he had grown to be the apple of his eye, but if she was like it with him, what's to stop her being with another bloke? He started to feel depressed. And what about his money? He had it hidden in several places around the house, and in the garden. He had told her there was more than enough to live on, that was if he should get a heavy sentence, but knowing Sal, she would get pleasure out of blowing the lot.
"Fuck it!" he said, beginning to feel irritated.
It might be the case that he could go home to nothing.

He had already began to dislike the sound of the keys going into the lock, for some reason it startled him.
The door opened, a skinny figure with a broad grin on his face was pushed into the cell, and almost landed on his knees. Then the door closed quickly behind him, with a look of bewilderment he peered across at Harry.
"Hello mate, I'm Jack, your new cell mate."
Quickly Harry perked up to see a smiling face and got off his bunk, and grabbed Jack's hand.
"I'm Harry, good to meet ya mate, I've not been long here myself. Where ya from then Jack?"
"Bethnal Green mate, and I tell ya somink, mate, I'd give me fucking 'art to be back there now, the only good thing to come of all this is, I hear me old mucker Frank's in here. I aint seen neither hide nor 'air of him, since we shared a cell at Brixton."
Harry liked him; he suddenly felt his spirit being lifted.

He gazed out through the bars of his cell window, the sun shone brightly through the mist on the crisp September morning. His thoughts were with Sal, he hadn't seen her since March and was expecting a letter any day, to let him know if the baby had arrived.
As he looked out wistfully, coming into view was the parish parson, galloping at a fair speed on his chestnut stallion.

Often Harry watched him gallop across the moor heading towards the prison gates, with his black cassock flowing in the breeze as he bounced up and down, when the horse's hooves hit the hard ground of the moor land. His black Stetson hat jolted from side to side on his head as if it was dancing.

He had been ordered to wait in his cell; the governor was due to do his inspection of the cells, and everything had to be as clean as a fine tooth comb. Jack had chosen the short straw; he had been given the task of cleaning the prison officers' toilets.
Their cell door had been left open, awaiting the visit from the governor, and then came a booming cheerful voice, "Good morning young man."
He didn't bother to turn, thinking it was the governor.
"Are you Church of England or Catholic?"

He turned; he was surprised to see a parson standing there.
"Well I went to a Catholic school, so I suppose you could say Catholic, but if you want to know the truth I don't really believe in any religion."
He waited to see the expression on the parson's ruddy face, but he showed indifference.
"Oh that's alright son, I usually pick randomly when I visit the prison, just hoping I can give just a little bit of comfort along the way."
Harry walked across to him, "I'm sorry father I didn't mean to be rude."

The parson was holding a bible in his left hand, and resting on top of the bible, what should have been his right hand, was a hook. Harry found himself staring at it, suddenly he felt awkward.
The parson caught him looking at him, "It's alright son, I lost my hand in the war, I was in the army, that's why I thank God each day. I only lost my hand, it might have been my body and soul."
Harry felt uneasy and shuffled from side to side, he was feeling pity for the man. Then he looked into his eyes, he thought no, he wouldn't take pity kindly, it was inner strength that peered back at him.
He put out his hand; the parson then put his hook hand forward and shook Harry's hand.

"Well I bid you good day, God bless you, and perhaps I'll catch up with you another time."
He watched him walk off along the landing, he had seen him many times strolling around the prison, this made him wonder why people dedicated their life to religion. He thought of Ruby, he once asked her if she ever regretted becoming a nun, even to this day he can still remember the look on her face, it was pure surprise, "No, no," she replied, "I would have more regret if I hadn't taken my chosen path."

He can remember the gentle smile on her face, as she touched his cheek, and said, "You know Harry, I just had a calling, and it's as simple as that."

He had waited patiently for days, for the letter to arrive from Sal, at last it arrived and he held it in his hand for several minutes, as he always did, just to savour the contents.
His rubbed his hand carefully over the envelope, a habit he couldn't break, then he counted up to ten and took a deep breath as he slowly opened the envelope, yes it was from Sal, it read.

Dear Harry,
Hope you are alright, we had another little boy, on the 14th August.
I called him Henry. I wish you could be here with me. Little George often asks for his Daddy, we both miss you a lot.

Love Sal. xx

He glanced over the short and to the point letter; and threw it on to his bunk.
"For fuck sake Sal," he mumbled.
He knew she was no letter-writer, but this he took as a personal insult, just a few lines. Why the fuck did she bother?" he thought.

After a year without Harry, Sal was doing her best to get on with her life, with two small children to take care of and a big house to look after she was kept busy.
Christmas had passed by, but this Christmas it had been different, with Jim and Harry away, her father now in poor health, there was no jovial celebration.

She walked across the bleak common, with her two small children she just had to get some fresh air with only her own adult company when she needed to escape the loneliness of the house.
 Little George held tightly onto the pram handles as she dawdled across the common, she was about to take a rest on the bench when she glanced over her shoulder, suddenly she spotted a familiar figure, locking his car door. George began to run off, and quickly she made chase after him, shouting, "George get back here at once!"
Finally she caught him and swept him up in her arms, to make her way back to the pram.
There standing at the side of the bench, was Eddie, he was dressed in what looked like an expensive winter overcoat.
"My dear, dear Sally, how the devil are you?"
She felt shocked that he made a point of talking to her.

"Yeah I'm all right, no thanks to you."
"Oh come on now, Sally no hard feelings, I hope."
He looked down at the pram, "I see you've got two now, Harry has certainly kept busy. How is the dear chap?"
She stared at him long and hard, surely he must know, or was he just rubbing her nose in it? Suddenly she was feeling angry.
"Well if ya wanna know about Harry, he's in fucking Dartmoor."
Now she didn't see any point in putting on airs and graces, he had led her on once, but now he was going to get the real Sally.

He stepped back looking surprised, "No honestly Sally, I didn't know a thing, I only got back from Spain a few days ago."
Inside she was feeling very angry, but this didn't stop her feeling weak at the knees, just being in his presence, was enough to melt her heart, she peered into those deep blue eyes of his.
He gently put his hand on her shoulder, "You look cold Sally."
Her heart was thumping; she wrapped her scarf, tighter around her neck, as if to protect herself from him.

"Sally my Love come back with me and have a cup of tea or something."
"No, no, it's alright I only live across the road now."
"Well in that case, I'll come and have tea with you then, shall I?"
Caringly he put his arm around her shoulder, and walked towards her house, she opened the door that led into an elegant wide hallway.
He took a step back to take in the surroundings, "Well, well Sally, you've certainly come up in the world, haven't you?"

A feeling of uneasiness came over her, she was slightly intimidated by him; he had an aloofness about him.
She took his coat and led him into the lounge; the log fire sent out a warm ambiance, she went over to stoke the fire. As George clung on to her leg, the baby slept on peacefully in the pram.
She stood in front of the fire, her cheeks were now glowing, he couldn't help but notice how good she was looking, dressed in a tight black skirt and pink sweater, longingly he looked at her pert breast that he had once fondled.

She picked George up, "Come on darling, its time for your nap."
Her heart sank into despair; would she ever be able to tell him that she was ninety percent certain that Henry was his son, and not Harry's?
"She shouted from the kitchen, "It's two sugars if I remember right?"
As if in a trance she watched the steam flowing from the spout of the kettle. Her body began to shudder, as she asked herself, what the fuck am I doing? for she knew it could only lead to one thing.

They sat in front of the fire; the grey sky put the room in semi-darkness, they chatted on and on about the past. Eddie was keen to find out how Harry ended up in Dartmoor.
She explained how a simple job ended in disaster.
"I think if it was just a matter of the break-in, they wouldn't have got such a heavy sentence, but they found traces of gelignite across the floor, you see Harry was going to blow the safe."
Eddie roared out heartedly, "Well Sally my darling, I see the old chap remembered all I taught him, it's so bloody awful the poor chap got caught though."

He looked at his watch. "My, my, how time flies, when you're in the company of a beautiful woman. Well Sally, I must be off, you will give Harry my regards when you're next in touch."
She stood up to get his coat, in her heart she didn't want him to leave. "I tell you what Eddie, if you're not doing anything, why don't you stay for dinner."
"Sally dear, I don't want to put you out."
She smiled, "You won't be, I'm as lonely as hell in this big house."
Not needing too much encouragement he sat back down, "Well you know Sally; I could never resist anything that you might tempt me with," he gave her a cheeky wink

She got out of bed to go to the bathroom and pulled back the bedroom curtains, dawn was just breaking. She felt warm and snug inside, once back in bed she put her arms around Eddie, the sound of him breathing gently as he slept made her feel secure. It had been a long time since she had felt like this; slowly she put her hand down and began to touch his dick, and he gradually woke up.
"Oh Sally what a pleasant surprise," he said with a warm inviting smile.
She giggled and lay on top of him.
"Oh Sally I don't know if I can summon up enough energy, after last night."
"Well I'm gonna make sure you do." She kissed him passionately, all over his body, yes this is what she had been longing for, just to feel a man's body close to her. Then after another pleasurable hour in each others' arms, came the unwelcoming sound of baby Henry crying, this brought their love making to a sudden end.

It had been two long years in Dartmoor; Harry was feeling desperate, with no visitors, and only a handful of inmates to confide in, and of course the odd courtesy visits from the parish parson. They had discovered that they both shared a love for some of the greatest poets from times gone by. They rarely, talked of religion, but at least they had found something they could share.

The damp mist that had settled on the dismal moor made it almost impossible to see your hand in front of you. They were under heavy guard as they were taken on to the moor to work on the stone quarry for the day. Due to the bad visibility this gave them more than a good chance to make their escape. They worked away at the quarry on the cold November afternoon, with the thought of freedom on their mind. The group of about thirty prisoners appeared cold, as they worked tirelessly with their sledge hammers and pick axes, breaking the rocks; the bitter cold was punishment enough in itself. Their knuckles were turning deep shades of purple; their red noses running uncontrollably.

Harry looked up at the bleak grey sky, and gave Jack a nod to indicate it was time to shuffle their way to the edge of the quarry. The sky had now got even darker with monstrous clouds rolling above them, almost like night was falling; little by little, they edged slowly away from the rest of the men.
They soon found themselves distanced a good way from the rest of the group. He threw his sledge hammer to near Jack's feet, and Jack turned to him, "Is this it Harry?"
"Yeah for fuck sake mate, run for your life."
As they ran over the uneven ground, the only sound to be heard was their heavy footsteps hitting the ground. They ran like they were being chased by wild animals, into the distance.

Then a mighty screech came from Jack, as he went down with a thud. Harry turned to him breathlessly, "What is it Jack?"
"Fuck knows Harry, my foot went down a pot hole, I just heard something crack."
He tried to get him to his feet, but it was no use, "Just put your arm around my shoulder Jack, we can make it."
The fierce pain showed blatantly in his face, and a tear ran down Jack's cheek, he looked up at Harry sadly, "Don't be fucking silly Harry; I'm done for mate, carry on without me."
He bent down to him, "I can't leave ya like this Jack."
"Of course ya can, they will find me in no time, just fuck off mate, and good luck."

He knew this was his only chance.
"Alright Jack; just tell them you came after me to take me back, when you saw me doing a runner, that will put you in the clear."
Jack smiled through the unbearable pain. "Go on fuck off will ya."
Harry shook his hand and quickly disappeared out of sight. Breathlessly he ran across the vast open moor land.
Now he was beginning to regret what he had done, somehow it didn't seem so bad when there were two, but it was different now he would be

alone, already he was feeling fear. He asked himself where could he possibly be running to? this open land went on for miles and miles, what chance did he really have?
He stopped breathlessly, falling to his knees he was doubled up with a stitch, and he held his side, trying to take deep breaths, but it felt like there was no air in his lungs.

A fine shower of rain began to hit his hot cheeks, this he was more than pleased with, but his body felt as if it was going to explode, at anytime. Steadily he stood himself up, and gritted his teeth, for he knew he had no other choice but to keep on running.
The lonely open space gave no sign of life. There was no sign of a building or a light; it was now pitch black, all he could feel was fear, taking over his body.
He found his footsteps gradually dropping, and seemed to be heading into some sort of ditch. Then he came across a small gathering of bushes; he decided to take a rest.

The cold night air now gave him a chill that ran through his body, and he felt himself start to shiver, it was difficult to control his body from trembling.
He rubbed his hands together trying to put some heat back into himself. It was difficult to muster enough energy to rise to his feet; he had to find somewhere a bit more suitable to spend the night. If he remained in the bushes, the chances were that he would be dead by morning.

Struggling with every step, he walked on for another mile or so, finally he found himself standing at the top of a steep hill.
He blinked his eyes several times, if he wasn't mistaken, in the distance there was a building. Wearily he walked along a small narrow winding road. When he came to rest at a small petrol garage, it was in complete darkness.

Beyond the two petrol pumps on the forecourt, was a roller shutter with a wicket gate. He went to the wicket gate it was secured with a padlock. He took a step back to assess the building, this, if he could get inside would be the ideal place to spend the night, he thought.
He walked around the back of the garage, there were two battered cars parked near another small outbuilding. He wrenched open the door of one, praying there might just be a key left in the ignition, but there was nothing; he felt around in the darkness, it appeared that the car had been stripped. Feeling anxious he tried the next car, it was much the same; he kicked the wheel hard, angry that it wasn't in working order. Feeling despondent he walked back to the front of the garage.

The smell of oil and grease in the night air was something he hadn't smelled in a long time, in the confined space of the prison odours of the outside world were soon forgotten about. He became more familiar with the smell of urine and male sweat.
What should he do? He rubbed his face, feeling agitated. He looked to his left, there was a mound of tyres.
Searching on further along, he found a ramshackle, old outbuilding, he opened the wooden door that was barely hanging on its hinges, but could not go any further. There was no room to swing a cat; it appeared to be stacked with car engines. This would have done him fine, just to put his head down for the night.

He looked down at his feet; there was a pile of tools. He picked up a Tommy bar, and then went to the garage, with hardly any strength needed he wrenched the padlock from the wicket gate, and in no time he was inside.
He stood near the door anticipating his next move, in the darkness, he could see a large object, he put his hand on it, it was a car in front of a ramp.

He walked to the front of the car; the bonnet was open. He put his hand across it; there he found a torch on the radiator of the car. Hesitantly he shone it onto the grey Morris Minor, he opened the car door and shone the torch inside. Instantly he searched for a key, "fuck it!" he mumbled, this could have been perfect for his getaway. He was more than pleased to see a blanket on the back seat; he rubbed his arms vigorously to get warmth into his body.
Everything was becoming too much for him, and he felt exhausted. He decided to take a chance, and settle down in the car, but before doing so he slowly went around the garage, to check for a quick way out, if anyone should find him.

With the aid of the torch, he came to a small room, on the table was half a packet of biscuits, and a bottle of milk, which he picked it up and smelled; hurriedly he put it down, as he felt bile rise in his throat, the stench was unbearable.
Then he came to a dirty old sink, he picked up a mug and filled it with water, he was that thirsty he felt he could drink a well dry.
He shone his torch at the clock on the wall, it was half past one, he felt like he had been running for days.
It was no good, he could not stand on his feet a moment longer, so he lay on the back seat of the car and covered himself with the blanket.
If the clock on the wall was right, he could have a few hours sleep.
Finally he felt himself drifting off, but with a sudden jolt he came back

to reality. In his heart he knew the chances of getting caught was almost certain.

Quickly he pulled the blanket over his head and reassured himself that he wasn't going to give up easily. He flitted in and out of sleep, every now and then, shining the torch at the clock.

Thoughts were coming back to him, when he was a young boy, lying in the big old cosy bed that he shared with Patrick. The warmth as their two small bodies huddled together, on cold winter nights.

As he opened his eyes again he noticed that dawn was breaking; he could now see the area around him more clearly. He opened the car door and started to shiver as the coldness hit him. Wearily he walked over to the sink, with the blanket still wrapped around his shoulders, and splashed the freezing cold water over his face.

He cast his eyes around the untidy small room, next to the sink was a primer stove, and a box of matches, he opened them up.

"No fuck it!" he cried as he threw them on the floor in temper, they were all dead. He looked down at the matches now strewn across the floor, but no, were his eyes deceiving him or was there one lying there that had not been used?

Slowly he went down on his knees, in the half light he could just about see it, he picked the match up and held it in the palm of his hand, as if he had found a diamond in the sand.

"Yes, yes you beauty, thank you," being very careful, he struck the match, and carefully put the match to the primer stove.

He couldn't believe his luck, but there on the window ledge was a bottle of coffee. He warmed his hands over the steam from the kettle; he was now feeling as if some life was back in his body. Feeling just a little happier he sat on the floor drinking the black coffee.

Further across the room hanging on a hook on the back door was a boiler suit covered in grease, and a dark jumper. Yes, he must act fast he thought, he put the boiler suit on, then the jumper that was full of holes, over the top.

He picked up the blanket, putting it round his shoulders; and stuffed the torch up his jumper, to prepare himself for another desperate day across the moor. He looked at the rough brick, wall there hanging on a hook was a bunch of keys, he felt a twinge of excitement as he grabbed them and moved quickly towards the car. His hands trembled as one by one he tried each key in the ignition, he felt his luck was running out as he only had two more to try; gently he put the next key in, his heart almost stopped as it went in perfectly, he tried to turn it but it wouldn't move; it was jammed, angrily he banged his fist on the dashboard.

It was no good, time was running out, he would have to make his way on foot. Slowly he opened the door; and gazed out on to the bleak moor, the wind was howling fiercely, giving out a sound like an animal screeching out in pain.
Vigorously he walked and walked, across the desolate moor land looking out in the distance at the occasional hamlet. He put his hand across the top of his eyes and took in the array of different shades of colours in the distance, they ranged from dark brown to almost black, yellow and green; the grey sky rolled gently on top of gathering clouds.

He came across half a dozen rocks, in them he found a small break, and gladly crawled in. Then he put the blanket over his head; with sheer desperation he tried to close his eyes.
Now he was thinking what an idiot he had been, this is something he should have given more thought.
Over and over again he told himself only an idiot would escape from the quarry and have no help of transport on hand.

The sky turned dark, night had fallen, and his stomach began to rumble. He came to a small copse, as he tried to struggle through the undergrowth; he suddenly felt his foot slip from under him. The freezing cold water began to rise up his legs, he was feeling shaken and disorientated, and he finally got himself to a more open, flat part of land, and the cold water ran down his thick grey prison trousers, and the boiler suit. He bent down, putting, his head in his hands, as he ranted to himself, "You fucking idiot!" he felt done for. He tried to carry on, but the weight of the water soaked into the bottom of his trousers; it felt like he had an anchor tied to his feet, this made it difficult to walk.

He looked up towards the moon, somehow this gave him comfort, and then he wondered what time it might be, he began to panic. Where on earth could he take shelter from the cold night that lay in front of him? He looked across the open land, and could see a group of about three houses, in the distance, when he got nearer the sound of a dog barking came from one of them.
Across the lane, there was another house; it was almost in darkness, with just a dim light, coming from beyond the front door. Slowly he edged his way around to the back of the house, there was now complete silence.

Dare he chance his luck? If only he could get something dry to put on, it would make it much easier to get on his way.
Keenly he tried the sash window, with no luck, he moved on to the next window. He put as much strength as he could muster, then came a creaking sound, it finally opened.

Hesitantly he shone his torch through the window; the first thing that came to view was a kitchen range. He waited a while, and then plucked up courage to climb in.
The instant warmth hit him, he touched the top of the range, it was still warm. Carefully he moved his hand further along; he felt his finger turn moist, he sucked it and could taste meat; to his delight he had put his hand straight into a meat pie. Without giving it another thought, he picked it up and rammed it in his mouth.

He put his hand over his body; and felt the wet clothes clinging to him. If only he get into something dry he consoled himself that he would then feel almost human.
Fear was rising in him as he opened the door that led into the hallway, in the dark silence he began to feel his heart beating fast. The last thing he wanted was to wake anybody, that would be the end for him. It was a chance he had to take, he crept into the room opposite and felt around, there was still a glow in the hearth from the fire. He put his hand across the solid wood furniture, awkwardly he fell across a bulky sofa; the room appeared cluttered with furniture.

He stood at the bottom of the stairs, dare he take a chance and creep up? He hesitated, and then put his foot on the bottom step, it creaked and he stepped back nervously. There was a sound, coming from upstairs, he listened carefully, was it someone snoring loudly?
This pleased him; he hoped this was the only occupant in the house, and that they were out for the count. Slowly he made his way up; and almost caught his foot in the thread-bare carpet. He could just about see, thanks to the dim light still on in the hallway.
Once on the landing, he felt more confident, the snoring became even louder.
Then without any warning, the bedroom door in front of him opened wide. It felt as if his heart was about to stop. There just a few feet away from him, stood a young girl, her long white night shirt and long blond hair showed clearly in the darkness.

He froze! He had to think quickly, and put a finger to his lips, to indicate for her to be silent. The last thing he wanted to do was to frighten her. Very slowly he walked towards her, and whispered, "I wont hurt you, please don't worry."
There was fear showing on her face.
He whispered, "Please just find me some dry clothes, I will leave straight away."
She turned to open a cupboard, and threw a pile of clothes in his direction, he scrambled to pick them up, and mouthed the words "Thank you."

Then he turned to go back down the stairs, then came a loud thud, and a light went on.
There stood a stout man, his grey hair almost standing up on end, he raised his hand, and in it he held some sort of tool. Quickly he grabbed the young girl, and put his arms protectively around her. A woman's voice shouted from the room in a distressed tone,
"What is it, what's happening?"
The man began to walk towards him shouting, "Stop, stop, stop! Who would that be?"

Harry froze, and turned to take another step down the stairs; he looked back at the man.
"I'm not going to hurt anyone."
"Bloody right you're not, you must be this escaped prisoner the police are searching for. Get out of my house right now, you can make a run for it if you want, but I'll tell thee now, I'm going to ring these here police, and bloody get you caught. Just who do thee think you be, coming in my house and frightening my family?"
The young girl looked up to her father, "Dad let him go, he done me no harm."

Harry jumped down the stairs, still with the bundle of clothes in his arms, and ran until his legs would carry him no longer.
Then he heard the sound he had been dreading most, the ringing bells of police cars, in the distance.
He sat himself down and rested his back against a mound of earth. Quickly he pulled off the wet clothing, and covered them with the damp earth; he wanted to leave no clues. Then he put on the trousers that the young girl had given him, they were much too big, but at least they were dry.

The sound of the police bells seemed to be fading. Suddenly he came to a narrow lane, he looked across to the road junction, there was a telephone box and a sign post which he could just about see. It read, 'North Bovey, one mile'.
He looked around, there were a group of houses in the distance, and complete silence all around him.
Then a thought occurred to him, the phone, yes he could ring Sal.
He stood in the warmth of the phone box, rain started to hit the windows, with his finger trembling; he attempted to dial the operator. To hear a voice on the other end of the line gave him comfort, in a chirpy manner the woman spoke, "Hello operator speaking, how can I help you?"
He began to stammer, "Yes, yes I'd like to ask for a reverse charge phone call to London."

"State your number please caller?"
He looked at the faded number on the dial, and could just about read it. After giving her the number, he wondered, had he done the right thing, after all it was the middle of the night.
The operator spoke again, "Caller your number is ringing for you."
A breathless voice came on the line, "Hello, hello."
He spoke quietly, "It's me Sal."
"Harry I don't believe this, what's happening?"
"I've escaped, look Sal, I'm going to have to be quick. I will get back to you as soon as I can, let me try and work something out. Perhaps you can arrange some transport for me, I'm getting fucking nowhere running across this moor on foot."
"Harry but why? I've had the fucking police here most of the day, they are searching everywhere for ya."
A sudden glare of headlights hit his eyes. "It's no use, I've got to go Sal."

He turned his face away, from the oncoming light that was hitting him in the face. Praying the car would carry on, he looked out of the corner of his eye; it had carried on slowly going up the hill to his right.
He wiped the condensation from the window, and breathed a sigh of relief. When suddenly he peered out again, it was making its way back again. His legs began to tremble, fear, panic, all sorts of emotions were going through his mind. He felt trapped, should he make a run for it? He wasn't really sure what to do next. Wiping the window again he still could not be sure if it was the police car or not, he pondered for a while. Keeping his back to the window; he heard the engine of the car, then it was switched off.

Then he heard the sound of footsteps heading towards him.
His heart began to pound, he mumbled, "No please God, no."
The door was pulled open; and he was confronted by two policemen. One grabbed his arm he lifted his helmet further back on his head, his face showed signs of tiredness and age.
"Alright lad, I'll come straight to the point, you have got to be Creedy."
He dropped his head down in disappointment, as he put his hands up in the air, "Yea that's me." Now he knew it was no use, his time was up. He stood in the dark cold air, as the handcuffs were put on him. Not a word was spoken, but he knew this was another of the major fuck ups, that he kept making in his life.
In a funny sort of way, as they drove back through the dark vast moor land, he was pleased he had been caught. The silence of his own company, and the wide-open land, had been playing havoc with his mind.

Once back at the prison and being severely reprimanded by the governor he was told he would be spending the next six months in solitary confinement, his heart sank.
He was taken below ground level; he looked around the narrow corridor, there were three cells, the small area appeared clinical.
The scrubbed floor shone like it was an ice rink, there was not a sound to be heard; only the jangling of keys as his cell door was opened.
When the door shut firmly behind him, he rubbed his face in his hands. He knew he must stay calm, panic would do him no good whatsoever.

There and then he made a decision, that he had his mind, and his vivid imagination, this was what was going to get him through the next few months.

A banging noise hit the wall, then a distant voice said, "Is that you in there Harry?"
He put his ear close to the wall, "Yeah, who is it?"
"It's me Jack; they've put me down here for two weeks. When they found me with my leg injury they didn't really believe I tried to stop ya going on the trot."
Harry banged the wall hard. "Sorry about that mate, goodnight mate."
He was in no mood for talking, he just desperately needed sleep.

Finally he was put back on to the regular wing, and life seemed to brighten up, being back with his mates Jack and Frank, helped the time to pass more quickly.

Then one day he received a letter from his old mate Jim, telling him that he was now back home, after serving his sentence and life was good; he had now met a new girlfriend called Jean.
He put the letter on the cabinet and smiled, so Jim had finally got himself a girl.

A light hearted feeling came over his body; he rubbed his hands together feeling delight, for the first time in almost four years; he was only days away from going home.
On a March morning, the sun shone bright, through the mist. Once again dressed in his civilian clothes, the feeling of deja vous came over him. Yes, he thought to himself, he was becoming an old hand at walking in and out of prison gates.
Happily he stepped into the dark van, with two other ex prisoners en route to Taunton station, to return at last to London.

FOOTLOOSE

He stepped onto the platform at Ealing Common Station, still feeling confused by the hustle and bustle that he had encountered on his long journey. He felt weary and exhausted, and had almost forgot about the fast pace of the outside world.
He looked across at the station clock, it was half past six, then he turned to look over at the station kiosk. The woman behind the counter was about to pull the shutter down. Quickly, he searched his pocket for the money the prison had given him to get home, and he pulled out a ten shilling note.
He shouted across to her "Hold on a minute Love, any chance of a packet of cigarettes?"
She glared at him as she passed them to him as if she was doing him a favour.
Suddenly he felt angry, if it wasn't that he was so desperate for a smoke, he would have thrown them back at her.
In his heart he wanted to shout, "You cow, don't you realise I've been locked away for four fucking years?"

Wearily he walked towards the common, puffing hard on his cigarette. The bright headlights from the oncoming cars gave him a feeling of unsteadiness.
The evening was calm; he didn't really know how he was feeling about seeing Sal again, after being four years without her. The uncertain love he did have, now felt even worse. He shook his head, hoping that once he set foot in the door and put his arms around her, some feeling might come back to him.

As he walked across the common, he stopped occasionally to gather his thoughts. A young couple passed him with their dog, they were giggling out loud. Yes he thought, how good it was to hear real laughter once again.
Nervously he opened the front gate and glanced across at the front window, it looked warm and cosy inside. Cautiously he stood at the front door; he could hear a small child crying, he took a deep breath before knocking on the door.

A light went on in the hallway; a voice shouted, "Alright I'm coming." Yes he recognised, it as Sal's.
The door opened; there she stood with a toddler in her arms. A bright smile came on her face, and she beamed, "Harry, its good to have ya home Love," and held out her arms.
He felt awkward, as if he was just a visitor.
She showed her excitement. "Oh come here you lovable rogue."
He put his arms around her and rubbed the little boy's face, "How are ya Love? You look good ,and this must be Henry."
"Oh yeah, that's him alright, he's a right bundle of trouble, I wonder who he takes after?" she said with a giggle.
He laughed, "Perhaps he takes after his Dad."

Sal put the boy down, she grabbed him round the neck, he pulled her up to his level, and she kissed him passionately.
To feel a woman in his arms again felt good, he glanced towards the doorway. There stood little George, who walked over towards him, holding out his arms.
"Hello Georgie boy, how are you son?"
George turned his back and ran into the room opposite; Sal could see the hurt in Harry's eyes.
"Don't worry he'll come round, he's been nearly all his young life without you, it's gonna take time, you know that don't you?"

He took his coat off and hung it on the bannister, Sal grabbed his hand. "Come on I've got a nice meal waiting for ya, you must be tired after the long train journey."
Suddenly he was distracted, he was about to walk into the dining room, when he caught sight of two long slender legs, he looked down at the black high heeled shoes. Then cast his eyes upwards, there sitting near the table was an elegant woman, reading a book.

She put the book down and smiled, as she said confidently, "You must be Harry, I've heard so much about you."
Sal interrupted, "Harry, this is Jean; she's staying with us for a while."
A smile came on his face, he was surprised, who was Jean, he thought? He leaned forward to shake her hand.
Sal started to explain how Jean came to be their new lodger. "Jean was going out with Jimmy; they met at a dance, she had come up to London from Sussex. To be honest I was pleased of the company. This all happened when Jim first came out of prison, since then, they have split up," Sal said.
Jean smiled, "Yes, I don't think I was outgoing enough for Jim."

As the weeks passed, Harry felt himself becoming attracted to Jean. She was intelligent and she liked to read. They would often while away the hours, talking about one book or another or topics of the world. This he could never do with Sal.

If he was honest, things were never really right for him and Sal, she was evasive about the years when he was away, somehow she never wanted to talk about it. Sometimes he wondered why, he knew it wasn't her fault that he had spent four years behind bars, but it was almost like she had shut those years out of her mind.

Sal had set off to visit Ma. Suddenly he heard the front door slam, a voice shouted out, "It's only me."
He felt happy it was Jean; she stood in the hallway, with a pile of books in her arms.
She looked at him sitting there, the bright September sun gleaming on his golden blonde hair, the more she got to know him, she felt herself becoming attracted to him, hoping the feelings would pass, but if anything the attraction was getting stronger.
He glanced at his watch, "You're back early from work Jean."
"Yes for some reason, the boss decided to close the office early.

He looked at her slender body standing in the doorway. Discreetly he touched his dick, thinking if only she knew how much he wanted her.
"Jean why don't you take your books upstairs and come back down and join me? I'll put the kettle on to make us a cup of tea. Sal won't be back for ages, once she's at Ma's she never wants to come back."

She returned looking refreshed, her short blonde hair emphasised her clear complexion, with no makeup, only a very pale lipstick, she looked young and pure. The pink blouse she was wearing looked crisp and fresh, the top button was undone, showing off her cleavage. He didn't know much about her, she kept herself very much to herself. He looked at her longingly, really wanting her, often he watched her walking around the house, and thoughts would go through his mind of her lying close to him, but he was determined to get to know her better first.

He opened the French window; the room was hot and stuffy. She stood by his side, he wanted to put his arm around her and pull her close. Yes he wanted to fuck her, right there and then, but he was frightened of spoiling their relationship as friends. He had grown to like the in depth conversations they often had about poetry and different parts of the world and such. He felt good when in her company.
She walked into the garden and sighed, "You know, Harry the garden is really delightful."

"Yeah but Jean don't you think it's sad this time of year, when everything starts to come to an end?"
"No not really," she replied, "I grew up in the country, I used to walk along the country lanes at different times of the year, watching the wild flowers grow, and then before long, they would die off. That's nature isn't it? Well let's face it every season as something to offer."
He stared into her eyes, "Do you ever wish you were back there now?"
She smiled softly, "I did until I met you."
He was surprised that she had said this; caringly he put his arm around her shoulder.
"I'm flattered; at least I'm making someone happy." He sat on the garden bench; she sat herself down next to him, "What is it Harry? You look sad."
"Oh it's just me and Sal; I think she spent too much time on her own, what with me being away for so long. It's wrenched us apart even further; it was never a very strong marriage, now its just going from bad to worse."
She touched his hand, "Yes, but your friend Eddie came to visit, sometimes to make sure Sally was alright."

A look of shock appeared on his face, his mind was working overtime. Then he thought to himself, not once had Sal mentioned Eddie visiting the house while he was away, he stayed silent.
She felt awkward; she instantly knew she had said the wrong thing.
Thoughts were now running riot in his head, why had Eddie come to visit her? Yeah he loved the ladies alright, but not Sal, she wouldn't be his type.

An early evening breeze started to blow up; Jean stood up, and clasped her arms in front of herself. "I think I had better get inside, I'm starting to shiver."
He put his arm protectively around her, "Come on lets get inside."
Once inside the room, he pulled her close to him and felt the warmth from her breath. Gently he put his hand under her chin, and kissed her. She could feel his body pushing hard against her, and was finding it difficult to control her feelings so she reluctantly pulled away.
"No we can't let this happen," she said hesitantly, for in her heart she wanted him more than anything in the world.

He looked lovingly into her eyes, "But Jean you make me happy, you're different, you're interesting."
"Harry I wanted this moment to come for a long time, but now it's come, I feel torn. It's just that Sally has been a good friend to me, and anyway she will be back soon."
He pulled her close to him again, "No she won't be back yet.

She felt herself wanting him more and more. He rested his hands on her breasts and fondled them gently.
Taking her by the hand, he led her up the stairs, once on the landing they began to kiss passionately. Frantically he kicked the door open to her bedroom; he could not take his hands off of her, it was difficult to let her go and he had waited so long for this moment. They fell clumsily onto the bed, his dick was hard, waiting to penetrate her, and he put his hand slowly up her skirt as she vigorously wriggled around the bed. Her breathing had become heavier, as she put her tongue into his mouth and yes he knew she wanted him badly.
Suddenly a voice shouted up the stairs, "Is anyone home? We're back."
He jumped up. "No; fuck it, its Sal."
Jean jumped up quickly, trying to tidy herself up. He looked at her, she was flushed, she put her hand to her mouth showing surprise.
"Quick, quick, quick, go," she said in a frightened voice.
He stood with his back to the door, trying to get his breath back, and then he shouted down the stairs, "I won't be long; I was just about to have a bath."

Jean sat in her room, for the rest of the evening, crying over what had almost happened. What had she done? She felt ashamed, she knew now there was no turning back; she had fallen hopelessly in love with him.

In bed that night Harry felt restless; he was lying next to Sal, but wanting Jean. He tossed and turned thinking about Eddie's visits to the house. It was no good, he would have to wake her and confront her about what was going on in his head.
He kicked the covers back, and went to stand near the window, he lit a cigarette. He gazed out to the sky, it was full of stars, if he could make a wish now it would be to with Jean, he desperately wanted to make love to her. Why couldn't things be clean cut, why was everything in his life, was so tangled?

He racked his brain, little George came a month early, and if he remembered right, it was only just about possible that he could be Henry's father.
He pressed the cigarette out hard into the ashtray anger was sieving up in him.
Ranting to himself, "Fuck it, and fuck you to Sal, you've been taking me for an idiot." The whole of his body began to tremble, he went over to her, tugging at her arm.
She sat herself bolt upright, "What is it Harry, what's going on?"
He leaned over to her, "You fucking cow, you've been deceiving me all this time."

She quickly got out of bed, "Are you having a nightmare or something?"
Yeah, yeah, it all a fucking nightmare alright, you was seeing Eddie when I was away."
She cried out, "No, honest Harry I aint."
"Come on Sal, you don't fool me; you've had more fucking pricks than a secondhand dartboard."
She slapped him hard across the face, "Is that what you think of me? That I'm just some old slut or something."
Tears began to stream down her face as she tried to explain herself. "Look I met Eddie one day on the common, he came back for a cup of tea, he didn't even know about you being away."
He retaliated, "Yes but, how about when he came to the house in Acton?"
"Yeah but that was for you, I didn't know it at the time but he wanted to sort out the money from the bank job. I was just trying to make him feel welcome, at that time."

He took a step back, "So ya let him fuck ya. Well Sal you couldn't make him anymore welcome than that, could ya? Do you honestly expect me to believe that nothing happened? Do you really think that Eddie would show you concern, about me being away? You stupid cow, he's a womaniser through and through. Where is he now then Sal? Well I'll tell ya, he's probably had what he wanted from you then shot back off to Spain."

She covered her hands over her face, she didn't want to hear this, and she knew he was right. Yes she knew it; he had used her once again.
She flung her arms up to him, there was no other way, she knew now she would have to admit it.
"Alright, alright I'm sorry, there was something going on, but let me tell you, I regret every minute of it."
"Its all too late Sal, I'm leaving, as soon as I get myself sorted out, I'll take my money, what's left of it, and you can have this house."
She started to beg him, "Please, please, don't go, don't leave me."
"It's no good Sal, it's not all your fault, I don't think I ever truly loved you."
She threw herself down on her knees. "I know, it's Ellen, you've always loved her. I always knew I was only second best.
He closed his eyes; a picture of Ellen came to his mind. Yes he still did love her but she would only ever be in his thoughts, not in his arms. He was more than aware of that.

After giving it a lot of thought he had decided to stay on until Christmas had passed. The main reason for this was for the sake of the boys.

There was a Christmas tree standing in the big bay window and the roaring fire gave the house a warm cosy feeling.
This all gave out a false impression, things were not right, the atmosphere between Sal and Harry was as cold as ice.
He had managed to keep his relationship with Jean under wraps. They made plans to move in together on New Year's Day.
He took a chunk of his hidden money and brought another house, in a nice select part of Acton. All he wanted now was to start afresh with Jean. Fear was continually with him, dreading the day coming when he would finally have to tell Sal the truth.

On New Year's Day 1960 he packed his case, Sal came out of the kitchen with tears streaming down her face. He stood at the bottom of the stairs looking forlorn, desperately wanting things to go as smoothly as possible.
He put his arm around her. "Look Sal don't upset yourself, we can still be friends. We have been through a lot together and if I'm honest, there were times when I don't know what I would have done without ya."
Not once through all this had he given a thought to how he had betrayed her with other women.
She buried her head in his chest, "But Harry I love ya; I don't want ya to go."

Then she caught sight of his case, surprise came to her face, there were two. "Harry, whose case is that one?" se asked with a look of surprise.
She glanced across, out of the corner of her eye, and saw Jean's long legs standing near the bottom of the stairs.
 Sal turned to her, "Are you off out somewhere all dressed up in your new coat?"
Harry pulled Jean towards him protectively.
Sal stepped back against the wall, as if to, need support.
"No please tell me no, not you two."
Jean stood there looking pale and feeble.
"I'm sorry Sally; I didn't want it to be like this, you have been a good friend to me and I'm truly sorry."

Sal now felt an inner strength coming into her body, and she stepped forward and looked her directly in the eye.
"You deceitful cow, so that's how you repay me is it? You stay in my house, and then have it off with my husband. Well I tell you what! You both deserve one another."
Tears began to flood down her cheeks again; she sat at the bottom of the stairs and cried until there were no more tears left.

In their neat Georgian semi, life became bliss. Harry was now thirty one years old, and had made up his mind to try and make this relationship work. Often he went back to visit the boys. Sal now had a new man in her life, and had almost forgiven him for hurting her so much. In her heart she blamed Eddie, if he hadn't come into their life in the first place, they might still be together.

In September that year Jean gave birth to a little girl, they named her Carmen. He felt overjoyed, at last he had been given the chance to cradle a little daughter in his arms; as Carmen grew so did his love for her, she became his pride and joy.
Sometimes he missed the life he shared with Sal; though he never really knew what was coming next with her, one minute they were lovers, the next minute they would fight like cat and dog. Jean had a great deal more intelligence than Sal, this he liked, it stimulated his mind, and she was loving and caring, but sometimes a bit too predictable.

Carmen was now one year old; he was gently pushing her on the garden swing when Jean called him from the kitchen window.
"Harry there is a chap at the door for you; he says his name is Graham."
He felt surprised, and went to greet him in the hallway. Graham stood there looking as dapper as ever, dressed in a tweed jacket and smart brown trousers.
He rushed to shake his hand, "Hello Graham how are you mate, how did you find me?"
Graham puffed on his pipe, "I went to your house at Ealing, and I was given this address."
She offered them a cup of tea, as they walked back out to the garden. She watched the two men talk, as little Carmen toddled nearby.
Harry's arms were waving about with excitement, and then came a broad smile on his face.

He took a sip of his tea. "Well what is it I can do for ya Graham?"
Graham tapped the end of his pipe, "Well it's like this; I thought who's the best man to blow a safe, now that Eddie's out of the country. It didn't take a lot of working out; there's no one better than you Harry."
A wide grin spread across his face, he felt flattered that Graham had come to him.
He lit a cigarette, "You know Graham, I've kept me head down for a while, after doing four years on that fucking moor, well that took its toll on me."
"Harry I won't push you, it's a few little jobs that I've got lined up, nothing major; but they will just keep us in the lifestyle that we have become accustomed to."

That old feeling was coming back to him, his stomach began to flutter, and he loved the feeling; he could almost smell the gelignite. Giving it some thought he knew there was no way he could refuse.

Harry beckoned her towards him, "Jean come over here; let me introduce you properly to Graham, an old mate, from times gone by."

She walked over sheepishly to shake his hand, half heartedly. There was something about him she didn't like, as she thought that this could be the end for her and Harry.

It was something she had been dreading - his past catching up with him again.

Harry stood in the drive, feeling optimistic about the plans that had been made. He waited for Graham's cream jaguar to disappear out of sight then returned to the house. The stern look on Jean's face put a damper on how good he was feeling.

She gently touched his arm, "You know Harry, I could never put up with the kind of life that Sally had with you."

He looked surprise, "What do you mean by that? Sally had a good life with me, she wanted for nothing."

"Did it ever occur to you, that it might have been you she wanted? Not the big house and diamonds. You in and out of prison all the time broke her heart, she told me so."

He felt angry, "Well why didn't she fucking tell me?"

He sat on the sofa, feeling bewildered, no woman had ever tried to rule his life before, and no way was he going to let it happen now.

The uneasy feeling was getting to him, there was nothing else for it, he had to get out of the house, he felt stifled. He would go and see his old mate Jim.

Yes he would ring him straight away. To hear Jim's chirpy voice on the line, cheered him up instantly.

"Hello Jim mate, how'd ya fancy a drink down the Vic tonight? I need to talk to ya."

A voice beamed back, "See ya about eight mate."

They stood at the bar, in the same spot where they stood all those years ago. Jim continually put his arm around him; nothing made Jim happier, than being with Harry.

"You know Jim I'm sorry about everything that's happened with me and your Sal and to top it off I went off with Jean, it all just happened so quickly."

Jim raised his glass. "That's alright 'H' as long as you are happy now; you know Jean wasn't my type anyway." He began to laugh, "Well let's face it mate, she's too fucking straight-laced for me."

Harry's head dropped forward towards his glass.

"I'll drink to that mate. Do ya know Jim I don't think I am happy with her."

Then he suddenly lightened up, a broad smile came back on his face.
"No Jim mate, what I'm really here for is to let you know there might be a bit of work coming up, I had a visit from Graham today."
Jim raised his glass. "Fuck me mate I'll drink to that. I could do with a few extra quid right now, but I'll tell ya this 'H' no way, do I want to end up, behind fucking bars again."

That night he returned home to Jean after a few drinks too many, he fell through the front door, and lay in the hallway motionless, with his arms stretched out, then a sudden stamp came down on his hand. There standing over him was Jean in her fur indoor slippers. Carelessly he pulled his hat from his head and looked up, at her very serious face, as she glared down at him with distain.
"I'll tell you this now Harry, if you think I'm going to spend my life with some drunken crook, you are very much mistaken."

Jean was no longer happy with her life with Harry, she was finding it increasingly hard to cope with his life of crime. Now she regretted that she had ever taken him away from Sally in the first place, she was a country girl at heart, and that's where she wanted to be.
When she looked back at the situation, she asked herself, were they truly suited to one another after all? Sally could quite easily pass as a gangster's moll, something she could never be, and didn't want to be.
The thing was now, it wasn't so easy to just, walk away, she had Carmen to think of, and she meant the world to him.

She stood near the window, and watched him read, this was the Harry she loved, the man that had first attracted her, he was a handsome and intelligent man as far as she was concerned. She walked over to him; and sat close to him resting her head on his shoulder. Finally she summoned up her courage, for what she was about to ask him was either going to make or break their relationship.
She kissed him gently on the cheek, he put down his book, and a smile came on his face.
"What's all this about?" he asked softly?
She cleared her throat. "Harry I want to move back to Sussex, this sort of life is not for me."
He looked surprised, "Well what's going to be different in Sussex?"
She tried to explain her feelings to him. "I can't carry on, life is so uncertain; I never know where you are, or what you're up to."
He became serious, "Well Jean I'll tell you right now, I've been a thief since I was six years old and moving to Sussex aint gonna change that.

You knew all about me from the very beginning. For fuck sake you were there the day I got back home from Dartmoor, it can't be made any clearer than that."

"The trouble is Jean, you don't know the meaning of excitement. You never let yourself go, in your world everything as to be so perfect."
She snatched up his book from him and threw it across the room.
"So do you call being behind bars exciting, do you?"

After lots of lengthy discussions, he finally agreed to sell the house and move to Sussex. He wanted his relationship to work with Jean, if only for Carmen's sake. There was no other way; he would at least give it a try.
He found village life tame, too tame. Jean was at her happiest in the garden, caring for Carmen, and tending the flowers. He became a well known character in the small village pub, as much as he tried to keep a low profile this proved almost impossible.
The day finally came when Jean confronted him, at the breakfast table. She picked up the local paper. "Oh no, no, I don't believe it."
He looked at her curiously. "What is it?"
She turned the front page towards him, the headlines read. 'Village drunk drives car in pond.'
Angrily she shook the paper in front of him. "Look, look, there's you standing next to that policeman."
He started to laugh, he hadn't realised that he had been photographed. "Don't worry about it; I'll just get a fine."
She put the paper down; no she wasn't worried, she was embarrassed. There were her friends and family around here, whatever would they think?
He handed her a cup of coffee. "You know Jean; you shouldn't take everything so seriously."
"It's no good Harry; I can't go on like this, I had hoped that the move might help, but you are never going to change."
He felt annoyed, and walked towards the door. "I tell you what Jean, I don't fucking want to change."
"Well in that case you had better leave," she said assertively, pointing to the door.
He suddenly felt relief, if he was honest there was nothing he wanted more than to get back to London.

He walked into the kitchen, Jean sat at the table, her eyes were red, she had been crying. All the time they had been together he had never seen her look so sad. Caringly he rested his hand on her shoulder. "Jean I'm sorry it has to end like this." As he walked out of the door, he turned to see Jean holding Carmen tightly in her arms.

BACK TO THE SMOKE

As he drove towards Acton his thoughts were with the last two years he had spent with Jean. What a fool he had been to think they could have spent the rest of their lives together. The only thing they had in common was their love of books, and now Carmen of course; how was life going to be from now on? He made his way from Acton High Street, he drove past the laundries and that same fresh soapy smell came through the open window of the car.

He breathed in; it took him back to his childhood, his heart began to lift as he drove through the narrow streets. He noticed that some of the familiar buildings had disappeared; in place of the neat little cottages blocks of flats were being built. Finally he stopped the car in the street where he was born, he got out and stood back in despair, all there was to be seen was flat building land.
His stomach churned, he didn't like what greeted him, he looked further up the road; a pleasing feeling came to him. Still untouched was the sweet shop on the corner, but how long for he asked himself? He thought back to all those years ago, when he would go in there with Patrick to steal their sweets, but in spite of all the changes, as far as he was concerned, he was back home.

He got back into his car and drove further up the road and stopped the car outside the house he once shared with Sal and her family. There was relief that it had not been demolished. He stood in the porch with his suitcase at his side; a strange feeling came over him. He waited in anticipation then knocked feebly on the door, hoping it would be Jim and not Ma that answered. He looked through the stained glass then saw a figure coming towards the door. He heard the voice shout, "Alright hold ya horses." Instantly he felt safe, for he knew it was Jim. The door opened; there as bold as ever stood Jim, with that same wide grin on his face. He held out his arms, "'H' mate, what the fucking hell are you doing here?"
He puffed on his cigarette, "I thought you might be able to give an old mate a room for the night."
Jim picked up his case, "Follow me mucker."

Once inside he noticed an unmistakable silence. He started to undo his jacket. "Where's Ma, is she going to be alright about me staying the night? You know what I mean, after all the business with me and your Sal breaking up?"
A solemn look appeared on Jim's face. "Oh of course, you wouldn't know, poor old Ma died a month ago, and the old man passed away back last year. I'll tell ya 'H' you just don't know how much your gonna miss them until they're gone, do ya 'H'?
Harry didn't want to show it, but all of a sudden he felt relieved, it was almost certain that Ma would have lashed out at him for leaving Sal.
"Yea 'H' I'm all on me tod now, it gets a bit lonely at times."
Harry smiled, "You still aint found a woman to put up with ya yet then Jim?"
Jim laughed heartily, "They come and go 'H' ya know what I mean."

The two men sat in the little back kitchen, that hadn't changed since the day him and Sal moved out. Perhaps a little bit more worn with age, but somehow he could still feel Ma's presence.
Jim put a bottle of whisky on the table. "Well what's gone wrong in ya life this time 'H'?"
"I don't know mate, I just can't seem to settle."
Jims face became serious. "You know mate ya got to get to grip with things, you're gathering a long line of kids behind ya."
He took a large gulp of his whisky; he didn't need Jim to remind him of this, things were bad enough as it was.
Jim felt the uneasiness, and jumped up. "Oh for fuck sake mate, don't let's get morbid. Let's get down that dance hall, and find ourselves a bird." They broke out into hearty laugher.

His head felt heavy as he stretched out his arm, he ran his hand across the soft silky skin of a woman's body. It was difficult to open his eyes; a ray of light came through the curtain, instantly he knew he was in a strange room, but where? he asked himself.
She slept soundly; he could just about hear her gentle breathing. Hesitantly he crept out of the bed, searching the floor for his clothes. Then things started to slowly come back to him, it was a long journey in a car, and a group of people, and very loud music.
He turned to look at the woman there was no doubt about it, she was beautiful, her long dark hair lay fleetingly across the pillow.
He gingerly walked onto the landing, his mind was now becoming much clearer. Yes he remembered, he parked the car and started to walk towards the dance hall with Jim. There was the sound of a car horn, and the screeching of tyres. It was Graham, in his Jaguar, yes that was it, he remembered now. Yes, him saying, "Jump in; I'm off to a party in Hackney."

They stopped at a pub along the way to meet a group of people. Then he got a sudden blur, he couldn't remember anything else.
The door was ajar to the bedroom near to where he was standing, he peeped in, the bold patterned wallpaper dazzled his eyes. On the bed lay a foreign looking man snoring loudly, his legs were spread across the double bed. He was wearing a bright floral shirt, and cream trousers. The unbuttoned shirt showed a mass of dark hairs on his chest.
Who could he be? he asked himself, was it his house? He mysteriously glanced around the room, on the side cabinet next to the bed lay a wallet, a set of keys and a gun. Suddenly he felt edgy as he wiped the sweat from his brow.
Who the fuck were these people?

All he could think of was getting out fast; waking up next to a woman he had never met before and a man with a gun, this only spelled trouble as far as he was concerned.
He crept down the stairs, the lounge door was open. There were people lying on the sofas, it appeared that everyone was out to the world.
As he peered in closer, to his relief, there lay Graham.
He walked over to him, hoping not to wake anyone, and shook him, then beckoned him out of the room. He walked back out and sat on the bottom of the stairs.
Graham appeared in front of him, his hair ruffled, looking bleary-eyed. Harry gazed up at him, "Where the fuck are we Graham?"
Graham started to laugh, "Don't you remember? We are in Hackney."
"Graham where's Jim?" He was feeling concern for him.
"Oh he went off with some bird in a taxi last night."

Harry stood up, and lit a cigarette. "Look all I know is, I got to get out of here quick. I woke up next to a beautiful woman up there and in the next room there's a bloke lying with a gun at his side."
Graham began to look serious, "Oh that will be Maltese Michael, known in the underworld as 'Mickey the Malt.'"
He puffed long and hard on his cigarette. "What do ya mean the fucking underworld and what about the woman, who's she?"
Graham looked him straight in the eyes. "Well did you fuck her?"
He rubbed his head, as if trying to think. "Yeah I seem to be getting some flash backs, yeah I did."
"Well Mickey the Malt he happens to be her pimp, you know he is one of these blokes that's got his fingers in many pies. I think you had better go and put a few quid up there. You know what I mean, pay her for her services, so to speak. Yes I would definitely do that before they come looking for you."
Graham watched with delight as he turned a deathly shade of pale, then he let out a hearty laugh.

"It's alright mate I'm only joking, I took the liberty of offering your services to a few of the chaps last night. If the occasion should ever arise for a safe to blown, I told them you were the best man for it. I've done business with them before, they are a good bunch. There's no panic, Mickey the Malt took a liking to you. He said she came free of charge."

Happily Harry breathed a sigh of relief as he rubbed his hands together. "Thank fuck for that."

They headed back along the embankment, the bright morning sun shone across the river. Today he felt good, at last the depression of his broken relationship with Jean seem to be lifting.

He looked across at Graham; he never spoke of Josie much these days, he wondered if all was well with them. Harry knew he had a young son but he rarely ever mentioned him. He shrugged his shoulders as he thought, perhaps he likes to keep his private life, private.

Days turned into weeks, weeks into months and he was still lodging with Jim. The two men couldn't have been happier. With no woman close to them to tell them what to do, it was wine, women and song, almost every day.

Harry looked out of the window; the snow lay thick on the ground, Christmas was almost upon them. He was about to turn away, when a car came to a halt outside. Graham got out wearing a long camel overcoat.

In the back of the car sat a dark skinned man. Quickly he began to tidy himself up, he felt a mess, he had spent most of the day in bed with a hangover.

Quickly he went to the door, Graham smiled cheerfully. "Merry Christmas mate, here take these."

He handed him a box of Havana cigars. This surprised him, the last person he expected to call was Graham.

"Well are you going to invite me in?" he asked in a pushy tone of voice.

"Yeah come on in mate, what can I do for ya?"

"Well it's like this mate I've got Mickey the Malt in the car, and he's got a big old John Tan safe to be blown. He said it's a big old fucker, and I told him there's only one man for the job."

He smiled that shy smile of his, "Oh right."

"Can you come on a trial run, right now Harry?"

"Where is it?" he asked feeling flustered.

"Somewhere in Bow I think."

"Alright give me a couple of minutes, I'll get myself together."

He quickly got himself into his smart clothes. On the journey Mickey the Malt filled him in on the details.

He handed him a sheet of paper. "Here you are Harry my son." His thick cigar smoke went into Harry's eyes, they started to stream. Harry waved his hand in front of his face trying to clear the smoke from the air.
Mickey stared hard at him. "You know Harry; there is nothing better than the aroma of a Havana cigar."
Harry closed his eyes, he's thoughts were drifting. Yes he could now see a Cuban beauty standing in front of him, gently rolling the tobacco leaf up her slender leg to the top of her thigh, to insure the perfect finish to a perfect cigar. He sighed as he thought, oh yes he could almost smell her body.
Mickey nudged him hard; to gain back his attention. He spoke in broken English, and showed signs of anger. "For fuck sake Harry, when I talk, you fucking listen."
He jolted himself upright. "Sorry about that Mickey," determined not to upset him.

Mickey smiled slyly, as if to forgive him.
"Harry my son, well what I've got in mind, it's fairly straight forward, and the groundwork will all be done for you by someone on the inside. All you have to do is follow the plans that I've drawn out. Then burn this piece of paper as soon as you have finished. You will need someone with you of course."
Keen to please, he put Jim's name forward.
Mickey gave it some thought as he blew another gust of cigar smoke in Harry's face. "Well whatever Harry, he comes on your recommendation."

"So when is this going to take place then Mickey?"
"Well I thought the sooner the better, like tomorrow."
"Fuck me you don't mess about Mickey do ya?"
"Harry my son, you know what they say, those who hesitate are lost."
"Yeah but Mickey how about, when fools rush in?"
"Alright, alright, don't try to be fucking clever with me, Mickey the Malt always knows best," he said in an aggressive tone.
There was silence in the car; he had now learnt that Mickey didn't have a sense of humour.
"When the jobs done Harry, I want you to ring me, I then want you to bring the money to an address at Dalston. This I will give you when you make the phone call; understand Harry? I know I'm putting this in good hands, you come highly recommended and you will be paid straight away after the job okay. Is that alright with you?"
"Yeah, yeah, this is safe with me Mickey."
They finally reached their destination and the snow was falling heavily.
"Well this is it, Harry."

He felt surprised; as he got out of the car, there was a line of lorries covered in snow.
"But what is it Mickey?"
"It's a coal yard, the offices are over there in the distance, I've had inside information, and the safe is loaded at the moment what with this cold weather, they're raking in plenty. Then there is the workers' Christmas bonuses of course, they are in the safe until the end of the week. As I say, the job's a doddle."
He shook Mickey's hand; "Alright I'll do it tomorrow, as long as I'm going to get no come-backs."
"Harry my son I can't see any, you've only got to blow the fucking safe, after all."

He lay in bed that night, wondering had he done the right thing? Was he getting out of his depth mixing with the likes of Mickey? He had met his type before, when he was inside. He knew there was no doubt about it, he could be dangerous. If he was honest, did he say yes because if he had said no Mickey might have turned nasty on him? After all it was better to Mickey's friend, than his enemy.

With all they needed for their night's work, they set off on their way to Bow. The weather was nothing short of a blizzard as they drove through the slush covered streets of London.
Jim passed him a cigarette, "Do you know 'H' we must be fucking mad, coming out on a night like this to do a bit of work."
Harry answered in a despondent voice, "Yeah I know mate, it's at times like this when I think I'd like a nine to five job."
Jim began to laugh, "Turn it in 'H' you doing a proper job? Never in a million years."

Once at the coal yard fear began to leave him, excitement kicked in. They parked the car, and went round to the side entrance. Burying their heads down they walked across the crisp untouched snow, he had studied the plan carefully throughout the day, determined that no mistakes could be made. Quickly he led the way, leaving Jim to follow with the hold all that had now been on many a job with them. They remained silent as they gingerly entered the big dark cold building, he had a good idea where he was heading, thanks to the plan that Mickey had given him.

With only the aid of a torch they went from one draughty dark passageway to another. Then finally they reached the small office that Mickey had marked out. The door was half opened; he peered around the door and shone the torch around the room, until he spotted what looked like the safe on the right hand side of the room.

Yes Graham was right; it was a big old fucker. Slowly he walked towards it and studied it carefully, before preparing to blow it.
Jim watched carefully, checking at the windows, he looked across the white covered coal yard, to make sure all was clear, he began to shiver he could almost feel the coldness. Carefully Harry wired the detonators and called across, "Any minute now Jimmy boy, it's gonna blow."
He was feeling good, there was nothing he liked more than to see the door blown open off a safe.

The loud thud always set his heart racing, the smell of the gelignite made him feel elated. Soon the big old fucker was open for them. Quickly he scuffed up the money, there was no time to count it, they bundled it into the bag, now only with the intentions of getting out of the building as quick as possible.

On their way to Dalston, they were both in a jovial mood; the hard part had been done; now it was only a matter of meeting up with Mickey. They stopped at the traffic lights, Harry gazed into the mirror, he clenched the steering wheel tight with fear, "No, for fuck sake, we got the Old Bill behind us."
Jim turned to check, "That's it 'H' we're done for."
The police car flashed its headlights for them to pull in.
"I've got to make a decision here Jim, either put me foot down, or try and bluff our way out of it."

It was too late, the car pulled up in front of them, a policeman walked towards them.
Harry wound down his window. "Can I help you officer?"
The policeman put his head into the car, "I don't know if you're aware of it sir, but you are driving with no lights on this vehicle."
He put on his posh speaking voice, "I'm so sorry officer, I was so busy clearing the snow off, it's a terrible night, isn't it? Somehow it must have slipped my mind, I do apologise."
"Well you do know it's an offence sir, don't you?"

He was just about to answer, when a loud screech of tyres, followed by the sound of two cars crashing into each other.
The policeman appeared startled, "Oh well, you had better be on your way, it seems I've now got something more serious to deal with. He turned back as he walked towards the crash, "Oh and get those lights on, safe journey sir, goodnight."
Harry drove off;with his heart still thumping fast, his hands were trembling, he turned to Jim, "For fuck sake how close was that?"
Jim rubbed his hands with delight,
"Thank fuck for that car smash."

They stopped at a telephone box, Harry hastily dialled the number to call Mickey and was surprised to hear a woman's voice at the end of the line. It threw him, he stumbled, thinking should he put the receiver down or talk? He changed the tone of his voice slightly.
"Hello, I don't know if I've got the right number?"
"Who did you want?" asked the woman, in a well spoken voice.
"His name is Mickey," he said hesitantly. The line went silent.
Then the gruff sound of Mickey's voice came on, "Is that you Harry, did it all go well?"
"Yeah, yeah, all done I'm on my way over."
"Okay my son, I will be waiting."
Mickey gave him the address, telling him to go straight down to the basement, he would be waiting for him.

They arrived at the narrow winding street, with three-storey Victorian houses on either side of the road. He drove slowly to identify the house number Mickey had given him. After going up and down the street several times he finally found the house.
They were about to get out of the car when they heard footsteps. It was a man and woman, dressed in winter clothing; they were huddled together as if to protect them from the fierce weather conditions. They seemed to appear from nowhere, they waited for them to disappear out of sight before walking down to the basement steps.
He looked down at the snow, he nudged Jim, as he spotted the footprints, on the steps. "It looks like someone, has been here before us."

He put his hand forward to knock on the door; it was already open, so he called out, "Mickey, it's Harry and Jim, is it alright to come in?"
There was no reply, he turned to Jim, "That's strange, he said he would be waiting for us."
He slowly pushed the door further open, and then opened another door, that led into a small room.
Jim tugged at his jacket, "There's something that's not right here 'H' he told ya he would be waiting."
Harry gazed around the dimly lit room; he could smell the musty smell of damp. Once in the room for a while, the aroma of Mickey's cigars came to him. He looked at the ashtray, there was a half smoked Havana cigar. "Oh well at least we're in the right house."
Jim peered out of the window; and looked up to ground level; he could just about see part of the street.

Suddenly he saw someone's bottom half of their legs walking by, he thought this might be Mickey returning, but to no avail, he carried on walking.
"Where the fuck could he be 'H'?"

Harry went over to the electric fire to warm his hands.
"It's no good Jim; we'll just have to wait for him, we can't go anywhere with all that money."
On the table was a bottle of brandy, and two glasses, "Look Jim, it seems he's had company." He picked up one of the glasses, showing it to him. "Look, lipstick marks, that woman that answered the phone, must have been his bird."
Jim began to get irritated, he felt uncomfortable with the situation. Harry poured himself a brandy, and handed one to Jim. "Here get this down ya; it will calm ya down a bit."
Harry looked at his watch, half hour had gone by, "Oh fuck this; everything was going alright, until now."
He looked across the room; there was a door slightly ajar, he started to laugh, "I bet he's asleep in there, or having it off with his bird and we've been waiting here like idiots."

Harry walked over, pushing the door further open, the room was in darkness, and he felt for the light switch. Finally he found the switch, when the light came on he stood back in shock, unable to speak.
"Well is he in there 'H'?"
He turned slowly around towards to Jim.
'H' what is it mate? You look like you've seen a ghost."
Harry spoke almost in slow motion, "He's fucking dead, mate."
"Turn it in 'H' he can't be, you only just spoke to him on the blower."
Jim walked over to the door, and gingerly peered in, "Oh no fuck me; I've never seen nothing like it, he's had his fucking guts blown out."
Harry put his arm across the door, "Don't go in there."
Mickey was sitting in a chair next to the bed, his eyes were bolting out of his head; the room was a mass of blood spreading from floor to ceiling.

Harry felt his body begin to tremble, "Bollocks to this, let's get out of here quick, and I mean fucking quick."
They were about to run out, when Harry stopped suddenly.
"No, no, let's stop and think, the glasses, they got our dabs on them, and wipe the door handles as well. Jim stop, and think of everything we've touched, or we're gonna get done for this mate."
They rushed around the room, wiping everything in sight to ensure there was no sign of them ever being there.
He bent down to pick up the hold all when he caught sight of something sparkling on the carpet.
He put his hand to it; and held it out to show Jim, "Look a woman's earring, it looks like he's upset that woman."
He put the earring in his pocket; then they quickly made their way out into the street.

The hazardous drive back across the snow-covered London streets seemed never-ending, and what they had just witnessed left them in shock.
They finally arrived at Park Road, Harry looked at his watch, it was half past one. They went into the back kitchen; Jim poured them both a stiff drink.
Harry sat at the table with his head in his hands, he rubbed his eyes, he felt exhausted, not only had he blown a safe, he was in the midst of a murder.
Jim handed him another drink, "Here get this down ya mate, we've got to think what to do about this whole sorry episode."

Harry stood up; and started to walk around the room like a caged animal. "It's no good I've got to ring Graham, we've got all that money, what a fucking cock up."
"Well 'H' why don't we just keep it, after all Mickey aint gonna come looking for us now is he?"
Harry began to laugh, "He'd have a fucking job; he's as dead as a dodo. Yeah Jim, I'm gonna ring him right now."
"I tell ya what 'H' he's gonna be well pleased he didn't come on the job now, aint he?"
"Yeah for some reason, he didn't want to know about it."

Graham answered the phone, "Hello," he said in a weary voice.
"Is it alright to talk Graham? It's me Harry."
"This had better be important; it's the middle of the night, you've woken my kid up."
"Graham, I need to see you right now in person, it can't wait."
Graham's voice now appeared agitated, "Right you've got my new address, you had better make your way over."
He went back into the room to Jim, "I'm gonna take the money over to Graham, I don't want it hanging about here, and we don't know who's gonna come knocking."
He opened the hold all handing Jim a bundle of notes, "Here take another bundle you'll be alright won't ya?"
"Yeah I'm gonna try and get a bit of shut eye mate, it's all been a bit too much for me tonight."

Once outside the big double-fronted house, Harry patiently sat there for a while, making sure all was clear. A light went on in a downstairs room, Graham pulled back the curtain to beckon him in.
He was led into a room with plush furniture; Graham appeared to be very edgy.
"What's happened Harry that can't wait until morning?"

Harry bowed his head in despair, "It's Mickey, he's dead."
"Dead? Are you sure"
"I'm sure alright."
Graham showed no emotion, "Yeah, but ya done the job alright?"
"Yeah of course, I've got the money here, but I can't keep it with me, just in case I'm tracked down, I don't know what the fuck I've got myself into here."
"Look Harry, leave the money with me for now, and come back tomorrow evening, I might know a bit more about what's going on then." Graham showed him quickly to the door.
He drove back home feeling relieved that he was no longer in the possession of the money, after all himself and Jim had already helped themselves to a tidy share, and as far as he was concerned it was in good hands with Graham.

The following day, he decided to lay low; he would wait until it got dark then drive back to Chiswick to see Graham. He had a nagging feeling, that everything might come a tumble on them.
Jim on the other hand couldn't care less, with a few quid in his pocket he was driving off to Brighton to spend the night with an old flame, way back from his army days.

Harry finally mustered the energy to get washed and shaved; he stood in the little kitchen, staring closely in the mirror, finding it difficult to keep a steady hand, as he ran the razor slowly over his face. He was still reeling with the sight of Mickey the Malt's blood-covered body, and he was convinced it would haunt him forever.
Gently he wiped his face with a warm towel, and peered closely in the mirror; he touched the corners of his eyes noticing the fine lines appearing around them. Well he sighed, he was now thirty five years old and he asked himself, where was he going from here?

As he stood alone with sad thoughts, there was no wife or family around him, yes he wanted to love women, but he wanted real love, not something he would become bored with after a few months.
Wistfully he combed his thinning hair and glanced back in the mirror and smiled. As he thought of his life, it had had its ups and downs, but definitely hadn't been boring.

After a downfall of rain the streets were clearing of snow, he sat nervously in the car outside Graham's house. He hesitated before leaving the car, he didn't know if he was going to like what Graham was about to tell him. A nervous feeling came over him, he rang the doorbell, no one answered, he rang again.
The door opened, to his surprise it wasn't Graham, but Josie.

This threw him; he had to think quickly, how he could approach her about the matter?
"Hello Love, I don't know if you remember me?
She answered assertively, "Yes I do."
"I've come to see Graham."
She threw her head back and started to laugh, "That might be difficult, he left me this morning."
He went silent. A more serious look came on her face, she opened the door wider, "Don't stand there in the cold, you had better come in."

He stood in the hallway and looked down, he heard the sound of a toy car, it was racing towards his feet, and there on his hands and knees, was a little blond boy dressed in blue striped pajamas.
He stared up at him, "Who are you then?"
He bent down to shake his hand, "Hello son, my name's Harry"
He showed him his toy car, "Have you got a car Harry?"
"Yes son it's outside, by the way, what's your name?"
"It's Greg."
Josie grabbed his arm, "Come on Greg let's get you up that wooden hill to bed." He rubbed his eyes, as he lovingly stretched out his arms for his mother to pick him up.
"Go and wait in the lounge Harry, I will just get him settled."

He waited in the room that he stood in the previous evening, and practiced in his mind how he could broach the subject of the money. Obviously she was upset about Graham leaving, but he couldn't put it off any longer. He paced up and down the room; he could hear her singing to her little boy upstairs. A picture came into his mind of her sitting on his bed, gently rubbing his forehead. A shiver went down his spine as he thought of his own childhood, what it would have been like to have a mother to see him off to bed.
Suddenly he shuddered and thought about the reason for being there; his body went cold as that terrible picture of Mickey came to him.
He wondered how Graham could leave a woman like her, he remembered the first time he set eyes on her, in the pub at Ealing, and he wanted her then, but he felt himself wanting her even more now.
No he told himself try not to rush things, appear cool; to put himself forward straightaway would be wrong.

She walked back into the room looking refreshed, "Do you want a drink?"
Yes she was confident, he'd give her that, she didn't wait for an answer, she was already pouring from a decanter.
"Look Josie I'm not going to beat about the bush, I got involved in something with Graham, and it went wrong, I left a hold all with him;

he was going to sort everything out."
"Is that what he told you? It sounds like the sort of thing he would say. He took it with him this morning, you don't have to tell me, I know it was full of money, I think he's taken you for a right mug. Did you know he's been having it off with a coal merchant's wife, from Bow; it seems she's been putting herself about with Mickey the Malt as well."

Suddenly he felt shocked, "How long has it been going on?"
"Oh a couple of months, he kept telling me he had business to attend to, you know the sort of thing I mean? But I'm not an idiot, and he's not as bright as he thinks he is. Graham saw an easy way of getting money, and he went straight for it."

He stood silent, the bastard had double-crossed him, his mind was racing with thoughts. Yes he had fallen right into his hands; Graham must have known that he wouldn't want to hang on to the money, after finding Mickey's body.
Then he asked himself, but who the fuck killed Mickey?

He held out his glass for another refill, he wasn't sure how much she knew, but he was almost sure she knew nothing about the murder. He didn't really care about any of it, as long as he didn't have any comebacks on himself and Jim. Hastily he drank his drink, "I suppose I'd better be going, is it alright if I come back in a few days? You know just to see how things are going?"
She smiled as she saw him to the door.

He arrived back at Park Road, the house felt lonely, usually he would hear Jim singing or whistling the latest song.
His thoughts turned to Josie; she hadn't changed much over the years. He pictured her standing in the pub at Ealing, her blue eyes and auburn hair, alright perhaps she had put on a few pounds, but this only added to her voluptuous figure.
He tried to work her out, he thought she came across as over-confident, but he was almost sure there was a gentle side to be found. Now he had decided to make this his mission, to find the real her.

He was getting anxious, Jim said he was going away for the day, it was now the fifth day, without hearing a word from him.
 His imagination started to get the better of him. What if they were being watched, by Mickey the Malt's associates? Poor Jim might be lying dead in some woods somewhere. Nerves began to take over, he began to find it difficult to breath, and felt his chest tightening. Who knows, it might be me next, he thought. As he put his hand to his throat there was tightness, as if he was being strangled.

Quickly he walked out to the back garden to breathe in fresh air, and looked up to the sky. He thought of his sister Ruby and wondered where in the world she could be. He had lost touch with her since she went off to Italy.
Nervously he put his hands together, silently asking her, 'Wherever you are Ruby pray for me, you always used to tell me that you would pray for me, whenever we parted company, please do it for me now'.
He gradually began to feel calmer; the sound of the telephone broke his thoughts. He ran inside to answer it, on the other end was the cheerful voice of Jim.
"Hello 'H' mate, how are ya?"

He breathed a sigh of relief, "Jim where have ya been, I've been worried sick about ya, I've almost been planning your funeral."
Jim started to laugh, "Turn it in 'H' your trouble is you've never lost that vivid imagination of yours."
He was right; it was doing him no good, being bolted up in this house all alone.
"Well when are ya coming back Jim?"
"It's like this mate," he stammered slightly, "I'm waiting on a license, I'm gonna get married in the next few days."

Harry was speechless, no surely not, Jim getting married?
"'H' Are you still there?"
"Yeah sorry mate, it's come as a bit of a shock, I never thought the day would come, congratulations mate, I never realised it was so serious."
"Well I've kept in touch with her for a long time, on and off, she's been married, her husband died.
It's only a registry office wedding, with a few of her family, a quiet affair. Once it's done I'll be bringing my new wife back with me."

As the days passed he began to feel more confident that the Mickey the Malt saga had passed, it was like a great weight had been lifted from him.
Until an unexpected phone call from Josie, asking him to get over there quick. Her husky voice was blunt and to the point, to him this indicated a problem.

As he drove across to Chiswick he looked into the car mirror, wanting to make sure he was at his best.
She opened the door, her auburn hair was swept up into a bunch of curls resting on the top of her head, she appeared elegant in a black top and grey checked skirt that showed off her shapely legs. He felt a flutter in his stomach, and was happy to be there, he had not felt like this towards a woman in a long time.

He hoped she was not going to shatter his happiness with some bad news.
She glanced along the street before showing him in. Wanting to show him hospitality she offered him a drink; he readily accepted.
"Well what's so important Josie?"
"It's the police, they were here earlier."
"What about? The robbery?"
She hesitated a while, "I wish, no, no, it's more serious than that."
He almost knew, what was coming.
She began to top up her glass; he noticed her hand shaking.
"They seem to think Graham might have something to do with a murder."

He acted surprised, "Who's dead?"
"Mickey the Malt, I just can't believe it."
He tried to act as if he knew nothing about it, no way was he going to admit to anyone that he had seen Mickey's blood-covered body.
The way he saw it, if he mentioned ever going into that basement, he could be a prime suspect.
A worried expression came on her face.
"The police said after they did some investigation, it seems this woman that they had both been seeing, well she may also have something to do with the murder."
He went silent, all he hoped was that the robbery would not be tied to the murder.

"They asked me if Graham was in all night on the date in question."
Harry paced up and down the room. "Well, was he in all night?"
"No he wasn't, I can remember because it was my mum's birthday, we were supposed to go and visit her but he said he couldn't make it, so we had an argument. He got back here about half past twelve, then not long after you rang, but I didn't tell the police that you came over here."
He walked over to the corner bar. "Is it alright to help myself?"
He filled his glass to the brim.
"So what did you tell the police?"
"The truth, no way am I going to lie for that deceitful bastard, I hope he gets all what's coming to him. I have not heard a word from him since that day he left."

Harry could not help but feel sorry for her, but she was showing no sign of weakening. As he walked over to her he knew he wanted to hold her close. "Josie what do ya want me to do?"
She put her arms on his shoulder, "Well can ya just be there for me?"
He felt pleased that she needed him and sat down on the sofa. "And do ya think he'll be back?"

"Well if he walks through that door, I'll tell him to fuck off; he's had his chances with me."
This pleased him, everything was going his way and it seemed she was adamant that Graham had shot his bolt with her. The other good news being that the police seem to be gunning for Graham.
She sat herself down next to him; he noticed a tear running down her face.
"Are you alright Josie?"
"Yeah, yeah, I just don't like being taken for a fucking idiot."

He studied her, she might look demure, but no way would he want to get on the wrong side of her, and he was almost sure that if she was upset she would fight like a tiger.
He put his glass down on the coffee table; he had made up his mind what he was going to do next.
Suddenly he leaned towards her and kissed her; the kiss lingered on, it felt like a hot flame coming from her body to his. Inwardly he was waiting for her to push him away, but this never happened, she took him by the hand and led him upstairs, not a word was spoken.

They lay on the bed, he spread himself across her shapely body, and slowly he started pulling off her clothes. She unbuttoned his shirt, and she threw it across the room, his breathing became deeper; she rubbed her hands across his bare back, as he put his cock inside her he sighed as he said, "I told you one day, didn't I?"
She wrapped her body tightly around him, "Do you know I never thought that day would come. Will ya stay the night with me?"

Wearily he opened his eyes and looked at his watch, it was six thirty. He turned, there lay Josie, she slept peacefully, her auburn hair lying on the pillow, he lay his arm across her body, she felt warm and he wanted to make love to her again. A feeling of contentment came over him, he hadn't felt like this in a long time. She turned her body towards him, her eyes gradually opened and she gasped with surprise, "Oh Harry, you're still here."
He ran his fingers through her hair, "Josie I thought that's what you wanted."
She pushed her breast into him, "I don't ever want you to leave me."
She put her hand on his cock. "Harry make love to me again, I never knew that love making could be that good until last night."
He kissed her passionately, "Josie you know I'll do anything to make you happy."

He walked into the kitchen where she was making coffee, "Where's your little Greg?"

"He's still sleeping."
He walked behind her and kissed the back of her neck.
"I'll have this cup of coffee, and then I will be on my way Josie."
She turned and flung her arms around him, a serious look appeared on her face. "Why don't you move in with me?"
He was shocked that she wanted things to move so quickly, "But Josie, Graham could come back at any time."
"Oh I don't think so," she said indignantly, "he's history."
He wasn't going to argue with her, every word she spoke was making him happier by the minute.

He drove back to Park Road, feeling on top of the world, he would get his things together and then leave Jim a note for when he arrived back. As he neared the house, he spotted a police car parked outside. His heart skipped a beat; he slowed the car down to give himself time to think.
The policeman got out of his car and was about to knock at the door. Harry walked up behind him and took a deep breath, before asking, "Can I help you officer?"
"Yes sir, you can, I'm looking for Harry Creedy."
"Oh right, what's that in connection with?"
"Why? Are you Mr Creedy sir?"
"Yeah, you had better come in."
They walked into the house it was cold and unwelcoming, he walked down to the little back kitchen, asking the policeman to follow him.

The policeman took off his flat cap, twirling it around in his hands.
"Well what it is Mr Creedy, we're investigating a murder. Do you know a man by the name of Graham Hunt?"
"Yea I do." As he answered, Harry turned towards the mantelpiece, and next to the clock he spotted the diamond earring he found at Mickey's place on the night of the murder. He felt his body tighten up as he went to stand in front of it.
"Well sir, it's just that your car has been spotted outside Mr Hunt's house on several occasions."
"The reason for that is officer I have been a family friend for a while, at the moment his wife is very distressed; he's left her."
"Well sir can I ask you, where you on the twentieth of December last year? It's not that long ago sir, so perhaps it will be easy to remember."
"I can tell you exactly were I was, I was in bed with the flu."
"It's just that on the night of the murder sir, there was a break-in at a coal yard and we're connecting the two incidents. There was a safe blown open, and it's come to light in our investigation that you have been imprisoned for a similar offence in the past sir."
"Yeah that's right, but like I told you, I was in bed with the flu."

"Is there anyone that can verify this sir?"
"Yea my mate Jim, he lives here, but he's away at the moment."
"Alright then sir, when he returns we'll get this matter cleared up, but in the meantime if you hear any word from Graham Hunt please let us know, as you may understand sir, murder is a very serious matter, yes very serious."
Harry showed him to the door, and watched the car drive down the street. Once he was back in the kitchen, he felt the sweat ran down his forehead, and realised how close he had come to being arrested for the robbery, but at least Graham appeared to be the main suspect.
He stood and thought about Graham and found it difficult to believe that he could actually be capable of committing a murder; perhaps it wasn't him, it might have been one of Mickey's villainous associates. As long as he was left alone he couldn't give a shit who it was that bumped Mickey off.
He decided to give Josie a ring, after all if the house was under surveillance, it might not look good him turning up with a suitcase ready to move in.

Nervously he waited in anticipation; it seemed she was never going to pick up the receiver, finally to his relief, he heard her voice.
"Josie, I don't think I better come back over just yet. I've just had a visit from the Old Bill, whatever happens don't mention that I came to your house in the early hours, on the night of the murder. They are connecting it to the robbery. I think I'm in the clear, I told them I was in bed with the flu. I don't think they have any proof that connects me to the robbery, it all went well. We done a nice clean job, and they wouldn't find any dabs on anything, we wore gloves all the time. Now with Mickey dead, and Graham on the wanted list, I think that leaves me and Jim in the clear."
"Well what ya worried about then?" she asked, showing concern.
"I just don't want the situation to get any worse."
She began to laugh, "Oh for fuck sake get yourself back over here, they aint going to worry who is shagging who, you're seeing too much in it."
He was beginning to feel relieved, just the sound of her voice had settled his nerves.
They lay in bed after making love, he was feeling content and weary, and it had been a long day. He felt his eyes becoming heavy, all he wanted to do was sleep more than anything, and being questioned today had taken its toll on him.
A sudden thought came to his mind; he sat upright blurting out, "No, no, for fuck sake."
Josie sat up and put her arm around him.
"What is it, what's the matter?"
"Oh Josie I just thought about the night of the robbery and the murder,

we got stopped at the traffic lights for having no lights on the car."
"So what? Why don't ya stop going on about everything."
"Well what if that copper reported it back at the station?"
"Did he take any notes?"
"No I don't think so, a car crashed in the snow; he went running over to that."
She smiled, "Look if that had come to light, they would have been in touch with you before now."

He kissed her, "You know Josie you're good for me, sometimes my mind goes wild, there's no stopping it, and I've been like it since I was a kid."
He lay back down, she gently rubbed his cheek, now he knew he had found his soul mate; he wasn't going to keep anything from her from now on. Yes he had now found the woman he had been waiting for. He decided he was going to tell her all, he took her hand. "Josie I got to tell ya something."
She snuggled into him, "What is it?"
"The night of the robbery well we had to take the money to Mickey's house, I don't know if ya remember it was a bastard night thick snow everywhere. After the job I rang Mickey, he gave me the address, he said he would be waiting for us, then he was going to pay us off."
She was beginning to look puzzled, and irritated, "Oh for fuck sake Harry get to the point."
"Alright, alright, if ya want it straight, we found him with his guts blown out."
She appeared unperturbed, "Well ya didn't do it, did ya?"
"No of course I fucking never."

She began to laugh heartily; he looked at her amazed, as she got out of bed and walked over to the linen cupboard.
She got back on the bed and sat naked and her legs astride him. A wide smile appeared on her face as she clutched a pillow case.
"What's in it" he asked, feeling even more confused.
She tipped out the contents; the notes fell all over his naked body like confetti. He began to laugh. "Where has this lot come from Josie?"
She waved a handful of the notes in the air. "They are ours now. Well when Graham went, I knew what he was up to so I opened the hold all; I see all the money, then I thought no way, so I took the money out and filled the bag with his dirty washing. Then I carefully laid a couple of layers of notes over the top.
"Well let's be honest," she said brimming with confidence, "he could hardly go to the Old Bill, and say he had been turned over, could he?"
As they rolled round the bed laughing, Harry knew he wanted to spend the rest of his life with her.

TARTS AND HEARTS

He had found true happiness at last. Finally Graham was serving time for helping the coal merchant's wife to kill Mickey the Malt. This didn't bother Josie none, she was pleased to be shot of him.
Her only concern was that this had distanced Greg from his father, and he was a good father, if nothing else.
All that Harry wanted to do was to make Josie happy, he had been living with her for five years, and Greg had become like his own son. Sal had finally divorced him but they remained good friends. His role with Henry and George seemed to suit everyone, he became more like their uncle than their father, but he knew that they were being brought up well, and that was his main concern.

The strong sunlight prompted Josie to get out the feather duster, as she dusted along the window ledge she sang merrily along with the radio. She watched the young man walk up the path to the front door, she opened the door, and screeched with delight; there stood her nephew Ronnie.

She threw out her arms, "Ronnie Love, what are you doing here?"
He hesitated slightly, and tossed his head back, then gave out a cheeky chuckle, "Auntie Josie, I just got out."
Josie couldn't be more delighted, than for Ronnie to turn up on her doorstep. He was her elder sister's illegitimate son, his father was the son of a wealthy Italian family who had an ice cream business, and they had settled in the East End of London just after the war.
She took a step back to look at him, his dark shoulder length hair rested on his brightly coloured shirt, she glanced up and down at his trendy clothes, and she began to laugh.
"So Ronnie is this the fashion, is this how they all dress these days?"
"Well I just been on a shopping spree up the West End," a wide smile appeared on his face.
As Josie leaned forward; she felt the material of his shirt.
"That must have been expensive, how much did that cost ya Love?"
He answered bluntly, "Nothing."

She lit a cigarette, concern was showing on her face.
"Oh for fuck sake Ronnie, you aint on the nick already, are ya?"
She was about to hand Ronnie a cigarette, when the sound of Harry's voice came from the hallway, "Josie I'm back!" She looked at her watch, about bloody time, she thought.

She pulled him towards her, "Come here you, give me a kiss."
He looked over her shoulder and saw the young man standing there.
"Are you going to introduce me Josie?"
"Oh yeah sorry, Harry this is my nephew Ronnie; you've heard me talk of him."
He ran his fingers through his receding hair as he weighed him up, and walked towards him to shake his hand, resting his hand on his shoulder he smiled, "It's good to meet ya son."
They sat around the table, It wasn't long before Josie began to feel left out of the conversation; the two men found they had a lot in common as they spoke about one prison or another that they had frequented. Harry gazed across at the young man; he could see a lot of himself in him.
In a way he envied him, he himself was now forty years of age and couldn't go on forever, leading his life of crime, but at least he was now happy, life with Josie was good, never a dull moment.

In the year that followed, Ronnie became a regular visitor.
On a hot summer's afternoon, in 1970, Harry lazed peacefully under the tree in the garden, to shelter himself from the hot afternoon sunshine.
The sound of the traffic hissed through the trees causing him to stir, to his surprise there stood Ronnie towering over him; he rubbed his eyes as if waking from a dream.
A half-hearted smile appeared on his face, he grabbed Ronnie's leg to pull himself up, and looked at him puzzled, "Who let you in?"
"Oh Josie, she's just popped out for a while."
"Well what can I do for ya son?"

He hesitated to speak at first then he pulled out a tobacco pouch from his trouser pocket, and began to roll a cigarette slowly, he licked along the edge to seal it, and then offered it to Harry.
"Here have you ever tried it?" Ronnie smiled, "It's only a little bit of grass man, and it won't hurt you."
Harry pushed his hand away. "No thanks son, I've seen enough idiots on that stuff when I've been banged up."
Ronnie began to puff on it. Harry watched on as Ronnie slowly unwound. He began to laugh, "Oh come on Harry, just give it one blow."
Harry took the cigarette from him, feeling slightly agitated.

"Oh give it here; I'll try anything once."
He sat himself down on the garden wall, the sun was getting hotter, suddenly he broke out into uncontrollable laughter, he felt good, yes he felt very good, he took another puff and put his arm around Ronnie, "Oh son, I aint felt this fucking good in ages."
Ronnie walked around the garden, he was feeling content, he was sure it was now the right time to ask about a plan he had come up with.
The sound of Josie's voice jolted him back to reality, she handed each of them a mug of coffee, as she looked at Harry curiously, "Have you been drinking alcohol?"
He started to laugh; she stood glaring at him seriously, she was not amused.
Ronnie stepped in to his rescue, "It's alright Auntie Josie, he had a little bit of grass, it won't do him no harm." Anger showed in her face, "For fuck sake Ronnie, I don't want that stuff around here.
Ronnie left the house with his head bowed, to be told off by Josie was bad news, she didn't suffer fools gladly, and he had learned that at an early stage in his life.
He had briefly laid out his plan to Harry before her return, now it was just a matter of time, to wait for him to make up his mind.

Over the weeks Harry gave Ronnie's idea a lot of thought, money was getting tight, and he had been keeping his nose clean of late; it had just been the odd small job here and there. Now there was just enough money for them to keep their heads above water.
From the day Jim returned with his new wife, things had changed, Jim had decided to go straight. After all the business with Mickey the Malt he considered they were lucky to get away without getting nicked.

He walked in to the pub that was situated on a small road at the edge of the common; it was busy with the lunch time trade. He gazed around at all the workers earning an honest living. As he looked to the end of the bar, there in a cocoon of blue smoke stood Ronnie. Quickly he walked over to him, he was always pleased to see Ronnie. He had got to like him, as far as he was concerned he was a boy after his own heart.
He slowly added more water to his whisky as he quietly told Ronnie he was up for the job.
After a while he began to unwind, then he waved his hand in front of his face.
"For fuck sake Ron, you aint smoking that stuff in here are ya?"
Ronnie began to chuckle, "Yea why not, do you want one?"
Harry took a step back and began to laugh, "No it's alright mate, I think I'm getting high just being near ya."
They found a table in a small alcove; it was here that he learned for the first time that he was to carry a gun.

He bent closer to Ronnie, "Well if that's the case, you had better fill me in on everything."
"Well I thought Harry we'd go somewhere like Oxford Street, on a Thursday night, you know when all the shops are open late for late night shoppers, some of these big shops must take plenty of dough; we will pose as plain clothes policemen."
Harry was about to take a gulp of his drink, when it spurted out of his mouth, he began to laugh, "Oh for fuck sake Ron, me a copper."
Ronnie's face appeared very serious, "So what's so wrong with that, you know the first time I met you, I thought you looked like Old Bill."
Ronnie grabbed his arm for attention, "Look all we have to do is wait until the shop is ready to close, and then get the manager to round up his staff in the office. We will say something like we are there because there is a lot of shoplifting going on in the area, then once we got them all safely together, and the doors closed, we will pull out the shooters, just to put a bit of fear in to them, you know what I mean, but we won't use them. I'll tell you what, believe you me, they will hand over the takings with no problem at all."
He raised his glass, "Here's to us then Ron."

All that week Harry was feeling edgy, he woke up early on Thursday morning; today was the day they were going to carry out their plan. Carefully he took the gun that Ronnie had given him from the bedside cabinet, slowly he ran his hand over it, he felt his body begin to tremble, his hand shook uncontrollably. Quickly he put it back in the drawer, and wiped his hands as if they had been contaminated, he buried his head in his hands.
His head was spinning, what if it all went wrong, and he was forced to use it? He could be done for murder.
That horrible feeling had never left him from the night when he discovered Mickey's blood-covered body. He rubbed his hand down his chest; it was wringing wet with sweat. He almost stumbled over to the window; he reassured himself that he must go through with it.
The days of robbing banks and jewellers were long gone, the security was too tight these days.
Alright the money was not so good, with the idea that Ronnie had in mind, but all he wanted was a few quid to have a decent living.
Josie began to stir, he looked across at her, he never tired of her, she was a breath of fresh air every day. He always told her everything that he was up to, but she wasn't best pleased about his latest venture - armed robbery, to her, this spelled trouble and lots of it.

At five o' clock as arranged, they met outside Oxford Circus Station.
" I see you're on time, I hardly recognised you Ron with that short hair cut. Ronnie stepped from side to side nervously.

"Well I got to look like Old Bill now, aint I?"
He looked at Harry and began to laugh, "Well look at you in those wire rimmed glasses." He pulled off Harry's trilby hat, and playfully tossed it in the air. "We must look a right pair of pricks."
Harry looked at his watch, "Come on Ron let's have a little wander about, we've got a few hours to kill."
As they sat drinking coffee in a small café just off Oxford Street, they ran through their plans for the final time.
Ronnie felt in his inside pocket, "Oh fucking hell Harry, I did give you your fake I.D. didn't I?"
"Yeah, yeah calm down Ron, everything is under control, remember once we've done it, no running, walk straight to the station, or if a black cab's about, jump in that, we've just got to lose ourselves in the crowd." He pulled out his fake identification card and studied it.
"Well this looks the business; I will introduce myself as Detective Inspector Ford and you as my aide by the name of Detective Sergeant Mason. The less you speak Ron the better; we don't want them to pick up on anything. It will be no problem, with me putting on my posh voice; we will make it quick and to the point, no hanging about, yeah."

They stood on the opposite side of the road, carefully monitoring the customers going in and out of the busy store that sold mainly jeans and leather coats.
Ronnie turned to him, "You know word has it they take a fortune in there, and it's all the latest gear."
Harry glanced at his watch once again, "Well let's hope so, all the better for us, right Ron it's time to move."
They darted in and out of the busy traffic. As they walked into the store, it began to empty out, and then a bell rang to indicate closing time.
A young man walked towards them dressed in a smart blue shirt with a brightly coloured patterned tie, his hair neatly combed back, he pointed to the clock on the wall.
"I'm sorry gentlemen, we're about to close the doors."
He pulled out his I.D. "I'm Detective Inspector Ford, and this is my aide Mason, are you the manager?"
The young man stood there looking stern, his nose pointing slightly up in the air, he appeared very proud as he answered assertively. "Yes I am sir, is there a problem?"
Harry pulled his glasses further down his nose, "Yes I'm afraid there is young man, there is a lot of shoplifting going on; we're doing our rounds trying to give people like yourselves some sound advice."
Harry stepped forward, now brimming with confidence, convinced he had won him over.
"If you could just lock the door young man, and round up your staff,

we would like to have a word with you all in the office."
The young man only to willing to please, firmly put the bolt across the door, he stood in the middle of the now empty shop, and called to the staff.
"Right, can I have your attention please, will you all stop what you are doing, and make your way into the office."
Four women and two men formed a line and made their way to the small office. Harry closed the door behind them, he glanced along the line, they all looked slightly nervous. He studied their faces, their ages ranged from about eighteen to forty. A smart attractive woman stepped forward.
"So what's all this about then?"

He had made up his mind he had no intention of prolonging the situation. They all looked nice people, the sort of people that he would bid 'Good Day' to, just everyday people, he thought.
He looked slowly along the line, "Well it's like this, we want your money." There was a loud gasp, a young blonde girl who stood near the desk, put her hands over her face and mumbled quietly, "Please don't hurt us."
He instantly put her at ease, "No we aint here to hurt you Love."
The manager stood indignant, "No I'm sorry it's my duty to guard the takings with my life."
Ronnie had remained silent through out; swiftly he pulled out his gun, and pointed it directly at them.
"Now look we aint fucking joking, hand over the money now, or this thing goes off, as he just said we don't want to hurt you, but don't fucking push us."
The manager quickly kneeled down at the safe, his hand shook uncontrollably as he fiddled with the dial and opened the safe and swiftly handed them two money bags.
Ronnie was still holding the gun and pointing it in their direction. He then asked, "Is there any more money in the tills?"

The manager rose to his feet, looking pale and shaken. "No, no, its only small change, we start emptying the tills about half hour before closing."
Harry looked at them all one by one he smiled, "Sorry if we've caused you much upset."
He asked the manager for the key to the door, as he put the money bags into the deep inside pockets of his trench coat.
He spoke assertively, "Right, don't panic we're going to lock you in, give us ten minutes then you can ring for the police."
They walked out onto the busy street; the bright lights dazzled his eyes, as they reflected on to the wet pavement after a heavy downfall of rain.

Ronnie whistled loudly, instantly a black cab pulled up at their feet. Harry nudged him, "For fuck sake Ron; don't try to draw too much attention."
Harry popped his head through the cab window, taking off his glasses, "Can you take us to Kings Cross Station please mate?"
As the cab weaved in and out of the heavy city traffic, they decided to part company at Kings Cross and make the final stage of their journey alone. It was decided that Harry would take the money to be shared the following day.

He arrived back at Chiswick at ten fifteen, soaking wet and tired.
Josie was sitting in front of the roaring fire; he walked over to her putting his cold hands on her cheeks, "It's all done love." She pulled him towards her and kissed him full on the lips, she put her tongue in his mouth, he felt himself already becoming aroused.
He pulled away; "Give us a minute Josie, I've just walked through the door."
She started to giggle, "You know how the thought of all that lovely money just turns me on."
He smiled, "Don't get too excited, I aint counted it, but I reckon it's about a grand, that's five hundred a piece, but not bad for a days work."
She walked over and poured them both a large drink, with a happy grin on her face, she raised her glass, "Here's to us."

A close bond had developed between Harry and Ronnie, they carefully planned their jobs to detail, they would check out the stores, the ones they were going to hit in and around the West End, and with each one they hit, they became more and more confident. They found it was easy to get lost in a crowd, and just jump on a train or a cab; there was no getaway car to worry about. They had now learned the skills of changing their appearance and accents, making it difficult for the police to build up a file on them.

That was until a fateful sunny august day in 1972 when they had just held up a shop in Knightsbridge, as far as they were concerned it had all gone well. They were making their way up the escalator at the station, unwittingly, they didn't know they had been tumbled.

As they stepped off the escalator, they were in a happy frame of mind, their pockets bulging with money, and then suddenly both men were grabbed by a group of plain clothes policemen, greeting them with those fateful words, "You're nicked."
Ronnie tried to make a run for it, but to no avail. Harry knew instantly time was up, it was the end of the line. The instant thought of more time behind bars sent a shiver down his spine, he wasn't a young man

anymore, he was forty three years old doing time now wouldn't come easy. Then there was Josie, the love of his life, how was he going to cope without her?

She sat in the court room, at the Old Bailey. Her mind was in turmoil, today was the day when sentence would be given. She looked across at Harry in the witness box, he was dressed in a smart grey suit, the little hair he had left was now turning grey, but there was no getting away from it, she still fancied him like mad. The thought of not waking up next to him each morning would be unbearable. She sat there with her hands clasped together as if she was praying to God that he would walk out a free man.
Then suddenly her thoughts were broken by a booming voice that seemed as if it was echoing through a long dark tunnel in slow motion. Her head began to spin as she heard the fatal words.
"I'm sentencing you to twelve years imprisonment."

She tried to focus on Harry, but everything became such a blur, then as her vision came back, she caught sight of him being led down the stairs. She sat rigidly in her seat, only to be dealt another blow when Ronnie, her beloved nephew, was sentenced to eight years.
In the confinement of his small cell, he would often think about his life, all the women he had been involved with.
Then there was Jim, his life-long mate, it was only last week when he came on a visit, with that same cheeky grin, trying to give him advice on how to lead an honest life. He closed his eyes he could see Jim sitting in front of him; he could almost hear his voice from their last conversation.
"Come on 'H' mate, don't ya think you've fucked your life up enough, aint you getting a little bit too old for all this? I tell ya what mate, you've pulled more strokes than you've had on your dick, and that's saying something."
Harry slowly rolled his cigarette, as he murmured, "Good old memories."

Life without Harry was hard. Josie found each day harder to cope with. Money was tight, it wasn't long before she and Greg had to give up their luxurious life style. She could no longer afford to stay in the big house in Chiswick. There was no other way, her only chance of getting by was to move back with her mother in the East End of London.
At least she could go out to work, and her and Greg would have a roof over their heads.
Throughout the year things began to settle, finally she got a job as a ladies cloakroom attendant in the posh Regal Hotel, off Clarence Street in the West End. The money wasn't good, but every penny helped.

Then she eventually she left her mother's house for a small Council flat in Aldgate, it nowhere compared to what she had been used to in recent years, but it was a home.
At seven o' clock every evening, she set off on her journey, often she sat on the train feeling that life had let her down, not a day went by when Harry didn't escape her thoughts.
Visiting him didn't make it any easier, tearing herself away at the end of each visit became harder and harder, as time went on.

She kept herself busy wiping the sinks clean, it was a case of doing anything to stop the evening dragging on. She caught a glimpse of herself in the mirror and put her hand to the root of her hair; she spotted grey hairs coming through, "Oh fuck it," she murmured. She looked at her tired eyes; she didn't like what she saw in front of her.
The door opened, a gushing young woman stood at the side of her, she watched as she applied deep red lipstick to her pouting lips.
Suddenly she felt a twinge of envy as she eyed her up and down, then she thought back to her days in Chiswick with the big house and expensive clothes. Never in her wildest dreams did she ever think things would come to this.
The young woman undid the top button of her blouse and then pulled a hair pin from her deep red hair, her shiny locks flounced onto her shoulders. Josie turned to her, and smiled, "You look nice Love, have you got a date?"
She began to giggle, "Yeah, I suppose I have, but it's one I'm getting paid for."
She threw her odd change into the tips dish, and walked out.

Throughout the evening, Josie couldn't get the young woman out of her mind; all sorts of thoughts went through her head. Obviously she was on the game; she wondered how much money she earned. She gazed down at her own cheap shoes and felt a tear run down her cheek. She stamped her feet, "Fuck it; I must be fucking mad, working here for peanuts," she uttered with contempt.
She wiped her face and took a deep breath and began to sing, as she always did when she wanted to cheer herself up.
She thought of Harry, how when he tired of reading he would put his book down and say, "Sing to me Josie, you've got a lovely voice." Oh how she missed him.
She looked at the clock on the wall, it was almost eleven o'clock, and she would soon be finished. It had been a long shift, very busy to start with due to a function in the main ballroom. She began to count out her tips that she had made for the evening, when in walked the young woman that she had spoken to earlier. She couldn't help but ask, "How did it all go Love?"

Happily she waved a handful of five pound notes, like she was fanning herself; she smiled cheekily, "Not bad for a couple of hours work, eh?" Josie made up her mind there and then she would come right out with it. "Do ya work for yourself?"
The young woman looked surprised, "Oh no, no, I have a madam, it's better that way, she vets all my punters, it makes it less dangerous. You know, you just go in do your trick, pick up the money and leave, it's as easy as that."
Josie found herself becoming more interested, "What, do you work from hotels?"
She smiled, "No not always, it varies from day to day, but I never work the street, that's far too dangerous."
She hung on to every word; well it all seemed easy enough, she thought. The woman took a pen from her bag, she began to write on a scrap of paper, and handed it to Josie.
"Here think about it, if you want to, ring this number and ask for Dina, just mention my name Susie, you're a good-looking woman, with a bit of makeup, you'd soon look the part. Anything has got to be better than spending your night in a toilet, surely."
Josie took the paper and put it in her overall pocket; she smiled without saying a word.

After her meet with Susie, her feelings were mixed. Yes this seemed like a good way of earning a living, but there was her conscience, most things she didn't give a shit about, but facing Harry on a visit was different. They had always been able to read each other like a book. Not only was she to become a prostitute, she would have to be a bloody good actress as well, if she didn't want him to know.

She sat on the train, the darkness of the tunnel brought on a more fearful mood; it was to be the first night in her new job. After leaving Greg at her mother's, she had spent a good hour in front of the mirror, combing her hair in different styles, and reapplying her makeup, time and time again. A smile came to her face as she thought of the temper she had gotten herself into, throwing her shoes across the room and nearly giving up on the whole idea. She questioned herself, how the fuck were tarts supposed to look?

She finally reached Knightsbridge Station; she took the piece of paper from her bag, to check on the address once again.
With a feeling of caution, she made her way around the crescent lined with smart three-storey townhouses overlooking a small green. Her mouth began to dry out, as her stomach done somersaults. Suddenly she stopped and looked up at the highly glossed black front door. She swallowed hard, taking a deep breath as she walked up the stone steps.

After ringing the door bell, she waited patiently. A woman in her late thirties came to the door; her mouse brown hair and impish looks surprised her, she looked like an ordinary housewife.
She stepped forward, "Oh I hope I've got the right house? I'm looking for Dina."
The woman's face broke into a wide grin, "Oh right, follow me, she has been expecting you."
She was shown in to an elaborate room; she gazed across to the big window draped in expensive curtains. There was a woman sitting at a desk who rose to her feet, her beauty was instant, her long blonde hair bounced like a dancing wave.
She walked towards her, her tight black dressed fitted neatly on her slender figure. Holding out her hand, in a confident voice she said, "You must be Josie, we spoke on the phone."

Feeling slightly uncertain she went forward to shake Dina's hand, she knew now she would have to make her confidence leap out, or she would be no good for the job. She started to unbutton her coat, as she replied, "Yes that's me alright."
"Well Josie there's nothing like getting straight down to it," she began to laugh, "In a manner of speaking, of course. I will spend five minutes giving you, the do's and don'ts before you go upstairs, your first punter is due at eight o'clock.
"Oh and by the way it's advisable to change your name when you are working. What would you like to be called?"
For once she was lost for words, "I don't really mind."
"How about Estelle?" Dina asked, as if wanting her consent.
"Yeah that will do fine," she answered with a giggle.
Dina pointed to the other woman, "This is Kim, she will show you to the room you're working in tonight, follow the rules and there should be no problem."
As she climbed the stairs, her heart began to beat fast, but there was no turning back now.

The room was plush, the soft lighting relaxed her slightly, and she looked at her watch, it was two minutes to eight. She murmured to herself, "For fuck sake hurry up, let's get this over and done with."
There was a gentle knock on the door. Kim put her head around it, "Estelle, Mr Thomas is here for you."
If she wasn't feeling so nervous, she'd break into a fit of giggles, as she thought to herself, "Estelle, for fuck sake."
She looked the man up and down, he appeared more nervous than her. He wasn't that bad to look at, in fact quite handsome, she almost wished he was ugly, it might have made what was to happen that much easier.

She asked him what he would like her to do; in a soft voice he replied "Just straight sex please."
It seemed to make it harder that he was so polite. She felt shocked by his courteous manner. She began to slowly undress, she felt good, she had spent almost all her hard earned wages from her cloakroom job on new expensive sexy underwear, 'speculate to accumulate', well that's what she had always been told.
He lay on the bed, it didn't take much to arouse him, and she had noticed his dick getting bigger as he watched her get undressed.
After such a long time, it was good to have a man lying on top of her again.

She began to feel pleasure, she tried to tighten her body, she told herself no, and this was not the man that she loved, he was a total stranger. The feelings that she was getting were not supposed to happen, it felt good.
Desperately she tried to blank everything out, but it was no use she had climaxed, she felt angry with herself. "No fuck it," she sighed under her breath, she wasn't supposed to enjoy it.
At last his heavy breathing had slowed down, his body now limp, he had come; a feeling of glee then came over her. Yes her first punter, and there was no mistaking by the amount of groaning coming from him, that he enjoyed it.

Oh yes, she reassured herself, next time would be a doddle.
He put his clothes on sheepishly, laying the agreed amount of money on the side. He turned to her, "I do pay you don't I, or do I pay downstairs?"
She smiled, "I don't know, they forgot to mention that, it's my first time."
He smiled shyly, "Mine too, and is it alright to book you again?"
She felt wanted, as she confidently answered, "Of course, just see Kim on your way out."
She returned home on the train later that evening, still with mixed feelings, but now a lot better off.

It had been a long journey; she hated the ferry across to the prison, she never understood why he had to be sent all the way to the Isle of Wight. Wearily she walked down the long lane heading towards the prison. The hot afternoon sunshine was hitting the back of her neck. Today she was feeling different, excited but nervous; she wasn't going to lie to him, but she had made up her mind not to tell him the full truth, she could not bear to hurt him.
She walked in to the visitors' room; there was lots of hustle and bustle going on with people just arriving.

She looked across to the window, the strong sunlight made it almost impossible to see, then her eyes caught sight of a tall slender figure, waving frantically, trying to attract her attention. Her heart began to melt, as it always did when she set eyes on him.
He pulled her towards him, gently kissing her on the cheek, he looked her up and down and smiled his shy smile.
"You look nice Love, is that a new dress? You know Josie, blue looks good on you."
She sat herself down, and sorted through her bag, handing him his tobacco.
Lovingly he looked her straight in the eyes, "How's Greg? How's everyone?"

The conversation flowed, as always, but her mind, kept drifting elsewhere, for she knew at any minute she would have to break in with what she had to tell him.
She coughed nervously, and then with a smile on her face, to make it look like good news, she blurted it out, "Oh by the way, I'm working, I've got another job."
She watched him roll his cigarette using just one hand, this always fascinated her.

He finally asked her, "What ya doing then love? I'm sorry ya got to work. It won't be forever, ya know that don't ya Josie?"
She cleared her throat, "Well the moneys good; I'm working as a maid, in a brothel." Well that was nearly the truth, she consoled herself.
He remained silent showing no emotion, he puffed hard on the cigarette, as he kept his head down. She desperately wanted the silence to break.
"Josie you aint gone on the game have ya? That would fuck me right up, knowing you was with other geezers, while I'm banged up in here."
"No, no, honest, I met this girl when I worked at the hotel; she put me on to it. All I have to do is book the punters in and out. It's all done right, the madam that runs it, her name is Dina, and she must be earning a fortune; it's all done very tastefully, it's not some old knocking shop."

He sat there watching the ash get longer on his cigarette, and he pondered, as if to give it some thought.
"Did ya say there's good money in it? Well Josie I'm surprised you aint thought about turning the tables, and becoming the madam yourself."
She breathed a sigh of relief, he wasn't angry; his attitude had always been the same, if you see a way of earning money, then go for it.
He then asked himself, well who was he to condemn anyone? He had spent most of his life breaking the law.

Her journey home that day was filled with thoughts of what might be. Her new role in life, of becoming a madam, yes she could see herself in that role and it would be fine by him. Alright she never told him the complete truth, but that was because she loved him so much, to hurt him would break her heart.

In the years that followed, life didn't work out quite as prosperously as she had hoped, after renting houses in different parts of London; it didn't take long before each brothel was closed down. The police were always ready to move her on. Alright she made a living, and if she was really honest, that's all she wanted these days, after all she wasn't getting any younger.
She was always thankful that she had kept her little Council flat, her very own little' bolt hole' as she called it.
Time was ticking away quickly. Greg had left home, with the intentions of travelling the world.
She had suffered through the years without Harry; it had been a long, long time.
Now she was nearing fifty years of age, and when she thought back over her life, she had no regrets for all the ups and downs; she considered that this is what had made her the strong character she was, to this day.
In spite of all this, nothing in the world could stop the butterflies in her stomach today. Nervously she waited at the station, she glanced across to the ticket barrier and there he was; he walked towards her, looking fit and well.

For on this August day in 1982, due to good behaviour, he was a free man. At last she was reunited with her soul mate. He pulled her tightly to him not speaking a word, and kissed her gently. She put her arm around his thin waist; she looked up into his eyes as she said, "I never ever thought this day would come."

TURN UP FOR THE BOOK

Harry was in a sombre mood as he walked along the tow path, heading towards Kew. The river was running high, and so was his feeling. This morning he had left Josie in a huff, he was finding being a free man difficult to cope with. Her life was busy, he wanted to be there for her but these days she didn't seem to need him quite so much.
The hot midday sunshine proved too much, he finally came to a bench, unbuttoned his blazer, and sat himself down.

Wistfully he gazed across the river, he took out his tobacco pouch and began to roll himself a joint, these days he would have the odd puff; this was a habit he formed in prison, on his last long stretch. He blew the smoke into the air, and slowly began to relax, and a grin appeared on his face, as he reassured himself that the odd smoke so far, had done him no harm, anyway, he thought ,what did it matter at his time of life? He took out his pen and note book, and looked up to the sky, he watched the birds glide above, how peaceful they looked, no one to bother them he thought. He began to write his thoughts down in his note book, knowing that at some time he would turn it to verse.

If nothing else, all those years behind bars had educated him to the very best in his knowledge of the English language. He had now read so many books and written so many poems he was beginning to think Josie was right, she was forever telling him he should have put his real talents to good use at a young age, and that today he would still be a rich man, instead of an ex con, who was going nowhere. Well that's what she told him this morning, and if he was honest, it hurt.
He smiled, oh yes she definitely knew how to turn the knife, but it didn't stop him loving her.

As he looked down to his side, there appeared at his feet a little black dog; it threw itself down hard on the ground, its tongue hung out as his body shook; it seemed the heat had got to him as well. He began to stroke him; he playfully rubbed under its chin and picked him up to cradle him. He rubbed his hands through his shiny black coat.
"Come on mate, I think you need a drink."

He walked towards the waters edge gently lowering him in, he held onto him as the dog let his long tongue hang out to gobble up the water. Gently he then put him back on the ground to let him run free.

With newfound energy he picked up his belongings, and started to walk along the towpath, with the little dog at his heels, the full summer foliage gave him slight shelter from the bold sun. He smiled to himself, oh well at least someone wants me, he thought.
It had been a long time since he had made his way back over to this side of London, he hated the East End, and somehow he never really felt like he belonged there.

When he first set off on the train heading towards Richmond earlier, he was feeling so angry, his intentions were never to return, but Josie was right once again, she had said he had become paranoid about everything.
Alright, yes, to some he might come across as a little strange, well who the fuck wouldn't be after spending so many years away?
It was only yesterday when he decided to wear his big Stetson hat, she stared at him and blatantly told him that he looked a fucking idiot.
But why? He had always been a little eccentric in his dress, why should it worry her now?
He sometimes wondered, did she still want him? Had he become old and boring?
When he came out of prison, the first thing he asked her was if she would marry him. After all the years that they had been together, it seemed the right thing to do. When she got her divorce from Graham, she vowed she would never marry again, but it seemed love conquered all, well she readily agreed to marriage. So what was the problem now, had she fallen out of love with him?

He kept walking trying his hardest to keep in the shade. With a great feeling of relief he sighed, in the distance he could now see Kew Bridge. He took his handkerchief, and began to wipe the beads of sweat from his forehead. Now feeling weary again he glanced across to the green, at last he was thankful to see a pub, if nothing else, he deserved a pint. He looked at his watch; it was two o'clock.
Should he forget all about the argument earlier, and start to make his way back home, or should he be adventurous, and make his way to Gunners Park?
It had been years and years, since he last went there. It meant he would have to walk another mile, in the hot sun, but if he didn't do it, he would have regrets later; he had got this far, no, he told himself, he must carry on.

He gazed up to the sky; there wasn't a cloud to be seen; he was now thinking how good it was to be alive. There had been lots of beautiful days like this in his life, when he was only able to peer through the window of his cell. Often he would break out in a panic, thinking he was never going to breath fresh air again. He sighed deeply, as he thought about all those days he had lost; there was nothing in the whole wide world, that could give those lost days back to him.
As he made his way along the busy street, he was just dreaming, dreaming, and dreaming.
Then suddenly his thoughts were broken by the tooting of a car. He shook himself and looked at the large metal object in front of him; the car was within inches of his feet. "Fuck it!" he shouted, as the thought of what could have been a near-fatal accident ran through his mind.

Finally he reached the park gates, his stomach began to flutter, like it did when he was a young boy. He stood with his blazer draped over his right shoulder; a funny sort of nervousness began to take him over. He almost had to force himself to walk through the gates, was it fear of the memories that might come flooding back to him?
He looked across at the never-ending open land, there were children playing, dogs running, but most prominent, were long rows of cherry trees to his right.

His eyes welled up; he hastily walked towards the trees, stopping at one in particular. Frantically he ran his hand up and down the trunk, hoping to find the carving that he had done all those years ago, but to no avail, it must have simply faded over the years, as things do. Consciously he closed his eyes; yes he could still see a clear picture of Ellen, on that March day.
He thought back to how they made love, in this very spot where he was standing now, still remembering the pure excitement and the entwining of their two young bodies. Yes she was the girl he wanted to spend the rest of his life with. Oh how he loved her then, and in his heart nothing had changed.
Yes, in spite of falling in and out of love several times in his life, for some reason this was the one relationship he treasured most.

Then of course there was little Laura, but the more he thought about her, he came to the conclusion that they were two lonely children that had found one another, and desperately needed each other to get themselves through those very early years, where they were surrounded by poverty, and the uneasiness of war.
He sat himself down under the shade of the tree. Yes it had been almost seven years since he was released from prison in the early eighties.

Alright these days, he was potless, with no car and living in a Council flat, so what! He had the good life once, but most importantly he now had his freedom.
He had managed to stay almost on the straight and narrow, perhaps a little bit of wheeling and dealing here and there, but nothing too major.

Eagerly he began to make himself more comfortable, resting his back against the trunk of the tree. He took out his tobacco, and began to roll another cigarette.
A smile came on his face, no life wasn't all bad, at least after years of trying he had finally got in touch with Ruby, unbeknown to him, she had been back in the country for ten years. He had finally traced her to a convent, in Lancashire. Nothing pleased him more when in her last letter she wrote that in the near future she would pay him a visit. She also gave him the news that Biddy was living a rich and prosperous life in America.
As for Kathleen, Nora, and Patrick, it was as if they had disappeared off the face of the earth. In spite of all efforts on his part, he could find no trace of them.

He gazed at his watch; it was five o' clock; he looked around, it seemed the whole world had deserted him. The park now appeared almost empty, he felt at peace, but it was no good, he would have to make his way back home soon. Josie might think he had gone and got himself into some kind of trouble, he began to chuckle, there wasn't much chance of that these days.

After a long journey through the rush hour mayhem, he was pleased to be turning the key into the door. For at last he was home, feeling tired and weary, it had been a long, long day.
He could hear the clattering of pots coming from the kitchen. Then came the sound of Josie singing, this reassured him that all was well.
He stood in the hallway just looking at her, that beautiful voice of hers always melted his heart, he went over and kissed her on the back of the neck.
She turned and kissed him, "At last, I have been worried sick about ya."
He smiled, "It's good to be home Josie."
Josie had now come to terms with the fact that after all the years since his release, she was going to be the bread winner. The money that she earned in her profession just about give them a comfortable life, no they wouldn't be dining at the Ritz, but she could still keep herself looking good, and there was enough to give him the little things in life that he required these days.
Yes their life style had changed drastically from the early years, when they first got together, but through everything, she still loved him.

The summer so far had been good, she made her way home in a happy frame of mind, and takings were good today. She had opened another house only last week, the business so far had been much better than she could ever imagine; after taking on two new girls from Thailand, she had been inundated with punters wanting to make bookings.
She handed the taxi driver her fare, and looked up to the window of her flat, and yes she couldn't wait to give Harry the good news. She opened the door, to be greeted by a pile of letters at her feet, quickly she picked them up praying to God that they weren't bills.

She walked into the kitchen calling out his name, there was no answer, she felt let down, she wanted to tell him that money wise, she had done well.
She swiftly put the kettle on, and began to browse through the letters, she threw them on to the table, two looked like bills the others appeared to be circulars. Then there was one addressed to Harry, who could that be from? she asked herself She tutted, and began to smile. Oh it could be from anyone in the world, he spent most of his time these days sifting through magazines and adverts, replying to people who were looking for pen pals and it had become his hobby.

She began to giggle, it was only yesterday that he received a letter from a prisoner, serving time in jail in America. It appears that Harry wrote to him, referring to himself as a woman, and a friendship had now been struck up between them. Oh I don't know, whatever will he be up to next?! she thought.
Her laughter was broken by his voice, she turned and there he was, looking tired and forlorn.
"Sorry Josie, I didn't expect ya back yet, it's lovely out there, so I decided to go out for the day. Do you know, I've walked and walked, I'm now feeling weary."

She held up the letter, "I wonder who this one is from?"
He looked at the post mark, he could just about make it out, it looked like Middlesex. He stared at it hard, "Well I don't know who this could be from, I don't remember writing to anyone over there."
Slowly he began to open it, for some reason his stomach began to churn, instantly he looked at the bottom.
It was signed Ken Swift, but who was he?
He began to read the letter.
Dear Harry,
I don't know if you remember me. I originally come from Acton, or you may remember my wife, her name is Lena, her name was Lena Keller before we married, she is related to the Todd family. I know you were friends of theirs in the fifties...

He couldn't make sense of it, but then the name Lena Keller hit him like a bolt of lightning: she was his baby, the baby he held in his arms briefly, all those years ago. Hastily he handed the letter back to Josie, his hands began to tremble. He sat himself down, and she put her arm on his shoulder.
"Are you alright Harry? You look like you've had a shock."
He couldn't answer; she began to read the letter. "Well who is this bloke?"
With a bewildered look he gazed up at her; "I think he is writing on behalf of my Lena." As tears rolled down his face, she put her arms tightly around him.
"Oh come on Love, don't get upset, I thought this is what you've always wanted."
He began to sob, he felt overwhelmed and frightened, "Why now, why forty years on?"

Josie glanced back at the letter, "Look here Harry, it say's if you would like to get in touch, ring the number at the top of the page."
His hand began to shake again, as he took the letter back from her. "No, no, Josie I couldn't ring her after all these years; she's a woman not a young child, I might have been able to cope with that."
She put a cup of tea in front of him, "Well the choice is yours."
He sipped his tea, as he gazed into space, he then looked up at her, for reassurance.

"Josie, I wonder what she looks like. I mean what does a forty year old woman look like? It's something I've never really thought about. Do you know Josie, I can still remember you at forty, yeah you were a right good looker."
Her face stiffened, "So what are you saying? That I don't look good now?"
"Oh leave it out Josie, I'm trying to visualize what she might be like, I mean she might be fat and ugly, or she might be tall and skinny, like me."
She began to chuckle, "Well if she looks like you, it would be sad."
He felt himself beginning to warm to the idea.

That night he tossed and turned in bed, he felt unsettled, the last thing he expected in all the world was to hear from his daughter.
Then his thoughts turned to Ellen, what would she think of all this?
He lay there, the stuffy night air began to get to him; he walked over to the open window, and gazed across the street. Suddenly there were signs of life as dawn began to break; he felt relieved, at least in the light of day he may be able to think more clearly.

Throughout the week, he read the letter over, and over again, he rubbed his hand gently over it, thinking to himself that this sheet of paper had also been held by his daughter. A shiver went down his spine, he knew he must do something soon, or she would think he didn't want to know.
Curiosity was getting to him, how after all this time did she manage to trace him? After all the years of him being in and out of prison, he couldn't think of one person from years gone by who would know of his whereabouts now, not even Jim; he had lost contact with him.

Josie arrived home; his dithering was getting to her, since the day of the letter arriving he had been staring into space,; it was no good, she would have to sort it out.
These days, as long as he could go for his walks, and spend the day with his head in a book, almost everything else went unnoticed.
This was different; he was now in a situation that he really didn't know how to deal with; after his last long spell in prison it somehow seemed to destroy him.
In a lot of ways he had lost some of that confidence that once bounced out of him. He always used to say, it wasn't having lots of money that made him feel good, it was the buzz he got from nicking it, and there was nothing he liked better back in the old days than blowing a safe open, but without the money, life had changed. He was now sixty-one years old and there was no way he was going to rob a bank now.

After discussing the matter at great lengths, it was decided it was going to be Josie who was going to make the phone call to Lena.
He just wasn't ready to hear the sound of Lena's voice, he might break down and cry, this was the last thing he wanted, no it would all be too much for him.
He watched her carefully dial the number; she turned to him, and smiled, but her nervousness, showed through. "It's ringing love."
He felt his body tremble, it was no good, he would have to leave the room.
He stood in the hallway, he just about heard Josie ask, "Hello is that Lena? This is Josie, I'm Harry's wife."
He could not bear to listen, and went into the kitchen closing the door firmly behind him. Soon he began to feel agitated, what the fuck was she talking about, why was it all taking so long?
Finally she returned, her face beaming with delight.
She looked at his worried face, "Oh Harry she sounds really nice, and guess what? You're a granddad; she's got two teenage children."
He began to feel at ease as she carefully unfolded the story about Lena. What he heard he liked, and reassured himself that he would give it a couple of days, and he would ring her himself.

He walked along the East End Market, feeling irritated by the crowds, he never really liked the hustle and bustle; he would rather be walking along a quiet stretch of the river, this is where he felt most at peace, just handballing along the waters edge, but Josie had left him a list to go shopping.

Today was different, he found himself looking closely at almost every woman, and he was trying desperately to build a picture of what a forty year old woman would look like. Then he thought back to when he was younger, yes a woman of that age would be regarded as old, but in today's world, they seem to keep themselves looking much younger than their years.
After filling his bags with fruit and vegetables, he decided to take a steady walk home, and yes he had decided he would then make the phone call that had weighed so heavy on his mind.

He lit a cigarette, to calm his nerves, and put a glass of water at his side, just in case his vocal cords became irritated by nervousness.
Nervously he held the receiver close to his face, he could hear the thudding of his heart against the sound of the dialling tone, he contemplated putting the receiver down, no it was too late.
A gentle voice spoke, "Hello who's calling?"
He began to stammer, "Could I speak to Lena please."
There was a silence, as if she knew who was on the end of the line, and then she answered, "This is Lena, is that you Harry?" She was making it easy for him.
"Yes Love it's me," he felt a lump begin to build up in his throat, for at last he had exchanged the first words with his daughter.
Immediately, she thanked him for calling, and he listened to her quiet voice, savouring every word.

She explained to him that it had been hard going trying to contact him, but she hoped it hadn't caused him any problems with his family.
He reassured her over and over that there was no problem, he was just so overwhelmed that she had bothered to get in touch after all these years. He realised that they had so much catching up to do, but he knew that they would have to meet face to face to catch up on so many lost years.
Now that he was beginning to feel more at ease, he would ask her if she would be prepared to meet him. She readily accepted, and he detected the keenness in her voice.
"When would you like to meet?" she asked nervously.
He paused to think, "How about we send each other a photo of ourselves, then perhaps we can make a meet for next week."

She replied, "That will be lovely, I will look forward to that. Oh, and thanks once again, Harry."

He knew he could talk no longer on the phone, the important things he had to say to her, he wanted to say in person, he lovingly said goodbye, then put down the receiver.
With an exciting feeling welling up in his stomach, he sat back in the chair; and raised his fist in to the air, yes, he had done it.
He now began to think about all the things he could have said, for example, how was Ellen? He shook his head, no perhaps not, he would wait for Lena to mention her first.

The picture finally arrived, it was of Lena with her husband, son and daughter, they were standing in a garden. Carefully he studied it, yes it was a nice family picture, but he felt disappointed, it was taken from afar, he could barely see their faces.
Eagerly he began to read the letter, she thanked him for his photo and letter and she agreed that midday, Monday the 13th of August would be a good day to meet.
He had chosen Kew Garden's station, as the meeting place, and she said this suited fine. He put the letter down, thinking just three more days and he could hold his daughter close.

He woke early, he felt jittery. Josie had already left for work, he looked at the fresh pale blue shirt that she had ironed for him, and his trousers hung neatly pressed on the hanger. He glanced at his watch, only four hours to go. He opened the veranda door and looked up to the clear blue sky; it looked like it was going to be another scorcher. Somehow the feeling of uncertainty wouldn't leave him as he sipped his tea, carefully outlining his plans in his mind.

Slowly he put his hand across the top of his eyes to shield them from the morning sun; he glanced across to the derelict land opposite, and beyond that a train sped by on the railway track. Nervously he touched his stomach, it felt as if it was rising up to his heart.
His thoughts turned to Lena and wondered how she would be feeling, he smiled, probably just as nervous as him.
What would he tell her if she asked about his life? What would she think of him if he told her that he had spent so many years in prison? She might think he wasn't good enough to associate with her and her family. He pondered; what should he do? No, he would tell her the truth, he couldn't lie.
If anything she deserved the truth after all these years, anyway, who knows what Ellen might have told her? No, he would take the situation as it came.

The train journey had been hot and stuffy, he was more than pleased to step foot onto the platform at Kew, throughout the journey he had been feeling slightly queasy.

He glanced at his watch, it was eleven forty, and he was early, nervously he began to brush himself down. He looked at his trousers, they had creased somewhat, he felt annoyed, he wanted to look his best for her. He straightened his tie, really wanting to take it off due to the heat, but he didn't want to spoil his smart appearance, after all Josie had gone to a lot of effort to ensure he was well turned out.
Quickly he flitted through the crowded station, he was more than pleased to breathe in fresh air as he walked into the street. He was taken in by the array of colour, from the women passing by, in their brightly patterned summer dresses.
He looked around him curiously, could one of them be Lena? It really was going to be hard to recognise her from the photograph he thought, as he stood there for a while, feeling like a little boy lost.

Then he caught sight of the station bar to his right, he pondered over what he should do next, he was almost sure if she was nearby, she would have spotted him by now.
Right there and then he made a decision; yes he would get himself a pint, and sit and wait at one of the outside tables.
He made himself comfortable, taking small sips of his beer; and then began to worry, if he smelled of alcohol what would she think of him? Once again he looked again around the small square, and then he cast his eyes down the street, no he didn't want to look at his watch again, it felt like he had looked at it a hundred times already today.

It was hard to resist, he took one more look, five minutes past twelve, perhaps she had second thoughts or Ellen might have said something to make her change her mind. His nerves began to get the better of him; anxiously he began to struggle with his tie, as he got hotter and hotter, thinking to himself if I could only take the fucking thing off, I would feel a whole lot better.
Yes he would read his newspaper, that would take his mind off of the situation; he had his head bowled down when he heard footsteps heading directly towards him. It was the clicking of high heeled shoes, that made him think it could be her. No, no he wouldn't look up, he would wait for her to approach him. A shadow finally appeared across his table.

Then a gentle voice asked, "Excuse me, are you Harry?"
He instantly stood up, holding out his arms, he smiled, "You must be Lena."

Without really looking her in the eye, he pulled her towards him, with his tall body towering over her petite frame he held her tight.
No she wasn't the child that he had a faded memory of in his mind, but it was the first time in a lot of years that he had come close to holding someone that was part of him. He looked down at her; and sadly watched the tears roll down her face, he pulled away and sat her down at the table, handing her a handkerchief to wipe away her tears.
He sat opposite her, he was lost for words, She began to compose herself.
She wiped her face, "I'm sorry I was just so overcome with emotion, I thought I would be alright, then just seeing you, started me off."

He smiled, "It's good to see ya Love, you don't know how long I've waited for this moment, let me get ya a drink, and then we can have a chat, what would ya like Lena?"
"Oh just a coke please," she said nervously.
She watched him walk into the bar, he looked nothing like she had expected, he was tall and slim with quite sharp features but appeared very agile.

Throughout the years there was hardly a day that had gone by when she hadn't tried to imagine what he might look like.
He handed her the drink and smiled as he said, "Do you know you don't look one bit like Ellen."
She was quick to answer, "But everyone says I look like my mum." She felt let down, almost disappointed, was she not what he expected?
Then he began to chuckle, "I can see a lot of me in ya though."
She had to agree; yes she had already noticed a strong resemblance between them, especially the eyes.

After the initial shock of meeting, it wasn't long before they got on like a house on fire. All those lost years were now beginning to hit home, he gazed across the table at her, there she sat a bright bubbly person, and yes a mother of two, and himself a granddad, he could hardly believe it..
Her short blond highlighted hair emphasised her summer tan. He was taken by her smart appearance, her white top trimmed with navy, with matching navy skirt and shoes, she certainly knew how to put an outfit together, he thought.
He couldn't help but feel proud, yes this woman who was now appearing to be full of confidence, was his long-lost daughter.
As the afternoon wore on, it was agreed that a walk around Kew Gardens would be nice. It was here as they sat on a bench under a tree that they spoke about their lost years.
He was more than surprised when she told him that Ellen knew nothing of their meeting, and that she had spent most of her younger

years living with her Nan and Granddad Keller.
"Well how did you know of me then?" he ask curiously.

"Well when I was younger I was told by my mum, that Jack Bunter wasn't my father, but I was never told who my father was, and that left me with years of uncertainty about myself."
He felt hurt; did Ellen really hate him that much?
"Then one day a friend asked me out of the blue, wouldn't you ever like to meet your real Dad? I was surprised when she asked me; I wondered why, she was more shocked when I told her I didn't even know his name. She began to laugh, as if I was joking, then she told me that he had recently been in the newspapers, so yes, of course, that made me even more interested. Not wanting to upset my Mum, I asked Dolly Todd very discreetly, if she knew your whereabouts, she told me all she knew about you, but too many years had passed. Then whatever line I went down in search of you, I always came to a dead end. When I got to my late thirties, I knew then if I didn't make the effort, then I never would.
"So with the help of Kenny my husband, we went down lots of channels. We began by looking through telephone directories, even with Kenny knocking at doors, with feeble excuses, asking if a man lived there answering to your name. I was beginning to think I would never find you, then over a year later, we went to Saint Catherine's House, here we came across birth certificates and wedding certificates belonging to your family, then bingo, there was your address, on your wedding certificate, to Josie. We drove to where you lived but no, we just couldn't knock at your door for the fear of putting you into an awkward situation.
"So Kenny came up with the idea to send a carefully worded letter, which we promptly did, hence here we are today."

He looked on in amazement and put his arm tightly around her shoulder and kissed her gently on the cheek, "Thank you Love, for doing all that for me."
Now it was his turn for the tears to roll, for he never thought he would be talking to his daughter in all his wildest dreams.
After a heart-rendering day, she stood on the platform, as she waved him off on the train, feeling happy and content, for at last the puzzle was complete. After forty years she had at last met her father.
Not knowing then, that she would have twelve happy and interesting years, with a man she can only describe as 'different from most'.
Together they grabbed the precious moments, until sadly, Harry passed away on the on the twenty first of July 2002.

The end.

ISBN 142512235-3